Lily's Cupola

Lily's Cupola

Bronwyn Tate

To Pat & Celia

A memento of your

NZ experience.

Bronwyn Tate

OTAGO

Published by University of Otago Press
PO Box 56/56 Union Street West
Dunedin, New Zealand
Fax: 64 3 479 8385
Email: university.press@stonebow.otago.ac.nz

First published 2003
Copyright © Bronwyn Tate 2003
ISBN 1 877276 59 6

Published with the assistance
of Creative New Zealand

Cover photo by *Otago Daily Times*
Printed in New Zealand by Printlink Ltd, Wellington

Spend time with us on the boulevards, the byways and behind the facades of the most absorbing, dynamic and powerful places on earth . . .

Ad. OMA Village

THE CONTINENT AT HOME

PAR

that only

how to

for Mike

[One]

3 September

Dear Iris

I was gorgeous once. You remember, don't you? Gorgeous. No one would believe it now, especially not my grandchildren. (I have three, by the way.) I can just imagine their reactions. *Here she goes. Off on one of her voyages of fantasy. Again.* Grandchildren are so good at exchanging pitying glances from beneath extravagantly pierced eyebrows, at rolling their eyes skyward, the irises adrift in such an expanse of unblemished white. As though anyone over sixty should be well past seeking out the mirage of their distant youth. And anyone past eighty might as well remain prostrate, filling the days with finger-tapping langour, resignation, waiting for God, dreaming of the only kiss likely to come their way, the kiss of Death. A kiss, in their eyes – depending on their prospect of inheritance, or the degree of boredom for those who have lived already – long overdue.

Do you detect a hint of cynicism? Perhaps I've been unfair. My grandchildren have never done me any harm. I doubt whether they've even wished it. That would involve thinking of someone other than themselves.

Now self-pity's creeping in. But I'm allowed to indulge myself occasionally. I'm eighty-three, Iris. Can you imagine that? I didn't think I'd even get past fifty. Back when I was gorgeous, even fifty sounded decrepit. Now I'd give a lot to be fifty again.

I know it's a long time since you've heard from me, longer than either of us would ever have believed, but it's part of being eighty-three, this yearning for things long gone, to plaster fissures that should never have been left gaping. Imagine the ticket on a new blouse, sewn into the side seam, an envelope of stiff embroidered irritation which never softens with laundering, scratching away at your skin for years. That's what it's been like, for me, this rift. I want to take to it with the scissors, to be rid of it. What will you think, I wonder? What will you do when you see this exotic postmark, open the envelope and smell the freshness of the Southern Hemisphere? The scent of lavender from my garden, of grass, just mown, the salinity of a gentle sea as the wind rolls in from the coast. Then at least you'll know I mean well.

Best wishes
Lily

[Two]

10 September

Dear Iris

Are you interested in quilting? I imagine not, considering your obvious lack of skills with a needle earlier in life. My pansy cloth has always made me think of those days, before the war, when I was trying to teach you stem stitch and lazy daisy. You were inept, Iris. We have to be honest. You could never stitch to save yourself. The needle was like a weapon in your hand. So much blood, the hems of your handkerchiefs were red, and there you were with fingers like pincushions, expecting me to pity you. I've never been so frustrated with anyone in my life.

But we can change. You might be a dressmaker now, for all I know. Seamstress to the Queen. Perhaps if I tell you a little, you might catch the quilting bug, the way I have. It's not something you can be mildly interested in, Iris. It takes over your life. The one-patch is the easiest to start with, a good quilt for beginners. You can use all your scraps of fabric this way, without having to buy a thing. Cut your pieces about one inch square, then sew them together in long chains. Then sew the chains together. You don't need to have any idea about colour. Just sew, sew, sew. Allow fate to be the designer and see what happens. Some accidents are divine.

Speaking of accidents, and of fate, and of grandchildren (which I was in my last letter, if you remember – do you have any, by the way?), something has happened. My grandson, Nat, has turned up, a bedraggled boy of nineteen. And self-pity? He puts me to shame.

There he was, Iris, across my chunky-legged oak dining table, drinking tea as though he'd been in the Sahara without water for a month. His elbows, exposed by the rolled up sleeves of his heavy checked shirt, stabbed at my poor pansy cloth as he passed his head from one hand to the other.

My pansy cloth is ancient now. The hem's been ironed so many times its edge is like a blade. As I sat there I imagined it cutting through the thin skin of my wrist, the blood gushing the way it used to from your fingertips.

Grandchildren have their own myths. They spend all of childhood building elaborate constructions from half-forgotten memories, snippets of overheard conversations (they *always* take the wrong meaning), and convictions formed in their minds and never questioned. Like a beaver's dam made from random sticks picked up along the way, their own personal mythology grows around them, a solid shell to encase them, a conception of the world, based on misconception.

And who am I to disillusion them?

I'm not fat any more, but you know I used to be. I had to lose the weight, or die. What a choice. My limbs still show the signs, great wads of flesh, capillaries as purple as plums, dewlaps under my arms like the pearly throats of Brahman cattle. My heart has been carved up and repaired by surgeons. And plainly, I live in a dream world, imagining that once I was gorgeous. Yes, who am I to disillusion them?

Nathaniel, the grandson in question, is now called Nat by choice, although I can't imagine why he wants to share a name with an annoying winged insect. As grandchildren go he would rate about five out of ten. He arrived belatedly in my life, because his mother had taken such exception to Hugo when their marriage failed. Nat was ten, already a gangly acne-ridden pre-adolescent, his awkwardness making affection difficult. And he's remained at that distance – table width – ever since.

As I sliced at my wrist with the hem of my pansy cloth, he sat across from me, grinning like a fool. He disposed of a banana and chocolate-chip muffin by thirds, gulping more tea to wash it down. 'The car wouldn't start,' he said in a pause between mouthfuls. 'Bloody thing. It was piss ... isting down, and I had ten minutes to get to work, and I knew I was on my last warning.'

My fingers scaled the precipice of the tablecloth's overhang and located a pansy in one corner, stroking the strands of violet and indigo thread that have worn away to whispers. 'What's wrong with it?' I asked him. 'The car.'

'Cracked bloody head, it turns out. Oops, sorry about that.' He covered his lips with a finger, grimacing. I don't know why he bothered.

Sound travels in the country. There aren't many profanities I haven't heard, over and over, drifting up from the valley while a handful of sheep misbehaved and some farm dog somersaulted backwards through hoops, trying vainly to please its master.

And I was married to Eddie for forty years.

Something Hugo said, most probably. *You mustn't offend your grandmother.*

Would it be ungrateful to want to be offended occasionally, for the sake of feeling included in life rather than living like the porcelain in a china cabinet, admired but never used? To want to be told the truth, however grizzly? To want to be consulted on matters of importance, pivotal points of life, deciding moments? Age brings an overview, if nothing else. The patterns become discernible eventually. Cause and effect. There is such a thing as wisdom after all, and it comes with age. What is the point, if the oldest generation is stored away behind leadlight?

'Is it worth keeping?' I refilled his mug, splashing in milk, executing with precision the move that he and his half-sister have labelled the *long pour*, raising the teapot high mid-stream, to aerate. I don't know where the action originated. Was it Ma, do you think? Or Grandma Olivia? One of those enigmatic semi-genetic acquisitions made famous merely by being remarked upon.

'I wouldn't get much for it,' he said, stirring in sugar. Stirring and stirring, staring into the whirling tea as though it would evolve into a prophecy. *You will find riches beside a fast-flowing river.*

'It's insured for more than it's worth. Dad pays for that. *I* couldn't afford it. Should write it off. That'd do the trick.'

It took a moment to arrange my features to display serenity. It pays not to express shock at suggestions made by the young. Half of their behaviour is for that purpose alone: to shock. The other half is stupidity. 'And how could you do that without maiming or killing yourself?'

'That's the problem. It's bloody indestructible, this car. I've been wanting to get rid of it for bloody months – sorry, Gran. Would you believe I've parked it on the bloody – oops, sodding – street every sodding bloody – oops – night for frigging months, with the fucking keys in it?' He slurped from his mug. 'Even joy riders don't want it.'

I'd never seen him so agitated, and then remorse at breaking the rule – *don't offend Gran at any cost* – forced him to jam a muffin, whole, into his mouth. I dragged a tissue from my sleeve and dabbed my nostrils, covering my mouth, which shouldn't have been smiling. I drew in a breath, exhilarated at being let into something that Hugo, with the best of intentions, had tried to exclude me from for years.

'Gurnard reckons it'll cost a grand to fix it. A f-f-f-freaking grand! I don't have that kind of money. Especially now.'

'Why especially now?'

'Because it wouldn't bloody go. And it was bucketing down. And I only had ten frigging minutes to get to work. And I was on my last f-f-freaking warning.'

'You lost your job?'

He nodded, abject, over his half-empty mug. Or was it half-full. (I forget sometimes whether I'm an optimist or a pessimist.)

'And my shitty flatmate said if I didn't have a job I couldn't keep the room, because she's not into charity. Or freeloaders.'

'What about your mother?'

'She's in frigging Fiji with Bruce, lying on a beach somewhere soaking up ultra-violet. Then she's got a conference in Seattle. Won't be back until November.'

'Couldn't you stay in the flat?'

'Can't stand bloody Bruce.'

'Then what about your father?'

'He's got a new girlfriend. Joanna. Has he told you?'

'I think he's mentioned her.'

'Did he tell you she's twenty-bloody-five? The fat old bastard can score chicks that wouldn't even look at me.'

It occurred to me then that Nat, at his most self-pitying, was an experience worth avoiding. I slid the plate of muffins across the table, trying to divert the tide of self-flagellation. Hugo would have reminded him that, at the same age, he was in some position or other. I don't remember now what model behaviour he was exhibiting at nineteen. Personally, I don't believe Hugo should hold his life up as something to be emulated. His first marriage was an unmitigated disaster. And his second. Jeannette, Nat's mother, was so bitter that she fled to the other end of the country with Nat. Hence his speckled, knock-kneed, late arrival, and the table width between us.

The other weakness in Hugo's argument, of course, is that it needs to be constantly revised, as Nat grows older. *When I was your age ...* is not an easy sentence for Hugo to finish without sitting down with pen and paper, and reconstructing his own history so that he can recount the relevant part for the occasion. He married Diane at twenty. Became a father, to Bree. Later he divorced and married Jeannette, Nat, and not long afterwards the acrimonious split. Numerous miserable years as a bachelor, followed by a ten-year engagement to Amelia, which could have worked if only they had not taken the ultimate step, and married. Hence, wife number three and the Boiled Egg – Hugo's name for his youngest child, Vincent.

And now, it seems, he has moved on again, to 25-year-old Joanna.

Perhaps this is too shocking for you, Iris. Antipodean life bears a strong resemblance to those pillaging Vikings of old. I'm too tired to show horror any more. Better to drift like a length of silk in a breeze.

'Things can't be that bad,' I told Nat. Compared to Hugo's life, nothing was that bad. But Nat's beaver dam has Hugo sticks. (Do you remember Pooh sticks, Iris, down by the canal?) I didn't like to disillusion him. 'How did you get here?'

'No,' he said. 'It's not that bad, I suppose. And I hitched.'

'Where's your car now?'

'Outside the flat. Keys in it. But no one's going to nick it, 'cos it won't bloody start.'

His pile of belongings was on the verandah, concealed until he had sounded me out. Two suitcases, a canvas pack, and a cardboard box. Not much baggage for nineteen years. And in their arrangement was the desperation which must have brought him here. How many options had he pursued before settling on me? He stood awkwardly beside me while I pondered, his arms seeming unable to find a space to fill, his fists settling at his waist, then falling again to his sides, opening into great fleshy spades then clenching again into balls of worry.

'You might as well carry it through to the spare room,' I said. I've never been good at saying no.

His arms wound around me, elastic as convolvulus, and he lifted me off the ground. I couldn't imagine what he was so excited about. He'd be bored within a day, pining for his city life, missing the flashing lights, the constant vibration of traffic, the heart-beat of pounding drum-and-bass, the clubs, the pubs, the sense of belonging induced by crowded streets, the scream of sirens, neighbours towering on all sides.

It was almost five o'clock when he took his pile of debris from the verandah into the spare room. I fed the chickens that free-range outside the garden fence all year round. The sight of the bucket always sends them into a frenzy, dashing towards me from every direction, full run, to be closed in for the night. They would even leave an egg half-laid if there was food to be had. The wheat fell all around my feet like raindrops, and peck-peck, peck-peck, it disappeared. I had a low opinion of chickens even before we came to this house. Their mindless scritch-scratching, their clumsy flight, and the tiny space between their eyes in which to house a brain. Looking into one eye, I can surely see daylight through the other. But eggs, those golden-yolked parcels of nutrition plucked warm in the mornings from musty nesting boxes, the chicken's ransom, more than make up for such deficiencies.

Eddie and I woke that first morning, threw back the curtains, and found ten chickens pecking madly at the fresh putty where broken panes in the french doors had been replaced in time for our arrival. The beak-nicks are still there, like the marks from miniature pick-axes, stabbed into the putty, painted over now (Brunswick green), a memento of our first week of country life, our first week of life in a new country.

Perhaps I shouldn't mention Eddie, but I can hardly pretend he never existed, that he hasn't been a huge part of my life. Rest assured he was a good man, Iris, for the most part. And without him I wouldn't have found Nat on my doorstep, or been forced to look away while he tried to make a good impression by chopping kindling while I tied the old dog, Paddy, to his kennel. I dug a few carrots and pulled some leeks from the vegetable plot, trying not to think about the way he swung an axe. It arced and bounced off the wood, and each carrot, each glossy head of beetroot, each stalk of rainbow chard, furnished my imagination with pictures of the gash the axe would open against the bone of Nat's shin. I scrubbed at the vegetables, water gushing from the outside tap.

I would have run to Hugo, snatched the axe from his hands, and pushed him to one side while I made light work of finishing off. And Eddie would have leaned against the verandah post, despairing of me.

I gave Nat chuck steak for dinner, braised for two hours in a moderate oven with herbs and vinegar, tomato paste, and flour to thicken. Vegetables too, the carrots and leeks from the garden, and great chunks of potato. The meat fell apart at the touch of a fork, tender as youth, and we mopped the gravy with slabs of home-made bread. The Breville crouched on the corner of the bench, unassuming – the best present Hugo ever gave me. Nat, across the table, closed his eyes in delirium, groaning and savouring each mouthful. His mother, he said, was on some silly low-fat diet kick. And his flatmate, past tense, ate out most nights. There was no point, he said, in cooking a meal for one. Then he realised what he'd said. That every night, I cooked for one.

'It's not the same, is it?' I asked him. 'If you don't have someone to enjoy it with.'

He shook his head, conscience salved, and helped himself to seconds.

His half-sister, Bree, is twenty-eight and vegetarian. She nibbles on dry crackers or bread and marmite. I made her a pot of soup once, but I used chicken stock. I didn't know they were so picky. It was like the Inquisition, spotlight in my face while she demanded a list of ingredients. She prefers mixed frozen vegetables to bacon and egg pie. Once she ate peas out of the shells and a stick of celery while Hugo and I feasted on leg of lamb with the vegetables roasted in the juices.

Hugo says it's rude to serve meat when I know only too well that it will offend Bree. You know me, Iris. I don't mean to be rude, only to tempt her to try something with a bit of substance. She looks anaemic. And much too thin. If we look away for even a moment, Bree might disappear.

In fact I think she has. I haven't seen her for months.

Regards
Lily

[Three]

12 September

Dear Iris

Have you noticed the date? The day after the anniversary. You'll still be in the midst of it. All day yesterday I expected planes to fall out of the sky. I expected something poetic, some kind of symmetry, another inconceivable tragedy. Promise not to tell anyone, Iris, but there was a part of me that almost wanted horror, death, destruction on a massive scale. What would they think of me here if they knew that? Could I hold my head up in the butcher's shop, the fans whirring overhead, the gutted plastic pig eyeing me with suspicion as the butcher's boy weighed out half a kilo of pork sausages? And my doctor? What if his instruments could see into my mind, his stethoscope revealing a callous revolutionary rather than a harmless grandmother-of-three? I would have to stare, as I have so many times, at his poster of the cross-section of a duodenal ulcer, rather than look into his rather alluring eyes. Am I a callous revolutionary, or did we all have such an inappropriate wish, smothered by years and years of behaving well? Part of me wanted the opportunity to experience that wordless shock again, that horror, as a contrast to the evenness of everyday life. The drawing together of strangers into some kind of community. It's as though emotion has been ironed out of life, the wrinkles and creases smoothed away. Is this the next stage of human evolution? Technology taking the place of exhilaration, despair. Or perhaps it's just my medication. A pill for every hour of every day.

Nat is still around. He's been here two nights, and he doesn't seem to be bored yet. I've discovered he's no good at lighting fires. He screws the paper too tightly, uses too many matches, too much kindling, and pokes and prods as though the fire is something dead he's found on a beach after a storm. I'd like to ask if he was ever a Boy Scout, but I don't want to intrude into those early years. Is he sensitive to the space, do you think? Or does it simply represent the misty void of early childhood, before accurate recall kicked in? Has Jeannette told him that she loved his father with a passion that turned overnight to disgust? That she fled to the other end of the country rather than face seeing him again? If it wasn't for her pre-Hugo travel qualification, the emergence from her first decade of motherhood, and the desire to be something other than the divorced daughter of a farming family, I might never have met Nat. Jeannette is so ambitious now it's a wonder it took so long for her to grow bored.

'Anyway,' Nat said last night, poking, blowing, prodding. 'It was a dead end job. I hated it. Panelbeating, for Christ's sake. Who wants to be doing that for the rest of their lives?'

'Leave it now,' I said. 'Put another log on, and close the door. Give it some breathing space.'

He obeyed. He obeyed, Iris. It was a tiny miracle. When did Hugo ever do as I suggested? (He was an obstinate child. You wouldn't have liked him.)

Nat turned down the vent. Turned it up. Down again. He's such a fidget. 'What's the story? This is supposed to damp it down.'

I was in the process of arranging my glasses on the end of my nose, little half-moons so I can flick between near and far without suffering an attack of vertigo. One leg has been snapped off and sellotaped on again, which is why the operation was so delicate. I picked up a scrap of fabric from the occasional table with a needle woven between the warp and weft. 'Your grandfather couldn't abide fires that ticked over. They had to roar. So he drilled bigger holes in that pipe.'

'Shit. I mean *shivery grass*. That's not the idea of it. It's for efficiency. You've got no efficiency now, Gran. You might as well have an open fire. I should get you a new pipe, the proper sort.'

'It's almost the end of the fire season anyway.'

'No sweat, though. The hardware shop would get one for you.'

My hands went on stitching, as they do every night. 'Have you thought about money?'

He paused while he prepared his answer. 'Dad'll send some.'

'I suppose he will, if he knows you're here.'

'You'll tell him, won't you?'

'If that's what you want.'

'Probably.' He picked up the poker, put it down again on the hearth, as though he could hardly resist the urge to torment the fire. 'I'd ring him myself, only ...'

I worked the needle through two aligned slivers of fabric, in and out, the line of stitching even and perfect. 'Only?'

'Well, you know Dad.'

'I do. I should, at least. Though I dare say there are any amount of others who think they know him better. Your mother, for one.'

'And Joanna. It was kind of about Joanna, you know ...'

'You've had an argument.'

'It was just, just that ...' Still on the hearthrug, he pulled his knees to his chest, encircling them with his arms. 'I mean, I'm nineteen, Gran.'

'I've decided,' I said, stitching, 'that I don't want you to call me Gran any more.'

He looked around, startled. (A log coming loose from the beaver dam?) 'What ...?'

'Lily will do. It's my name, after all. No one calls me Lily any more. Only Mum, or Gran, or Mrs Lusk. Vincent tries (the Boiled Egg, remember), but he doesn't have all his consonant sounds yet. It sounds more like Weewee.' Nat giggled. 'I think Fred from next door is the only person alive who calls me by my name.'

'Doesn't Mum?'

'Your mother doesn't call me anything at all. *Hey you,* I think she'd find acceptable. Or *she,* you know, the cat's mother. Besides, I never see her.'

Nat screwed up his face. 'I don't know if I can.'

'Just try. Anything's got to be better than Gran.'

You remember, Iris, how Ma insisted on calling me Lil, as though she had gifted me with a beautiful name, only to snatch it away again. It was as though she begrudged me any small pleasure in life. Lil, like some nail, hit on the head. Lil, dull and drab and lifeless. Perhaps she hoped it would mould me within its dimensions, and she wouldn't have to be envious of my youth, my beauty (because I was gorgeous once), and the chances that were still ahead of me in life. In a way I think it worked, you know, Iris. What did I know when I was a girl, when I lived under Ma's roof?

It was fashionable back then to be named after flowers, or jewels. My friends were all daisies or poppies, rubies, pansies or pearls. What a sparkling lot we must have been, vibrant and semi-precious. No wonder Ma despised us.

Nat cleared his throat. The fire roared while he basked in its glow. He stretched out his legs, acres of them, and they seemed to take up the whole floor. He leaned back on his elbows, as though sunning himself. His trousers were baggy, striped like pyjamas, and his jumper was ancient, one I knitted him years ago: dark green, fisher-rib, holed at the elbows. His hair was long, straight, parted in the middle, hooked behind his ears. I watched him, lolling like some lumbering zoo animal, as I sewed, feeling a sudden rush of matriarchal pity, anger at girls of Joanna's calibre for never looking twice at him, and suspicion that there might after all be a similarity between Nat and his inauspicious winged namesake.

'So,' I said, 'if not panelbeating, what is your dream career?' That's what the young talk about now. Careers, not jobs. There has to be not just income and toil (preferably no toil at all), but fulfilment. No wonder they are so miserable. Their expectations are so unrealistic.

'I don't know about *career*,' he said, leaning his head back so his hair dangled almost to his elbows. Then he looked up suddenly. I thought something had just flown in and landed on the wall behind me, an exotic dragonfly or an alien. But he was looking at *me*, his eyes penetrating my own beaver dam, my shroud of wisdom and complacence. It was unnerving. I've been working on that armour for years.

'I don't know about *career*,' he said again. 'But I know what I want to be doing. I want to be making a film, Gr ... er ... Lily. I want to make a short film.'

In my day, is the kind of phrase which springs to mind when someone not even past their teens is grappling with the complexities of life that I laid to rest decades ago. But too many old men have said it already, to the point where the young are parodying them. *In my day, son,* coming from the mouths of babes on television advertisements. *We didn't have ...*

Nat needed more from me than confirmation that there is a generation gap. Or in our case, a gap of generations. 'A film?' I said. 'I don't believe I've ever seen a short film.'

'It's a snippet,' he said, eyes growing passionate. 'A glimpse. A vignette. You've read short stories, Gr ... Lily. It's a short story compared to a novel.'

'And what's the purpose of a short film?' The red and green fabrics in my hand battled for supremacy, so similar in tone that the eye can't be sure which advances and which recedes.

'It's art,' he said, as though it was the simplest and most natural conclusion in the world. 'Think of it as a moving painting. A poem. A fairy tale. All rolled into one.'

I gazed at the da Vinci cartoon above the fireplace and tried to imagine movement, speech. A madonna study, her skin translucent gold, her lips barely sketched. 'I think my taste in art goes back too far to imagine it as video footage.' The Renaissance is my period, because of all those weekends with Dad, wandering through London's National Gallery. While other children went fishing or made trolleys out of old crates, I was learning about Raphael, Tintoretto, Dürer. Saturday morning could never come quickly enough for him, or for me, and we scuttled out the door and down the steps to the Underground. I was a form of tax, Ma's insurance policy. Why should he follow his own desires when Ma had the house to scrub? At least he should be burdened by an over-inquisitive child. And just in case he had any thoughts of visiting a private address instead of a gallery, I would prove a dampener to the libido of any lonely widow.

I smiled at this. His course never wavered. He would drag me through the gallery door and the hushed rooms, choose a work, park himself before it, and scratch away feverishly with a pencil or stick of charcoal until he had replicated it. *What will it be today, m'darling?* he would ask me. *Rembrandt? Giacometti?* And he would bend his head over his work.

It's not a da Vinci cartoon above the fireplace at all, but a Bill Symes original copy. My walls are smothered in them. Each birthday I had another framed. Then I wrapped it and wrote on the card. *Love from*

Eddie. At least there is no need to constantly redecorate, when the wallpaper is barely visible.

I've only now recognised the tragedy of it, that Dad should be so passionate about something so out of his league.

'I don't mean it in a literal sense,' Nat said, creating a sudden and frightening parallel. He was still staring intently, still poised as though to strike at any moment, but instead of prey, it was my interest he hoped to capture. 'Not art in a two-dimensional sense, but three-dimensional, four-dimensional.'

Eloquent, for a panelbeater, you might think. But Nat is no ordinary panelbeater. No ordinary high school failure either. He has a brain inside his head, and book learning that would have surprised his teachers if they'd suspected its existence. But Nat has only ever been able to apply himself to that which fascinates him. And that which fascinates him has hardly ever coincided with the curriculum as laid down by the Ministry of Education.

'Yes, four-dimensional. I like that.'

I looked away, intimidated, back through my plastic half-moons. It's all very well for the young to have dreams. The future yawns ahead, a bolt of silk which has never had the scissors to it. I've cut so much from my own, it's little more than a cobweb, barely holding together. It will never be whole again. The original pattern is no longer discernible. But the design of the quilt is coming together.

The image in the mirror doesn't interest me either, and I don't know about you, Iris, but I avoid it while I undress for my bath. Last night I lay back, surveying my flesh, wrinkled and dimpled and magnified by the water. Far off my pallid toes with their square cut nails (Maree, my home carer) pressed against the end of the bath, old ladies' toes, hooked and heavy-knuckled and pointing the wrong directions. How can they be my feet, so ghastly and gnarled, so misshapen and undeniably old? I was so proud of them once, shapely dancing feet which hardly made contact with the ground, strapped into glamorous high-heels, tapping and skipping and jiving. I was vain, unpalatably so, especially about my ankles.

There's nought worse, Dad said as his charcoal scraped the page and a pair of legs began to form, *than a dame with fat ankles*. I came to think of it as the ultimate sin, and judged Ma's overcoated and bescarfed friends who entered the house by the state of their ankles. It seems pathetic now, but it took me years to stop despising some of them.

Now all that remains of my own is an expanse of flabby, swollen flesh between my feet and my calves, and my knees are no more than padded hinges, otherwise invisible. I can hardly bear to remember how I used to draw seams up the back, in the days when there were no stockings. Unwavering lines in eyebrow pencil, before the Americans came to London. I loved the feel of my hem against my skin as I danced. How I could dance, Iris.

Now they're stumps, kauri stumps the young boys here would call them, though they don't bother to call me names now. Because I'm eighty-three when I'm in public, which means I don't exist.

From the bath I watched the steam rising towards the old board-and-batten ceiling, misting the curving chrome rail with its plastic shower curtain rings gathered at one end, depositing minuscule dew drops on the webs of the daddy-long-legs, gone on Wednesdays after Maree has been, back again by Saturday nights. I dream sometimes of a silent procession, like ants, or the crayfish I saw one night on a documentary, from the vacuum cleaner pipe tucked away in the hall cupboard, back into the bathroom and up the wall to their same corners.

By an effort of contortion I turned on the hot tap with one bubble-encrusted foot, knowing there wouldn't be many more baths. Once the equinox blows through, rainfall is unreliable. There is either too much or not enough. One day the garden is a soggy mess, the next rock hard, and it stays that way until autumn. The flag on the tank descends by the day. At half-mast even showers must be rationed.

I sank down with my ears under the water, listening to Nat's movements around the house. Tossing a log into the fire and winding the useless vent. Creeping to the kitchen – was he hungry, the poor boy? Back to the lounge, careful steps across the creaking rimu flooring, as though apologetic.

Finally, the water hardly above blood warmth, I hauled myself out, tidal waves threatening to spill over the lip of the old bath and puddle on the cracked lino. I got ready for bed, catching sight, by accident, of my image in the misted mirror. It's always a shock to see a geriatric staring out, a stranger.

The ornate and intricate feats of engineering I remove from my mouth each night are reminder enough. Suspension bridges with flying buttresses to impress any architect. They grinned out at me from their pink effervescent glass, gappy and insincere.

'Goodnight,' Nat called on his way past the bathroom door as I folded my dressing gown across my chest.

'I won't be a minute if you want to do your teeth.' The sight of my own would terrify him, so I hid the glass in the overhead cupboard.

'It's okay,' he said.

Hot and cold running water, glassed-in shower cubicles and fluffy towels warmed by heated towel rails. And still the young don't wash. Is it too much trouble? 'What do you mean, it's okay?' I swung back the door to confront him, remembering too late – the teeth. I'd protected his sensibilities by hiding them from sight, but had forgotten the spaces they formerly filled, my half-empty mouth and the adjustments my face had made to compensate. He was scared speechless, and I was forced to choose between scuttling away in embarrassment, or braving it out.

'You're not to go to bed without washing,' I said, ignoring his horrified stare. (There was never really any choice.) 'Not in this house, anyway. What are you staring at? Haven't you see a witch before?'

He laughed then. And I laughed. We were suddenly helpless in the hallway, plastering ourselves against the walls, gripping our bellies.

'Jesus,' he said, recovering. 'You're scary.'

I made to slap him across the head. He ducked.

'Goodnight, Gr ... Gran.'

'I hope you wake up with better manners.'

He went to reply but thought better of it. Perhaps he was learning after all.

Good night, my love.
Lily

[Four]

30 September

Dear Iris

Having Nat around has reminded me how I used to dream of grandchildren in the days after Hugo left home. The house was so quiet, and waking in the mornings was like being immersed in a cold ocean. Every day I remembered again that he was gone.

This will make you laugh, Iris, but I milked cows for twenty years. Can you imagine it? Coaxing the essence out of a hundred and forty-five temperamental dames, and all before breakfast. I came back to the house while Eddie finished off, to get breakfast and to get Hugo off to school. I milked cows for twenty years so Hugo wouldn't have to. And once he was gone, it was over. I had put on my last set of cups. Eddie moaned and grizzled and said he'd have to get a boy, and I said he'd have to sell some of the cows. He took his little thundercloud to the cowshed and I lay in bed wishing that Hugo was still asleep through the wall, wishing that I still had a reason to get up and milk, so that I didn't have to be lying in bed wishing away my life.

And then I thought of grandchildren, a clutch of them. (What is the collective noun for grandchildren?) I imagined them growing into – and out of – each other's cast-offs, miniature Hugos, with his Splendour-apple cheeks, his wide-set blue eyes. And perched on gaudy plastic ride-on bikes, tumbling over each other, fat-bottomed from layers of nappies. Babies crying in a chorus, scrambling, grubby-faced, runny-nosed, onto my lap for cuddles or stories. Falling asleep on my armchairs, sucking fingers, eyelashes laid like hand-made lace on cheeks while all around them the room settled back into place, the dust motes tornado-ing upwards in the whisper of still turbulent air, a fanlight of sunshine creeping, sundial-slow, across the ancient floral carpet while the babies slept, and I watched the precious rise and fall of their chests, desperate for them to wake again.

An extravagant image, and one I've had to abandon.

Nat, arriving so late, forged no such fat nappy-bottomed memories. No joyous tumbling, or first words uttered for me alone. Even so, living with him has been more harmonious than I anticipated. So far. He is endearingly thoughtful, sleeping till almost eleven every morning, to allow me to complete my morning tasks without interruption. He showers – yes, he does wash, all his ablutions in one sitting – until I'm forced to check the flag on the tank from the kitchen window, and then he demolishes great slabs of toast for breakfast while I eat a sandwich for lunch.

'What's he after?' Fred asked me yesterday as we drank tea on the back verandah, watching Nat chop firewood down by the shed.

'What do you mean, what's he after? He's not after anything.'

'An inheritance?'

I almost choked on my tea. 'An inheritance? Where's he going to get that from? Is there some hidden fortune I don't know about?'

'You might have something stashed away.'

'I don't, as it happens. But if I did, it'd be none of your bloody business.'

Fred's face creased into corrugations, and his eyes disappeared. How many times over the years have I seen that smile? Yet I still wondered at how few teeth he managed to display. Just a hint of worn plastic ivory – his top lip, even when stretched tight, still concealing all but the edge of some long-dead dentist's handiwork. 'Methinks the lady doth protest too much,' he said, still laughing.

'Of course I'm bloody protesting. You'll be spreading rumours next that I've got a nest-egg. There's only just enough to get by on. When that blasted rates bill comes I do some serious thinking about this place. Whether it's worth staying on.'

'Where would you go, eh?' Fred scratched behind one ear, never fazed by my threats of leaving. His thin hair was Brylcreemed into place, still displaying the tracks left by the teeth of his comb. I imagined his pillowcase, stained yellow where he lay his head. 'Where could you go that's half as good as this? Eh?'

'Nowhere much, that I can think of. Not those retirement villages, that's for sure. Might as well shoot me first.'

Fred laughed. He took a gulp of tea. 'Bloody oath. Me too.'

'Sometimes I think I might like to go back home to England. Just once.'

He laughed again, a slow, even, expellation. A Frank Bruno laugh. *He, he, he.* 'You and your bloody dreams.'

'I could,' I said, indignant. 'If I sold up this place. It'd be nice to see it all again. The house. Number Thirty-two. Wonder who lives there now. And The Black Bull, our local. The Angel. How many times have I been up and down those stairs, eh, Fred?'

'They have escalators now,' he said. 'Escalators a mile high. One look and you'd get bloody vertigo. You'd have to go and lie down.'

'Get on with you,' I said. England seemed so close, as it always is when I remember, just a hair's breadth away, as though I could step through some invisible barrier and be there. Like youth, and memory, the boundaries seem almost tangible.

'It wouldn't be the same,' Fred said, wistful, remembering too the old haunts. Our lives, even after all this time, are like layers of sheer fabric in two different colours, creating a third where they overlap. Our old stomping ground. It has kept us together all these years, friends separated by a boundary fence. The shared knowledge of what things were like, once. The war. The high times in London, trying to forget, even for a moment, what was happening all around us. 'You'd be disappointed,' he said. 'You'd go all that way, spend all that money, and it wouldn't be the same as you remember it.'

Nat swung the axe. The tea in my mug was gone. 'I know that. I'm not completely daft. But a girl's allowed to dream.'

Fred laughed at that. *He, he, he.* Laughter comes so easily to him, even after everything. 'That boy'll have his foot off in a minute,' he said.

'Don't tell me that. I worry enough as it is. Besides, he's learning. And look at me. I've still got all my extremities, and how many years have I been chopping wood now?'

'Too bloody many.'

'Too bloody many, all right. But no one could've known less about chopping wood than me when I first arrived.'

'You're right there,' Fred teased.

I swiped at him with an ineffectual hand. 'Oh, go on.'

'The Queen.'

'Eh?'

'The Queen. Bet she's never held an axe in her life.'

Ah, the Queen. What was it Ma used to say? *There but for the grace of God ... I could've been her, and she, me, if only we'd been born inside different skin.*

'I bet she hasn't,' I said. 'But neither would I, if I'd had anyone else to do it. So you just leave my boy there alone. He's all right, is my Nat.'

We ate corned beef for dinner, slow-cooked for four hours with garlic and brown sugar and peppercorns. Potatoes done with butter in the microwave. Carrots, freshly dug. Scarlet runners, blanched and frozen at the height of summer. Afterwards I stitched and Nat poked the fire. We watched a documentary about the waterfront strike of fifty-one.

'Where were you,' Nat asked during the ads, 'when all that was happening?'

There it was again, the invisible line, the sidestep into another time, as though it existed on a parallel plane just waiting to be summoned. Nineteen-fifty-one. You remember it, don't you, Iris?

'On the other side of the world,' I said. 'I'd never been to New Zealand then. I thought it was a little island off the coast of Australia, and everyone lived in grass huts.'

Nat's brows rocketed upwards. 'Then what made you come here?'

'Ah, now.' The tip of my needle descended into the fabric, and re-emerged with perfect spacing. 'That's a long, long, story. And one I'm sure you can't be bothered with.' The sweet thing. He moved on straight away.

'Were you a war bride?'

I laughed. 'Hardly, since your grandfather was as English as I am. But I suppose you could say *he* was a war bride, in a way.'

Let me tell you, Iris, about my quilt. It is constructed of blocks. The first, for the lower right hand corner, has a row of houses. Not the traditional house motif of folk quilts, but London houses, Islington houses, Victorian terraces four storeys high. The central house in the row of three has a red door with the number thirty-two embroidered, as though printed on a ceramic medallion. Thirty-two Barnsley Street. I've read recently that the fossils of crocodiles have been dug from the mud beneath Islington, hinting at a tropical prehistoric connection. In all my childhood back garden digs, I never found anything vaguely resembling a fossil, but there were coins, a stirrup once, shards of broken china discarded over the century into the pit at the back of the garden.

I used to watch squirrels from my bedroom window, skittering along the branches of the oaks on the back boundary. You remember the garden, hardly wide enough to lie across, and terraced into three levels. And from my window I watched Dad install the Anderson shelter, his precious artist's hands blistered and splintered by the coarse wooden shovel handle. I watched as he mounded dirt over its roof, and planted lettuces and cabbages. Its door was like an open mouth, a shadowy orifice, mocking me as I tried to pretend there wasn't a war. And every time it rained it filled with water.

Once it was in, squirrels would dart down onto the mound amongst the brassicas, tumbling like acrobats while Dad threw stones and I stared into the mirror. It was my friend then, reflecting that gorgeous girl my grandchildren can't begin to imagine. The dark curls, the high round forehead, the sensuous lips.

Of course I didn't recognise my own beauty. Instead I agonised about that small mole on my cheek, a pimple which might have erupted overnight; the way, when I smiled, wrinkles appeared underneath my eyes.

That's all I can think of for now, Iris. Thinking of home fills me with frustration that I can't make that sideways step. It reminds me of my own mortality.

Lily

[*Five*]

4 October

Dear Iris

Believe it or not, Nat is still here. Last night he read the paper while I finished embroidering onto the dark blue rectangles of Number Thirty-two's windows, tiny white chain stitch, dividing the blank shapes into ten panes each. There was one window below the street (remember?), one beside the red front door, two above, where Ma and Dad slept, and at the top, the small gable with casements opening outwards onto the roof garden.

Every night I slept underneath Olivia's hand-stitched quilt, a simple nine-patch, which cocooned me, sending me to sleep while my fingers caressed the silks, calicos and cottons which had clothed her life. The design seemed random, apart from the yellow squares which criss-crossed the quilt from corner to corner, the two lines intersecting across my body, keeping me safe as I slept.

'Your grandmother died making that quilt,' Ma used to say when my bedmaking was less than perfect. And it was true. To a point. Ma had finished off the last few squares, and backed it with a coarse blanket. At night my fingers found and explored the ungainly stitches, so at odds with Olivia's immaculate needlework, the love and care stitched into each seam. Ma's stitches told of nothing more than a desire to be done with it.

'What are those bits you're doing there, Gran?' Nat asked as I worked on my own quilt, giving me such a fright I stabbed myself.

'It's a pohutukawa.' I held the two spears of colour flat where they joined, showing how they would lie side by side.

'Christ ...' he said. '... ipes. Cripes. Shouldn't they be, well, hexagons, or something? Diamonds? I know. Triangles. Shouldn't they be bloody tesselations of some sort? How the hell will you get them to fit? They're all skew wiff.'

'What are you saying?'

'Skew wiff, you know ...' He bit on the end of a pencil he'd been using to complete a crossword. (*What's another word for damson, Gran? Or piety, or intermittent.*) 'Random,' he said.

I told him it wasn't a traditional quilt, appraising the red and green, enjoying the juxtaposition. 'The pohutukawa, at Christmas. It's not exactly a traditional image for a quilt, so it needs to be shown in a contemporary way. It's going to sprawl across the top of the quilt, like an embrace, holding everything together.'

'Okay, I get the colour thing, now that you've told me what it's supposed to be. But how are you going to get the pieces to fit together?'

I demonstrated the *sew and fold* technique, and how each seemingly random piece joined to make up a parallelogram, and how the parallelograms fitted together to complete the top quarter of the quilt.

'Shit,' he said. Strange how the young show admiration. 'It's bloody maths. I was never very good at maths.'

I laughed and stitched on, more comfortable with the thought of him staying since the money had arrived from Hugo in the morning post, a cheque which seemed overly endowed with obese zeroes. (Hugo's script has always resembled Hugo himself.) Two thousand dollars. Nat drove us to town in my car, an experience that terrified me. Without the security of the steering wheel to cling to I even grabbed the handbrake at one stage, which almost finished us.

'Shit, Gran,' Nat howled, pulling over and bounding from the car. 'You frightened the fucking life out of me. Charriisst!'

Not to be outdone, I leapt out too. 'You're not alone there, boy. Who taught you to drive? Michael bloody Schumacher? You're a bloody menace! How did you keep your own car in one piece for so long? The way you drive, it's a wonder you didn't write it off the day you got it!'

'Christ,' he said again, still recovering, tugging his hair back behind his ears, gripping it into a slick pony tail, then releasing it. 'We nearly went into that bloody ditch. Handbrake slides are a good way to lose control on loose metal. You should know that by your age.'

'I'll tell you what I should know. I should know bloody better than to let my grandson drive me anywhere.'

'Gran,' he said, suddenly pleading. 'Please, Gran. Please, Lily. I'll slow down, I promise.'

I walked around the car and opened the driver's door.

'Come on, Gran. Come on, Lily. You can't ...'

'Oh yes, I bloody can. Now, are you coming or are you bloody walking?' I arranged myself behind the steering wheel and started up the engine. Nat, posturing in the middle of the metal road, thought I'd change my mind. I closed my door, adjusted the rear-view mirror, started the engine, and engaged first gear.

'Okay, okay.' He ran across in front of the bonnet and leapt into the passenger seat, scowling. 'At least put your seat belt on,' he said, gazing intently ahead as though he could hardly bear to look at me. Which caused my clutch-foot to slip, and the front wheels to spray metal onto the underside of the car in an inverted hailstorm as they slid sideways in the loose drift on the side of the road.

The journey home was just as bad. 'I don't think he meant you to spend it all on something like that,' I said, glancing across at the silver box cradled in Nat's palm. 'I think it was meant for living expenses. You know. Food and stuff. So *I* don't need to be out of pocket.'

He rolled three twenty-dollar notes into a tube and inserted them into the empty ashtray as I drove.

'The amount you eat, that won't last long.'

'There's more where it came from. Don't worry. I didn't spend quite all of it.' He squinted into the eye-piece, panning from the left of the windscreen to the right. 'He's a soft touch,' he said. 'Always has been. If I spend it all in a week, he'll send more. It's guilt. Buying me off, so he doesn't actually have to spend time with me.'

'And what would you know about guilt? In order to feel guilt, you need to have a conscience. And to have a conscience, you need to have some inkling of what things might be like for others.'

'You sound just like Mum.'

This shocked me, having no desire to emulate – or even be compared to – Jeannette. Nat is so phlegmatic that I find it too easy to grow harsh with him. His placidity breeds a desire to elicit some response. Rudeness bounces off him. Insults veer off course and strike somewhere above or behind him, striking an innocent tree or rose bush or fence post. His comment caused me to slide a degree closer to understanding him. His sullenness. His lack of belief in himself. His willingness to concede defeat in arguments, to admit to his own ignorance. Jeannette, like me, has been unable to resist wounding him, though her hurt has been inflicted over his entire lifetime, mine over only a matter of weeks. Less. I would never have treated Hugo with such scorn. I was the opposite with him, fussing around, offering protection from imagined dangers; liaising between Hugo and his father, Hugo and his teacher, Hugo and the child down the road who had shown reluctance to attend Hugo's birthday party or committed some similar slight.

Looking back now I can see I was not a good mother. My efforts to compensate for the harm Ma had inflicted with her sharp tongue, her hammered-in nail shortening of my name, her *Your grandmother died making that quilt* left me as ineffectual as she had been. Despite my good intentions, I did nothing to redress the balance. The seesaw swung too far the other way. Hugo grew up irresponsible, self-centred, anti-social, careless of the love behind the over-nurturing. He resents me, but that's all right, because I resent him back.

'Nine hundred and ninety-bloody-nine dollars,' Nat said, spying me through the lens as I drove. 'Six free tapes. That's eighteen hours of footage, Gran-Lily. And if I can't get a short film from eighteen hours of footage, then there's something bloody wrong. And if that's the case, I don't need to despair. I'll just tape over the top of the whole lot. I'll just start again.'

Later, in front of the fire, while my hands flew back and forth with needle and thread, I watched Nat, sprawled across the rug at my feet, reading books about film-making. He had a vulnerability as *Coronation Street* warbled from the television screen, which made me want to gather him up, to cradle his head in my lap, stroking the hair back from his forehead, tucking it behind his small ears. Hugo's ears. The rest of Hugo was out of proportion; his feet, his towering shoulders, his girth. But I was always fiercely proud of his tiny tucked-back ears. In the era of school-boy short-back-and-sides, school photographs displayed ears at alarming jug-handle angles, ears which, if flapped, could have lifted entire football teams off the ground, ears which could have been used to open Camden Lock. There, amongst those aurally over-developed boys, was Hugo, with his gaping shirt front, his round cheeks and double-chin. But his ears were perfect, hardly visible to that all-seeing camera lens.

Nat filmed the flames, zooming in and out at the touch of a button. He filmed Bill Symes's immaculate copies of masterpieces, and my hands as they worked with the red and green cloth. As if anyone would want to watch such things on a screen. What do you think, Iris? The high points of my life depicted. Enough to put the world to sleep.

Lily

[Six]

Floss

Shopping, Floss writes with an old fountain pen, its nib scratching a blue-black scar onto the page. *Two pounds of carrots and some greens. Brussels sprouts have come down. Twenty-four-and-a-half weeks to go.*

She pauses to stare from the window. Her words don't come near to describing the bleakness of the day. Brussels sprouts may have come down, but that's only to be expected as the season progresses. Brussels sprouts, for all their price fluctuations, have nothing to do with her despair. They are symbols, that's all, part of her code. She will only have to glance at those words on any long gloomy day in her future of long gloomy days, to recreate today in every detail: the lift broken, as usual, the stiff cold wind and dripping nose, the hole in the sole of her shoe, letting in water, the climb, laden with her purchases, up five flights. Today, in all its aspects, is inherent in a single sentence. *Brussels sprouts have come down.*

From the window she sees the walls of the neighbouring estate illuminated, alive, coruscating with sunlight, while her own windows are in shadow. She has never been able to decide which is best. Cheerful, watery, apologetic morning sunshine, or the brazen distracting glare of the afternoon variety. She ponders momentarily, as she has so many times in her life, knowing all the while that the answer is simple. A house with four walls and four corners. A north wall, a south wall, an east wall and a west wall. Her life could be divided into quarters. Morning dishes washed while gazing out into a sun-drenched garden. Lunches eaten in a cosy south-facing windowseat. Letters written in the afternoons as the sun begins to dip. And evenings spent tugging at weeds, the cottage and its garden rendered gold in the sunset.

She wipes the corners of her eyes with a lace-edged handkerchief, transparent from years of laundering. Her eyes, always watering, bidden, unbidden. Crying the tears of disenchantment, exhaustion, age.

The issue of the sun, she tells herself, is immaterial. It doesn't shine enough anywhere in England for her dream to come true. The reality would be a weak beam of sunlight while she washed breakfast dishes, and rain by half-past ten. Or worse. Sleet. Snow. And the countryside is no haven for lonely old women. The air alone could kill her, even without the factory chimneys, the nuclear spillage, the foot-and-mouth pyres. At least the city makes no attempt to disguise its diseased environs. The countryside puts on a green face, a rolling hills, see-a-hundred-miles, face. Chocolatey ploughed fields, verdant pasture, the shimmering gold of acres of rape.

Acres of rape. She laughs. As if it can be measured like that.

The countryside. Quaint cottages with diamond leadlight, drawing from a water table infected with bacteria from the excrement of farm animals, or from rain-water tanks tainted by sea birds blown off course, pausing to rest on roof tiles, shitting poison before they leave. And the air. She's heard on the radio that some bacteria can live in the nostrils for up to a week. Imagine that. Nostrils teaming with micro-organisms. Every one of her lace-edged handkerchiefs, embroidered on the corners in her youth, could be contaminated. She might wipe her eye, then hold little Daniel's hand. He might suck his fingers and hold his marmite sandwich, leaving the crusts for Julie to finish off. And Julie might blow her nose and the tissue might fall out of her bag while she looks for her keys, and blow away down to the street, into the window of a car with three children strapped in the back, and one might give it to the baby to shut him up, who would put it straight into his mouth, and here we go again.

But infection aside. Four-walled houses aside. And England's temperamental sun too. What her longing is really about is choice. Having the choice whether or not to sit at a sunny window, instead of the choice being made for her. An east-facing building or a west-facing building. Even then, it wasn't a choice. It was, *This flat's empty. Number 537. Take it or leave it.* That was the choice. A home. Or no home.

A loud knock on the door makes her jump. 'It's Julie,' calls a voice. For a moment Floss is confused, guilt-ridden that she could have been so careless as to strike Julie down, and little Daniel too, with some indeterminate disease while they put on coats and hats and boots in preparation for braving the elements.

'Are you there?' Julie calls.

Floss parcels up her imaginings. There always were too many. *You're in a dream,* her mother always said. So long ago. Not kindly, either.

'Just coming.'

'Anythink you need?' Julie asks as the door swings back, inviting in the cold. 'Only I'm going down the market.'

It takes Floss a moment to remember that she has been already. So often it happens like this. She could have saved herself the trouble if only she'd waited. But just once or twice she has waited on the off chance, and no one has come near her for days.

Julie waits, the only sign of her attempt at patience a booted toe rubbing against the concrete. Her ears are pierced. Her nose is pierced. Her eyebrow and her lip and even, she once showed Floss, her tongue. Her navel is pierced, and she has hinted that her nipples are pierced too. Floss found her terrifying to begin with. The black under her eyes. The coloured nails like claws. The clothes all strung with chains, layers of silk and lace and stretchy man-made things. The hobnailed boots. The tattoos. But then Floss saw Daniel in his snowsuit, a sleeping face amidst the fur-trim, and soon afterwards she noticed Julie's gentleness with him: the sweet, kind, loving side Julie was so reluctant to exhibit.

'I've been already,' Floss says, a sense of failure causing her voice to waver. As though she has let Julie down somehow. Shouldn't age offer more in the way of foresight? To minimise inconvenience for others? But it seems there is only hindsight. Hindsight with bells on. Hindsight until madness threatens. 'I'm sorry,' she says.

Julie chews her gum, her expression stoic, unchanging. 'Shouldn'a,' she says. 'In't I told you? The lift stuffed, 'n'all.' She swivels Daniel's pram around while his little hand waves bye-bye, and Floss is left standing in the door-frame with her too-brilliant smile and her knees going weak from the effort of pretending it doesn't matter, and the knowledge of all the lies she has spun Julie in order to appear in control of her own life.

She wants to take it all back. She wants to say, 'Once there was a little boy ...' And then perhaps Julie would understand everything.

But she closes the door, locks it and bolts it, and threads the safety chain into its slot. She comes back into the room, lit vicariously by the reflection from the windows of the building across the street.

[Seven]

10 October

Dear Iris

I'm writing this on my verandah. My view takes in three muddy paddocks, the curve of road as it heads down the hill and, beyond, swathes of diminishing hills stretching away to the sea. Sitting here in the afternoons, looking across the collage of hills and valleys at the line of the horizon, gave me the idea for my first pictorial quilt. Do you know what that is, Iris? Quilting-as-art, rather than quilting-as-craft. A picture you can recognise, rather than traditional motifs. Three fluffy black steers grazed in the foreground, with an embroidered barbed-wire fence, and rough totara posts carved from watermarked taffetta. I used silk in six shades of green for the hills, layering them one on the other and hand-quilting them with a multitude of curving lines like the contours of a map, curls and spirals, representing the ferns unfurling in the bush. The sea was brilliant white, a single stripe of satin, and the sky made from every fragment of pale blue I could find – poplin, cotton, satin, floral or plain. It was my first exhibited quilt and it sold within an hour of the opening of the Masonic Hall doors. It broke my heart, Iris. All that work. They say love is stitched into a quilt, and I think it's true. I'd lain awake so many nights, buzzing with excitement, my mind crowding with images. I gave in sometimes, got up, impatient for daylight, and worked for hours, not even noticing the sun coming up, the roosters outside the window duelling to outcrow each other.

But I don't miss the quilt as much as I thought I would, just as I don't miss others I've sold since. I have the real view, the original, to imbibe whenever I feel the need, and the image of the quilt is superimposed onto the landscape, with its textures and haphazard framework. I can almost touch it.

If I sewed it now there'd be a boy in it, chasing the steers into the bottom paddock. There are eight, as many as the land can maintain. I don't have the money for expensive top-dressing treatments, and I'm not up to spreading fertiliser by hand. Paddy, the old dog, is trotting at Nat's heels, willing but unable. He is in retirement, and about as much use to Nat as a poodle. Like me, he's ancient, moribund, waiting out his days, sunning himself whenever possible, dreaming of past pursuits.

In one hand Nat brandishes a stick, while his other arm waves madly at the churlish group as they approach the open gate. Bovines are not as stupid as many believe. They have a sense of humour, at least, and sufficient intelligence to deduce what it is a human wants them to do. They are mischievous, and enjoy making a simple task as difficult as possible.

Heads down, they eye Nat as he approaches, sinking into the mud by the gate. He thinks he has them, but one cuts free, galloping up the fenceline, kicking up its heels in delight. Nat turns, swearing, seeking support from Paddy. But Paddy is occupied with a difficult bowel movement which refuses to dislodge itself. He squats stiffly, shuffling his hind legs as though it will help, thrusting his tail up and down like a pump handle. Then his mission switches to visual intervention. If he could just see what was happening, he might be able to remedy the problem. But his eyes are milky with cataracts, and his spine seized with age and arthritis. He only manages to circle pointlessly, probably forgetting in the process why he started.

Nat cuts the renegade steer off further up the paddock, but the others are jumpy now and skittish, stamping hooves and dropping their heads to study him from beneath their lashes. They're in the mood for a game. Nat, by the language drifting up the hillside, is not.

Three times now he's had them within a few feet of the gate, and three times they dashed off at the last minute. I am trying not to laugh out loud. It's usually me there in the mud while it tugs and farts, trying to swallow my boots. And every time the steers tear past, another shower of filth hits like hailstones – another cardigan, another frock, destined for the laundry pile.

Nat is half-wild, screaming and waving his arms, darting about like the male lead in the Bolshoi ballet. Plié, leap, pirouette, pas de chat. A tangle of harsh masculine consonants whirlwind towards me.

Paddy's blockage has been cleared and he's investigating a rancid object. He is not as agile as he once was and ends up cast like a ewe, all four white limbs pointing skyward for a full minute.

On the fourth attempt the steers trot through the gate, as though bred for it. The grass in the bottom paddock is long and juicy, and within moments they've forgotten the excitement, the miles they have covered. Nat latches the gate and turns homeward, struggling up the hill, gasping for air, his cheeks blazing red.

Later: I had to stop, or he would have noticed I was writing about him. It's one thing for him to film my every movement, but he wouldn't like to think I was recording his unfortunate moments.

'Bastards,' he said when he climbed the verandah steps.

'I think you did really well, for a city boy. Come and have a drink, and a chocolate biscuit or two.'

'Only two? I think I deserve at least half a dozen.'

'Go on then.'

'Who did this before I came, Gran? Tell me it wasn't you.'

'Who else is there?' Sometimes it went smoothly, sometimes not. I've learned some things over the years. If they don't go through on the first attempt I abandon the mission until the next day. Or leave the gate open for them to find their own way through. Sometimes Fred helps, or Maree, the home carer, who's supposed to attend solely to domestic cleaning and matters of personal hygiene. The bathroom, the vacuuming, the oven, the windows. The toenails. Sometimes I drag her out in the pouring rain or in the heat of summer.

'Stand there with your arms wide.'

'What if they come at me?'

'Jump up and down. Shout. Wave your arms.'

Blanched to paper whiteness, Maree prepares. 'Shouldn't I have a stick?'

'If you can find one.'

Fred tells me I have a morbid sense of humour, but I play the innocent. After it was over I always gave Maree tea and biscuits, and she wrote in the little home care diary. *Washed sheets. Scrubbed kitchen floor.*

'Shit,' Nat said. Admiration again.

'It's not an everyday job, Nat. Only when the paddock they're in needs a rest. When there's more grass to be had elsewhere.'

Paddy struggled up the verandah steps and collapsed, panting, in a square of sunshine. Within half a minute he was asleep.

'You've worn him out, poor old soldier.'

'Fat lot of use he was. But he's not the only one who's worn out.' Nat helped himself to more lemonade, more biscuits.

'It was fun watching. I couldn't help thinking, well ... It would have made a good short film.' My laughter was too sharp, and too loud, but it gushed out like spring water, too plentiful and impetuous to control. Nat was not amused.

Roasted marinated chicken with a full complement of roast vegetables: potatoes, kumara, pumpkin, yams. Broccoli too, and beans. Peach cobbler for dessert, with custard, the peaches bottled last summer. Golden Queens from the orchard, peeled in the cool of evening, blanched around midnight in a pot of syrup, and crammed into the jars, the syrup avalanching down the sides as the lid went on.

Afterwards Nat was fat and useless and I massaged cream into my hands before taking up my needle. Sewn into the narrow black strips which will join the blocks of my quilt, next to the houses, is a meandering track of red which splits, then rejoins to create a tiny black enclosure. Inside are three small white ovals and a curled pink shape, like a fish or a lizard, with barely formed fingers and toes. The red trail will descend to the lower edge of the quilt, widening as it goes, white eggs falling too, out of the tube and away into infinity. The block beside the fish-lizard is an explosion of hot colour, orange, yellow, brown, pink, black, vermillion – all cut into diamonds as sharp as javelins, radiating from a chaotic centrepiece of white – its jagged, random heart.

Take it to mean what you will, Iris. For me it is the gaping chasm of war, reaching towards those quaint Islington row houses, and on the other side towards the trunk of a beach-side pohutukawa.

Lily

[Eight]

15 October

Dear Iris

My friend Marjorie is the sort of woman who cleans under the fridge and could slap up a dinner for twenty-one at a moment's notice. Her kitchen benches are polished wood, so glossy they can be used as mirrors, and cause anyone nearby to grow self-conscious about what might be found in their noses, as they sniff deliriously at the vanilla-scented air or lift the corners of tea towels to glimpse the home-baking cooling underneath.

Marjorie has a shelf instead of breasts, and skin immaculately powdered right down to the base of her neck. Her hair and nails are cared for by others, and her fingers have more sparkle than effervescent vitamin B. Her husband, Jim, has adored her since school days and gives her a new ring every year on their anniversary. He would never dare not to. She is a terrifying woman, so capable that she induces clumsiness in everyone within a radius of ten feet. Her house is a hundred years old, though the piles would never dare to sink, or the roof to leak. Her garden path is straight and bordered on either side with box and French lavender. She may not even need to clip the box. One look might be enough to cause new growth to conform with the sharp edges and flat sides she desires.

On alternate Wednesdays Marjorie invites the Hill Quilting Society into her home, where we stitch for two hours in her front room, drink tea, and discuss life. I am the society's token octogenarian, admired simply because I am not yet dead, when so many my age are. Or they would be my age if they weren't dead. It's a dubious honour, and it is too complex to explain that I feel the same inside as I did at fifty. Forty. My mind is the same, and my heart ... perhaps a little tougher. Perhaps not. I have such perspective on life that I can see two sides to everything. Perhaps that makes me not tougher but more vulnerable.

Suzanne is our youngest, at thirty, and her two hours per fortnight at the society are the only two away from her pre-schooler and younger twins. She quilts in symmetrical designs, in pastel florals, the most traditional of all of us, yet one of my favourites. Serena works with hessian, canvas and string, and Bernie appliqués complex serpentine vines and huge cupped flowers. Jane, a beginner, is working on a simple nine-patch, and Barbara, a purple wall-hanging in crushed velvet and satin, with sequins and swansdown and embroidered words. Marjorie is creating a quilt for an as yet unconceived grandchild. Red with rows of houses, sailing ships, trains, and farm animals.

'I live in hope,' she says, with two daughters living in London, each intent on a career in the world of finance. 'No time for babies at present,' she says. 'But perhaps one day soon ...'

'No time for men either,' says Barbara, 'by the sound of it.'

Marjorie's third daughter, Waverley, the surprise, came along when the others were in their teens. She is in her last year of school and is plain and dull, with homework spread across the dining table every time we arrive. She has no interest in us, and hardly looks up if we call hello on our way down the hall.

Last night Nat insisted on coming, sitting through the wall in the kitchen, inflicted with Waverley's company because he said he was frightened by the handbrake incident, and is convinced that I am a menace on the roads. His own driving has improved, at the threat of me taking the wheel. He is careful to stop at intersections now, to look both ways. And he changes gear before the gearbox is screaming. No wonder his own car developed problems. There are benefits from cautious driving.

'He'll be bored witless,' I told Marjorie, as a form of apology. It does nothing for my image to be chaperoned by an over-protective grandson. It was only after I'd spoken that I realised Marjorie might misunderstand. She is sensitive to criticisms of Waverley, and since Waverley and her homework were sharing the kitchen table with Nat and his film-making book, criticism was implied.

Marjorie swallowed air.

'I mean, not by Waverley, of course.' This made it worse, as though Marjorie hadn't previously considered this shade of meaning. 'It's just that, well, he doesn't usually go for intelligent girls.' Now I had Waverley shut in a room with a promiscuous purveyor of air-headed tarts. 'Actually, he's not interested in girls at all, really.' At least, he hadn't produced a girlfriend for my approval for years.

'You mean he's gay?' Marjorie asked, teapot in hand, paused mid-pour until the matter was cleared.

Why does age not eliminate the predisposition for causing ambiguity? I should be able to say exactly what I mean by now, but the more I said, the more obscure my meaning became. Would he have been less of a threat if he were gay? Would it be fair on him to have the entire society believing it, even if it wasn't true? 'Not gay, as such.'

'You mean bisexual?' Barbara asked as she opened her quilt.

I paused to inhale, biting back the comment that had sprung to the front of my mouth, snapping the life from its spine with my expensive and elaborate flying buttresses. This session of the Hill Quilting Society was in danger of ending before it had really begun.

'I'm his grandmother,' I said with deliberate slowness, my accent as strong again as when I first stepped off the boat. 'If he has sexual preferences other than the norm, I don't know of them, and neither do I wish to. All I meant was that I hardly need him to tag along with me, and that I hope he'll find the experience dull so that he won't bother to come again.'

'It doesn't bother us,' Suzanne said, smiling, while Marjorie's teapot tipped and spilled golden steaming liquid.

'Two sugars for me,' Serena said. 'Now, can we see what everyone's been doing since last time.'

Mine was not ready for the chaos of crimson and green that will form the crown of the pohutukawa, although fine strands on the ends of the roots will be appliquéed between the bricks of the row houses. Crochet, perhaps, worked in dull brown.

There should be a word, Iris, for the meaningless sentences at the end of letters, the excuses which break the news that the end has arrived. I read a book recently where odd place names had been adopted and given humorous meanings. So I will give the matter some thought, to make the process of signing off less painful. There isn't always a reason to leave, a pressing engagement, an appointment, a red letter box clearance. Sometimes I simply run out of words, as I have now.

Lily

[Nine]

24 October

Dear Iris

The Trip Around the World is a variation on the one-patch quilt I've told you about already. Your pieces are the same size but arranged differently. You start in the middle and work your way out, each row made up of one or two different colours. So you get a concentric design. It's simple, yet has the potential to be striking. Mine has brilliant yellow at its centre, and works its way through shades of green and blue to violet at the edges. Keep it in mind, Iris, as this is one I think you could manage.

Quilts aside, I suppose you're wondering why I have this belated urge to spill my life onto this musty old writing paper. I've been wondering too. I was poking about at the back of my wardrobe one day when I found it in a shoebox, packets and packets, all nicely wrapped in cellophane, with floral borders of every gaudy colour imaginable. And then I remembered all those years as a parent helper at school. They could hardly have functioned without me – cutting out shapes at the back of the classroom, mounting pictures, running cake stalls and raffles, cooking at school camps. And at the end of every year came the thank-yous, songs the children had practised for weeks, and hand-made cards. *Mrs Lusk, your the bigest and the BEST! Thanks for helping us. from Michael. Dear Mrs Lusk, Can my mum have the recipe for your chocolate cake? love from Shannon. Dear Mrs Lusk, Hugo is so lucky to have you at home. Jimmy Dodd.*

And with the letters a flimsy packet wrapped in hand-coloured newsprint. The same every year.

'Go on,' Eddie said the first year. 'Send her a note, at least. Let her know you're still alive.'

I tried, Iris. I sat down with a pen, so many times, but those first words just wouldn't come.

Nat is settling in. His bedroom smells like a lion's cage, and his clothes lie like dead wrestlers on the floor. He even went out the other night, waving as he opened the driver's door of my car, preparing to drive forty-five minutes into town to see a film. The Hill township once had its own cinema, a hideous pink Art Deco construction that still sports strings of coloured light bulbs – long dead – the building abandoned except for the monthly meetings of the Farm Discussion Group and the Senior Citizens' Drop-In mornings on alternate Wednesdays. Once air-conditioning and multi-screenings became commonplace, and once a new corporate-sponsored multiplex was built less than an hour down the road, our cinema suffered a fatal financial infarction. (Do you like that word, Iris? I have part ownership of that word.)

From the verandah I watched the tail-lights disappearing down the road towards town, hoping the standard of Nat's driving wouldn't deteriorate in my absence. It was barely dark. The days are lengthening and the mud is drying out in the sun, and as I stood there the breeze was a warm kiss on my skin. I sometimes think spring is my favourite season. It's a promise and, as I get older, that promise becomes more meaningful. That life will go on. Thorny skeletons of roses give life to the velvet tissue of new leaves and tight green buds promising rose petals and a scent to equal none. And here – you wouldn't believe it, Iris – jonquils and daffodils have long since exploded from within their green striated pods. Curled up and died too, most of them. Farmers don't bother waiting till spring for the lambs and calves to be born. They try to nullify winter by bringing their animals on to breed in July and August. So on the verandah I was thinking of the beginnings of spring, and the lambs were half-grown already in their paddocks. Spring unfolds by degrees in England, a gradual teasing entrance which can hide again behind a sudden veil of late snow. Here, Iris, it's over in the blink of an eye. If you sleep in one morning, you might have missed it.

I wonder if I'll see another spring. I intend to, but with so many friends under the turf now, it's harder to argue with the haphazard nature of death. How does it choose? Here am I with my fat-lady arms and legs, my carved-up heart, defying the odds, and yet Eddie is gone, who walked the length and breadth of the farm every day since we first arrived. Six hundred acres of rolling hills. That's what it was then. He would weep if he saw the five-acre blocks now, the modern stucco monstrosities erected by commuters who want a better life for their kids, but are too busy travelling to work and back again to enjoy it.

Eddie. Gone. Can you imagine it, Iris? His strong arms and the way he could haul a cow out of a bog. He was always there, in the background of my life. At least I thought he'd be. The only man I ever loved. And I did love him, Iris, whatever you might think. I did love him.

And Maisie, Fred's wife, thin as a grape pruning and hardly a day sick in her life, keeled over on the back doorstep while Fred was at the sales. He thought she'd left the laundry basket outside as he drove up in the dusk. But it was Maisie's frock, her cardigan, and inside them Maisie herself. Maisie's body, at least. No life left. Gone, just as though she'd taken off her body at the end of a long day, and discarded it until morning.

Morbid thoughts. It's all behind now. But it frightens me how vividly it can all be recalled: dashing through the hedge, down the paddock after Fred's call, the track well worn by our feet as we trekked to each other's kitchens over the years. Maisie's journey was the more difficult, up the hill, although she never complained when she arrived for a cuppa in the mornings, not even out of breath. My walk to Maisie's was always more leisurely, a couple of stops along the way to talk to the cows or take in the view. And afterwards Eddie would arrive in the ute to drive me home.

Maisie went first. Eddie was later. Long and slow. Months. In the end, too ill to leave the bed, the sheets sodden and messed every morning, the bed crackling when he moved, from the plastic sheet.

Hugo had never been close to his father, but he came for the occasional weekend. The sight of his car climbing the hill was enough, at the time, to cause a minor collapse of my coping mechanisms.

I went in from the verandah and picked up the phone. Hugo has phases of trying to drag me into the twenty-first century. My hideous clear plastic telephone thing with neon tubes inside which light up when it rings is testament to an otherwise forgotten attempt a year or two ago. It did nothing towards simplifying my life, but I do think of him

every time I use it. *It's got a perfectly adequate microphone, Mum*, he says whenever he rings me. *You don't need to shout.* 'That you, Fred?' I shouted.
'That you, Lily?' came the reply.
'Just making sure you're okay.'
'Honky dory. Went to town. Got some food in. I was getting a bit low.'
'You've had dinner?' I asked, thwarted mother, as Nat says. Not that he complains. I think it's nice for the boy to have someone fussing over him. His mother has done little enough over the years.
'Fried up a couple of snarlers,' Fred said. 'And some spuds from the other night.'
'Shouldn't have fried food, Nat says. Bad for you.'
'Horse-shit.' Fred laughed. *He, he, he, he.* 'Anyway, you don't need to worry because I had some greens. Boiled up a few frozen peas. So there you go. A good healthy meal.'
'See you then.'
'See you, Lily.'
I was glad to be finished with the phone. I've never felt the need to understand how things work, not that the telephone's transparency reveals more than a few rows of soldered dots. I'm too old now to understand electronics. Too old to even try. Television I can cope with, when it's as simple as an on/off button, a plus or minus of channel or volume. You can either embrace change, Iris, or resist it. Embracing it keeps you young. I fear that I embrace resistance.
With Nat away I could begin on the next block of my quilt without having to explain too much. He knows about the pohutukawa tree and he'll know about the rest, in time. Deep in my quilting box was a soft kid leather glove – mine, during the war. My hand doesn't fit into it now. I can hardly believe it ever did. I was rubbing the soft leather between my fingertips, remembering, when it fell onto my knee, and from there to the floor. I was gorgeous when I wore that glove. Nice girls would never be seen with freckled knuckles. When I reached down for it, a pain like a javelin pierced my chest. I had joked about the dangers of fried food. Joked about hearts. Karma, I've been told before, is swift. My heart had overheard. My arms ached, and my neck, and my shoulders. Every inhalation was agony, and before long I could hardly

breathe at all. I slid down against the arm of my chair, my cheek against a cushion – a simple nine-patch design in blue gingham, sunflower yellow, and a blue floral print. One of my first efforts. Tears rolled into my pathetic wispy old-age-pensioner perm.

I was frightened, Iris, wondering if I would die like that. Would Nat come home and tiptoe to bed, thinking I had fallen asleep in front of the television, and not wanting to disturb me? Or would he think me a pile of clean laundry, waiting to be folded? How would Hugo take the news? Even through the pain I could hear him. *I told her she should move into town.* As though moving house had the power to alter fate. My heart had only so many beats inside it from the moment of birth, and I knew the last was not far away.

It's strange the things you think about when you're dying. I regretted not labelling the china in the cabinet. Stickers on the underside is what Marjorie has suggested, each with a name. My three daughters-in-law would be into the house like vultures, each thinking they had more right to my belongings than the others, while Hugo stood helplessly by, as always. And what of Joanna? Would she participate, even though she and I had never met? What could they want of mine anyway? *A pile of trash,* Hugo calls it. I should have written a personal will. One bedroom quilt for each of the daughters-in-law. The houses for Jeannette. Thirty-six houses in different shades of blue. She has lived in at least as many. The Trip Around the World can go to Diane, and the Log Cabin for Amelia, always my favourite, the most genuine and the least grasping of the three, deserving of a sturdy and cosy home, for her sake, and for the sake of the baby, the Boiled Egg. His name had vanished into the pain, the letters distorting, as though in some psychedelic dance.

Bree. Bree could have some of the china. She'd have a home one day too. Perhaps she'd allow her piercings to grow over. One day she'd have a navel she didn't particularly want to display.

And Nat? The house? Would he want it? Would Hugo allow it? It had been difficult enough with a mother who refused to move to a more sensible location. Did he need a son intent on following suit?

By then I was starting to wonder why I hadn't died yet. The pain went on and on, but when would I take the final breath, that famous one that got everyone in the end? I thought it would have come and gone already, left me in a rush, the last movement generated by the woman who was Lily. Still it went on, a frantic gasping and pumping, in and out. Or if not the last breath, surely I could have unconsciousness.

Not much to ask, wouldn't you say, Iris? I'm too tired to write more now. You will have to wait to find out the rest.

Lily

Ten

The Fat Boy

From the corner of the cloakroom, through a hole in the old cladding, the fat boy can see the other children at play. He calms himself by sliding a hand into his pants, encountering the familiar rubbery dimensions of his penis, which hardens as he begins to massage. He leans against an old black oilskin raincoat, Jimmy Dodd's, which hangs on a hook beside him, smelling of stale milk and cat's piss.

Through the hole he watches as Jimmy Dodd launches a rugby ball into the air with an arc of his skinny arm. At the far end of the quadrangle, Peter Boyle prepares to receive the pass, positioning his body, aligning it with the ball's trajectory. His hands ascend as though in adulation, and he plucks the ball from the air, the leather fitting perfectly into the oval dish formed by his hands. His fingers splay, as though webbed, to grip the ball, and he dances. A hop, a skip, a half-turn. One arm slingshots behind his waist and releases the ball into the air in a rainbow curve, over the heads of dozens of squealing, oblivious children.

Jimmy Dodd takes the catch cleanly, and throws again, glancing suddenly towards the shelter shed, the boys' toilets, the cloakroom. The fat boy's cheeks burn as he assures himself that he is invisible, pressed against the oilskin, his fingers holding and twisting, gently, gently, stroking away the fear. Jimmy Dodd is no X-ray Man, no superhero of any description. Though why is his stare so intent, so focused, as though he can see the scabby hole in the weatherboard, and the overpowering blue of the fat boy's iris.

'Jimmy!' shouts Peter Boyle, jettisoning the ball again, watching it rise, higher, higher, into the empty sky. Then fall. Jimmy reaches out, snatching it, curling his body around it, like an egg, a bullet, pirouetting dramatically.

The warble of the handbell sounds, and the fat boy catches sight of its tongue clacking against the brass lip, as Fletcher – Sir – the head teacher, shakes it. The boy withdraws his hand, inch by inch. He peels his cheek away from the grip of the painted wood, and leaves his oilskin nest. He is first into the classroom, first to slide between desk and bench seat, and take out a text to read silently. His fingertips reconnoitre as he reads, across the pitted landscape of the desktop, a phalangeal moon landing. The desk's surface is familiar, the craters and riverbeds, initials and messages carved with compass points to combat boredom.

Next into the classroom is Jimmy Dodd. 'Skunk,' he whispers, curling his lips. 'Cowshit.'

Others file in, breathless, red-cheeked from the sun and their energetic lunchtime pursuits. Sir replaces the hand-bell on its shelf above the store cupboard, while the students scuffle and twitter, finishing conversations in whispers, rifling through untidy desks for reading matter, passing notes.

'Your old lady done it with an elephant,' Jimmy Dodd whispers across the aisle. The squeak of chalk signals Sir's preoccupation with the afternoon's arithmetic, and Jimmy Dodd fashions a circle with thumb and forefinger, extending his other arm, trunk-like, from his nose. He makes a frenzied attempt to jam trunk into circle, then throws his head back in silent, hysterical laughter.

The fat boy, seeing the movement from the corner of an eye, expels an exaggerated sigh and licks his fingertip to snare the corner of his page.

'Disgusting,' whispers Jimmy Dodd, swinging into his seat at last, leaving his bare foot in the aisle, stained green from the freshly mown grass, wide and spongy like a camel's, and giving off an aroma of hot boy. A reminder. That he isn't far away at all.

The fat boy's skin is soft and white. Blubber, Jimmy Dodd calls it. A single ray of sunlight can turn it ghastly pink, and an entire lunchtime in the playground can result in an afternoon in the sickbay, where he rolls on the bed, nauseous from sunstroke.

'You're my little English rose,' his mother says, stroking his hair back from his porcelain forehead. 'Have another peanut brownie.' He invariably obeys. His mother isn't one to be disobeyed. She can be easily upset, and he hates to see her cry. Her face seems to turn inside-out, the flesh from inside her lips rolling outwards, her eyelids reversing, her nose dribbling pints of sticky liquid.

It is beyond him to confess to despising his English rose status, that his aspirations involve bare feet and freckles, arms that can throw rugby balls halfway to eternity, legs that can run miles. He wants to swear without the fear of somebody hitting him from behind. To fart out loud in class. To wear old grey hand-me-down jumpers, with egg-noodles of wool hanging from each elbow, and holes the size of small islands in the Pacific.

'What's the story, Dumbo?' Jimmy Dodd asks, staring at the fat boy's feet, encased on the hottest day in grey woollen socks and polished black leather. 'Got hammertoes? Dumbo's got hammertoes! Dumbo's got hammertoes!'

The fat boy takes his shoes off to walk up the hill from the bus stop in the afternoons, waiting until the bus has ground the gears and slung the door shut with a bang, faces pressed sweatily against the glass, tongues out, fingers waggling, nostrils stretched to porcine dimensions. Peter Boyle, on the back seat, reserves a gesture as first gear screams and second is engaged, so that the fat boy is left with an image, before stooping to tear at his laces, to flip his shoes from his feet and roll his socks into twin American doughnuts. As though an unseen act of defiance at the end of the school day can make up for what has transpired since breakfast.

'Shoes off before you come inside,' his mother calls from the kitchen.

He stoops, pretending, banging the hard soles against the wooden porch floor for added effect. Rolling his socks back onto his pudgy calves.

'You look famished,' she says, stroking a cheek, pink from the effort of climbing the hill. 'You'll be wanting home-made lemonade. And look what's just come out of the oven. Your favourite. Ginger gems. Sit down, pet. We can't have you going hungry.'

The butter melts onto his fingers, running down through the gaps, onto his palms. He can devour a gem in a single mouthful, and licks as much butter as he can before his mother swoops in with a cloth napkin.

[Eleven]

28 October

Dear Iris

I have been in bed four days, hardly able to lift my arm, all the while listening out for the creaky floorboard in the hallway, a muffled conversation on the neon contraption – Nat ringing his father. I'm not a witch, Iris, though a few hundred years ago I might have been burned for one. You may beg to differ. You, of all people in the world, might have been the one calling the loudest. 'Witch! Witch!'

Why did I start on about this? Because of Hugo. Because he is my son, but I'm not sure I like him much. What kind of mother does that make me?

If only I hadn't put Nat through this. His coming in late, finding me in some pose like a beached sea elephant. Have you seen them, Iris? Great blubbery things. No one but a poet could see them as beautiful. That's what I must have looked like to Nat.

'What the dickens ...?' he shouted from somewhere. 'What the ...?'

When I opened my eyes I was still alive. Still in pain. I hadn't for a moment thought it was over, that I was dead. It hurt too much. I tried to say that I was wondering when he'd be home. Across the room, the minute hand of the chiming clock approached the twelve. The hour hand was already there. Midnight. The witching hour. That word again.

I was rushed down the hill by screaming ambulance, an ancient woman with chest pains. No time to waste. I could imagine Fred's bedroom light flashing on. Someone would have seen the lights, the spacey blur of gleaming white. Phones would begin to ring, further and further up the hill, until Fred's jangled beside his bed. *Who do you think it is?*

I don't know. Perhaps Lily. I can't get any reply there.

Meanwhile Nat followed in the car, convinced he had been given permission, for once, to disregard all rules.

'Why aren't I dead?' I asked the medic.

Instead of answering he put an oxygen mask over my mouth. 'Don't try to talk, love.'

Who was he calling love? I was no love of his.

I've told you already, Iris, that I loved Eddie, but there was someone else too, someone I've come to think of as the love of my life. I know I've told you different, but you can't always trust the memory of someone past fifty. Don't be too shocked. It is possible to marry one man, and love another. Especially if the other one is dead.

His name was Billy Brydon, and I met him on the doorstep of Number Thirty-two one night during a raid. It was past midnight when the siren sounded, and as Ma and I scrambled down the stairs there was a hammering on the door. There stood Dad, rain pouring off his Local Defence Volunteer helmet, running down the creases in his face as though they'd been made to channel water. Beside him stood a soldier.

'Go through with the women, lad,' Dad said, full of importance, unreasonably proud of his handiwork on the Anderson, longing to show it off to someone. But a soldier, who could dig his way to China in a morning?

Dad rushed off to usher any other unfortunates caught on the street, mid-raid, to safety. Only it was still the Phoney War at that stage, so we were probably just as safe where we were.

The soldier's eyes were soft feline brown and his hat brim gushed a gallon or two down his sleeve when he took it off in greeting. I didn't mind being introduced to soldiers, but having been dragged minutes earlier from deep sleep, I could focus only on my patched, cobweb-thin cotton nightgown. Gradually I became aware that my hair was tied in rags and my lips were bland and washed out, as they were every night when I cleansed away the last traces of lipstick. Vanity again.

'Come with us,' Ma commanded, no less mortified but able to take control. She jammed her feet into her shoes and gathered up the old Thermos, filled every night before bed, left on the corner of the bench, *just in case*. Wrapped in Olivia's quilt, cocooned within the fragments of debutante satin, bridal organza, matron of honour silk, and housewifely floral, I followed, hearing his boots behind me as they descended the last flight of stairs, crossed to the back door, and mounted the flagstone steps in the rain towards that gaping Anderson orifice.

Once inside he lit a match, and Ma produced a candle. The interior filled with flickering light. In the cold dimness we waited for the bombs. Of course they never came, but Billy Brydon proved himself an invaluable air-raid companion. He performed card tricks and regaled us with stories of his faraway homeland. 'Roight then, you'll loike thus one, eh,' he said, launching forth into tales about falling from horses, running barefoot over sand, creek-side childhood adventures which almost, but never quite, resulted in death.

We laughed until I thought the cabbages would vibrate from the earthen roof, until I thought Ma would collapse. Early on, her lips had been tight, as though she couldn't wait to confront Dad, to tell him just what she thought of having antipodean soldiers delivered onto the doorstep at midnight. But she was roaring by the end. Rocking and crying and holding her sides, begging Billy Brydon to spare her, to take pity, to stop, for God's sake, before her heart gave out. By the time the All Clear sounded, she had invited him to dinner the following evening, he and I had exchanged more than one coy-yet-meaningful glance as my fingers caressed the tiny squares on the quilt, and I had fallen dramatically in love.

He told us over dinner that he was on leave, wandering home to his digs in the starlight when the siren began to scream. That he was grateful to Dad, even if there had been no danger in the end. It was one thing to come halfway across the world to fight Germans, but to die needlessly, wandering lost around London at night, would seem a waste.

He slipped so easily into our lives, filling the empty chair at the kitchen table (your chair), finishing off the last boiled potato no one else could manage, adding a bass harmony to the piano-side singalongs. Sometimes he produced eggs or sugar or clothing coupons, which made Ma smile, and he filled our heads with a bottom-of-the-world dream, conjuring a land of green and blue, of wide open skies, white sands, tepid seas, and impenetrable bush. There were vines, he said, thick as my arm, and he circled my wrist with his fingers. I was not easily thrilled in those days. At least that was what I'd come to believe. But everything

Billy Brydon did thrilled me. Even leaping out from shop doorways, scaring me half to death, or shaking overhanging branches so that the raindrops suspended amongst the leaves saturated me. He told me there were wingless birds where he came from. Some had been nine feet high. But they were extinct now. He told me that the summers lasted for half of every year, and every family had a backyard as big as a cricket oval.

'Lie still, Mrs Lusk,' the nurse said while she taped electrodes to my doughy ankles. 'Don't move a muscle. Just relax. Think about a place you love. Someone who makes you happy. I want you to be as relaxed as you can be.'

She had a blonde plait to her waist and her name-tag said *Valencia*. A place I loved? I could only think of two: my own garden with its tangle of roses and overgrown perennials, and that place Billy took me so long ago, the place with no name.

'You have a lovely name,' I said, thinking Valencia might be apt.

'My father was a romantic. He'd never been anywhere near Italy. His family came to New Zealand more than a hundred and fifty years ago. So it's a flight of fancy, really.'

'I suppose my father was too.' Ma never let him hang his sketches in the house. They lived, rolled one inside the other, at the back of the spare room wardrobe. But she was always quick to shoo him out of the house on Saturday mornings, me in tow, bound for the tube station and the National Gallery, a paper bag under his arm containing pencils and charcoal and sketching paper.

'Your name's lovely too,' Valencia said, attaching the last of the electrodes.

'No one ever calls me Lily these days.'

'Have you ever had an ECG before?'

'Darling, I've had everything.' I remembered those two weeks in my London bedroom, the tumbling squirrels unobserved, the Anderson shelter, mocking still, Ma hovering with a cool cloth at the bedside. Enough to put me off illness for life.

And the weeks in hospital after my quadruple bypass.

But sometimes the body overrides the mind's desires.

'Then you're to be congratulated,' the sweet nurse said, adjusting the machine, one eyebrow flickering. My age, of course. I should be dead.

The nurse studied the machine and it was over in minutes. There on a strip of white paper, a wavering line spelt my destiny. It revealed a regular rhythm. The doctor was nervous. He frowned, unable to fathom such foolishness, that I should ever have allowed myself to become so carved about, so unfit, so old. He studied my notes, a great wad of multi-coloured papers compiled over the years. He read about the bypass. At the time I realised that seeing Hugo on a regular basis was a much simpler matter than I'd always thought. All I had to do was have major heart surgery. He visited me every day.

'I thought I was dying,' I said.

The doctor studied the scar on my chest. I told them at the time they should have put in a zip. It would make it so much easier the next time. 'We'll be keeping you in for observation, Lily,' he said. 'I'm not sure what's happened. I think you've probably had a small heart attack. Best to be safe. There is a possibility that it's muscular. In which case it'll be painkillers and anti-inflammatories. In a few days, I hope, we'll have you as good as new.'

'I'll never be as good as new, doctor,' I said, laughing. 'No matter what you prescribe.' He laughed too.

Do you remember the nightmares of childhood illness, Iris – Ma at the bedside, half annoyance, half concern? I haven't outgrown them yet. There is still the same ghastly contrast between bulk and sinew, the same terrifying quality of the blackest of black, and blinding white. Chiaroscuro, Dad called it, showing me how his charcoal could trace the darkest of shadows to draw attention to the whites. Is it those weekends in the Gallery that have visited me ever since on feverish nights? The Book haunts me still – the Book of Nightmares, we called it – its massive pages and spindly arms and legs, chasing me down the length of our Islington garden. And finally, somehow, I snare it, bury it under the oaks and flee back towards the house. But when I reach out to open the back door it's there, looming towards me again. I'm caught in a loop, an eternal circuit of pointless repetition. I know what it feels like to be a goldfish.

So far, by the way, Nat hasn't made the dreaded call. Instead he has come with soup and tea and thinly sliced bread from the Breville, buttered and spread with my favourite lime marmalade. And I have smiled, weak with need and self-pity and gratitude, dosed up with painkillers, feeling a far deeper trepidation than he could ever imagine, with the knowledge that I have escaped death by a whisker, by a stroke of good fortune I probably don't deserve. My bed, with Nat hovering, is far nicer than that mysterious whirling land of wind, the next place, wherever and whatever it might be. It was a muscle spasm, Iris. Not my heart, which has undulated so dutifully since the bypass, numbering its beats while I sleep, while I garden. And soon it will reach the last beat of its allocation, the approximate ten years of grace promised by the operation.

I know I should tell Nat about it, but it was in those dark days before Jeannette re-entered our lives, before he emerged, as though from a chrysalis, a fully-fledged ten- year-old. He has seen my Smartie-bright assortment of medications lined up on the kitchen windowsill, driven me obligingly to the doctor for my regular visits, assuming the regimes to be simply part of the cost of ageing. Underneath everything I know he would leave if he knew. The responsibility would be too much, and the peace he's found over the past weeks would evaporate. So my decision not to tell is philanthropic, while at the same time pure selfishness.

He has done his best to care for me. If cameras were a cure, I'd be dancing again. His silver fish-eye lens has travelled the length of my quilt, my favourite to date of those I've kept – my Log Cabin in shades of red and brown.

'Thanks for not telling,' I said this afternoon. The lens scaled the alpine ridge thrown up by my legs, and leapt to the window and beyond. Sunlight was angling in, painting white-hot squares on the far wall, and Nat paused to raise the sash, leaning out over the sill and activating the record button.

'No danger of that,' he said. 'Not talking to him. Remember?'

'I might be stuck here in bed, but I'm not mentally impaired. I remember only too well having to phone him to grovel for money on your behalf.'

'What if he visits?' Nat asked, swinging around until the camera's eye was aimed straight at mine. In the beginning I protested, or hid. But I'm used to it now. It's the only taste of movie-stardom I'll ever get. 'He won't, anyway,' he said, answering himself. 'He hasn't got time for things like visiting his mother.'

'Thanks for reminding me.' As though I needed reminding. All those years of caring, of loving, of anticipating his every need. And now this. Three visits a year, one at Christmas, and a paternal attitude that makes me want to vomit. 'Anyway, you're wrong,' I told Nat, more harshly than I intended. 'You're angry with him, so you're finding it hard to be generous.'

The camera stopped whirring and Nat's face appeared from behind it.

'Oh, is that what you look like?' I said, quick enough to silence any response he may have been formulating. 'I'll be out of bed in a day or so. You know what the doctor said.'

Nat sat down beside the bed, tracing the Log Cabin rectangles with a fingertip. 'You had me worried,' he said.

'I had myself worried. I still can't believe it wasn't my heart. But I'm going to be fine in a couple of days. So there's no need to dwell on it. And *no* need to tell your father. He'll only send more brochures about retirement villages. Can you imagine me in one of those places?'

Nat plucked a grape from the bunch he had brought from town – he was taking a liking to convalescence – his eyes crossing as he imagined his grandmother, gumboots and all, amongst manicured lawns and two square feet of allocated flower garden.

'But how would you have managed?' he asked. 'If I hadn't been here?'

'Fred would have done the honours. He's good like that.' Exhaustion descended suddenly, the way it does when questions are too hard. And from the pain, from the effort it took to appear always able to cope. Making the best of a bad situation. Sooner or later the pretence falls away. 'I think I'll try and sleep,' I told him. 'And just in case I can't, can you bring me my sewing basket? Somewhere inside is a kid leather glove, and my special fabric scissors. Put them on the bedside table for when I wake up.'

They will make two soft leather suitcases, which will be sewn into the block just above the explosion.

I still haven't found a word for this line, Iris, but I'm signing off anyway.

Lily

[Twelve]

Floss

Twenty weeks to go, Floss writes with her fountain pen, which threatens to run out of ink as she carves the word 'go' onto the paper of her journal. Twenty weeks, and then what? Wishing away her days, until there are none left. Still, there can't be any harm in a practice run, just to get the feel of the journey. Beside her on the table is a map of the London Underground. Her fingertip traces a line from the edge to the centre. Somebody once told her it was a work of art, that it won prizes when it was designed. And that somewhere, in some art gallery, it hangs on a wall alongside masterpieces by Constable, Picasso, and Gainsborough. It seems inconceivable. Someone was stringing her along, gullible old bird that she is. *I know, I'll spin this old bag a line. Just for a laugh. She won't even suspect it's cobblers.* She wipes her eyes. The London Underground in an art gallery. Bollocks. That's what Julie would say. Bollocks. Bollocks. Bollocks.

Her finger traces the black Northern Line through Tooting Broadway, Tooting Bec, on and on, station after station, all the way to Holborn. She would have to change there, to the Central Line, then three stops, and there it was. St Paul's.

She feels pain in her chest, a tight fist squeezing the blood from her heart, forcing it upwards into her brain where it queues at the narrowings of her arteries, like cinema-goers on a Friday evening. She is drunk all of a sudden. Her breath rasps in and out. Perhaps she'll have to lie down.

But within five minutes the cinema queues have dispersed. She feels well again. Chirpy. In control. She ties on her headscarf, smoothes on her gloves and wraps herself in her coat. She opens the clasp of her brown handbag, checks her purse for coins. How much does the tube cost? It's so long since she's been on it. Still, she deserves an outing.

At the ticket window her nerve deserts her. 'Richmond return,' she says, handing over money, receiving a magnetised ticket in exchange. The platform is quiet. She peels the wrapping from an indigestion tablet and pops it under her tongue. Already she is angry with herself.

'Coward,' she thinks. 'Can't even bring yourself to say *St Paul's*. What is so terrifying about those steps?' She imagines they will be smothered in tourists anyway – Japanese and German, French and American, snapping away with cameras, trying to take home a smudge of the greatest city in the world.

The train pulls in. *Mind the gap*, chirps the loudspeaker. *Mind the gap*. There is a yellow line on the platform which some authority has painted, trying to protect people from their own stupidity. She looks at the scuffed toes of her black lace-up shoes, placed carefully behind the line, only stepping over it once the doors have swished open. She can't help imagining the crunch of bone between the wheels and the track. Halfway in the door she shudders, the hair on her forearms prickling against the sleeve of her blouse, her cardigan, her coat. She fusses with her umbrella, trying to jam it into a corner of her bag, which gapes suddenly open, showing its contents to a bald and bespectacled businessman sitting opposite. He hardly bothers to glance up from his newspaper. Ungrateful, she thinks, given the level of intimacy she has unwittingly offered. The secrets of her soul lie within that bag. Not that she wants him to know them. Plainly, he doesn't deserve to.

The train begins to move before she is ready, and her thin buttocks come down on a diagonal, hard against the seat's plush violet covering. She gathers the handles of her bag and embraces it on her lap, as she would a child. Then she looks again at the businessman, wondering what age he might be. He's obviously important, or thinks himself so. Someone's son, no doubt. His mother will never be left to fend for herself, to arrange her belongings in a cupboard of a council flat. He looks kind behind the glasses, which are thick and ripply, distorting his eyes as he moves his head. They are like blue fish swimming in two oval bowls, back and forward as the carriage rocks. She imagines that he buys his mother flowers, that he takes her to restaurants, and gives her expensive toiletries for her birthday. At Christmas his wife delights in preparing a feast, and he seats his mother at the head of the table.

There are children – three – tall and handsome and articulate. They call her Gran with undisguised affection. They hug her and plant wet kisses on her cheeks. They telephone her when they win trophies at sport, or gold stars in their handwriting books.

The man's cellphone rings and he fishes it out of a coat pocket. 'Shit,' he says. 'Shit. The bastards.' He looks at his watch. 'I should be there by eleven. Don't let him leave until then.'

Reggie would never have spoken like that. *Pardon me*, Reggie said if anything as vile as *blast* left his lips. *Pardon me, my darling. Forgive me, sweetheart. How coarse I am. And in the presence of ladies too.*

Reggie. Reggie.

You've nothing to fear, Reggie said. *I'll always be here to look after you.*

Floss stares down at her gloved hands perched on top of her bag, holding it firm, closed, safe. She notices how neatly they fold together. From many years of practice, she supposes. She has always folded her hands in idle moments. They were folded like this when Reggie came into her life.

'Do you mind if I share your table?' he asked. She had been waiting half an hour for a friend who plainly was not coming. She had drained two pots of tea, trying to appear at ease, self-contained, only glancing at the door when the overhead bell tinkled. She had seen Reggie come in, brown-suited and immaculate, with a subdued blue tie, and hair cream holding down his curls. 'I've just driven all the way from Hull, and I tell you, I could do with some company.'

'I don't know that I'm much good at that,' she said.

He smiled, surprised. 'You're pretty enough for a man not to care. In fact, let me be presumptuous enough to say that silence with you would be preferable to the liveliest chatter with somebody else.'

She felt herself blushing.

'There now,' he said. 'Prettier than ever.'

'A travelling salesman,' her mother said, as though she could think of no worse profession. *She* could talk. *She* had married a bus conductor, with grimy fingernails from the filthy money and his back bent over from the hopelessness of it all. He hadn't even been to war on account of his wheeze. Reggie had come back decorated.

'Never mind me,' her mother said, sitting on the side of Flossie's bed, stroking back a curl. Flossie could never resist being coddled. Her mother stood up and went to the landing window. 'Ooh, will you look at that? That's the third night this week the eldest Tilbury girl's come home with that fella. She can't be more than sixteen.'

There was always a dig. Other girls in the street could get fellas, and there was Flossie, twenty-five. She looked at her mother's outline as she came back into the room, the hair in curlers, the shapeless floral shift and pinny, the cigarette cupped within the curve of her right hand.

'I were like that once,' her mother said. 'Sneaking out at night without me ma knowing. Creeping up them stairs past midnight, and there was always one that creaked. The fifth one, I think it was. Or the sixth. Can't remember now. Was it worth it? I ask myself now. All for thirty years with your Dad. What a catch, eh? And what a life. How did it happen, eh? That Tilbury girl's got a shock coming, that's all I can say.'

If only it was, Flossie thought. But her mother wouldn't stop there. She'd go on and on until Flossie's ears were numb, and her brain was knotted into tangles.

'I'm having a bath,' Flossie said, grabbing her dressing gown and dashing downstairs, wondering how long it would be before her mother noticed. In the bath she ran a fingertip over the contours of her cheek, her forehead. She drew a line down her nose, bisecting the cupid's bow, the dimple in her chin, her neck, and descending between her breasts, to her navel, and beyond as her body readied itself for Reggie.

Reggie turned out to be the kindest man who ever walked on earth. He wooed her with tickets to films, walks around Richmond Hill and Hampton Court, picnics beneath the spires of country churches, kisses in Kew Gardens. They married without fuss in a dour Islington church, with no more than a dozen in the congregation, and afterwards had sandwiches and cakes in her mother's front room while the men drank too much and her mother looked with envy upon the smart frocks of her sisters.

Reggie would never have let her catch the tube on her own. He would have been there, steadying her elbow, steering her with a hand on the small of her back, carrying her bag with its awkward umbrella, sheltering her from the profanities uttered by balding businessmen. *You'll never have to worry about a thing,* he said.

'Wanna come over for supper?' Julie asks, the metal in her face glinting. She stands in the frame of the doorway. Her hair is purple today. A predatory wind from off the North Sea finds its way into the flat.

'I was just going to have a biscuit and a cuppa,' Floss says.

'That's not enough to live on. I been doing cooking classes down at the Community Centre. I've made a whacking great pot of soup. No crap in it, either. Just veges from the market, and stock 'n' stuff.'

Floss draws air in through her nostrils, catching a hint of soup aroma. Just like in her mother's kitchen on cold winter afternoons after the war. She imagines the taste on her tongue, the warmth seeping into her joints. She thinks about the plain biscuits in her cupboard, the milk on the point of curdling.

'I've got heaps,' Julie says. 'A whacking great pot. Like I said. And Daniel – well, he'd love to see ya.'

'Are you sure?' Floss asks.

'Abso-flamin-lutely. Or I wouldn't ask. C'mon then. Grab ya coat.'

Floss is aware, as Julie waits outside the door, of how much she fusses. Checking that the kettle is off, the gas is off, the kettle again. Getting her keys and counting them, to make sure they're all there. Checking the kettle, the gas, counting her keys, rummaging in her handbag for her bankbook, her plastic cards. Checking the kettle, the iron, while Julie waits at the door breathing steam, and the cold invites itself in and settles in corners and on the furniture for the night.

'D'ya want to throw your electric blanket on?' Julie asks. 'So's your bed'll be warm when ya get in.'

'Oh no. I couldn't do that. I don't like to leave anything on when I'm not here. What if it started a fire?'

Julie frowns. 'Just a thought.'

'Of course. Of course it was.'

The soup is ambrosian, thick and scalding and full of chunks of vegetable which melt in her mouth. 'I went to Richmond Hill today,' she says between mouthfuls, trying not to smirk, trying to sound as though she does it all the time, forgetting momentarily that she could hardly get up the stairs to her flat afterwards, that she fell across her bed and slept for two hours.

'Did ya?' Julie asks, the tilt of her eyebrow betraying a sliver of envy.

'I used to go there a lot,' Floss says. 'When I was young.'

'Did ya? What, in the war 'n' that?'

'Well, I was only your age in the war. Younger. I was only a little girl. I got sent out of London for the war. Evacuated. I went to stay with this awful aunt in Cornwall. No, it was after the war. That's when I did my courting. In the fifties.'

'The fifties. Wow. My mum weren't even born then. Even my gran weren't.'

'My Reggie used to take me there. Sometimes we'd have a picnic. Sometimes we'd go to a tea shop or a little pub. Sometimes we even went to Hampton Court. *Walking on the same sod that Henry VIII used to walk on.* That's what my Reggie used to say. I'd never really thought about it, till then.'

Afterwards she sat on Julie's couch, hard and blue. It hadn't occurred to her earlier that people like Julie would have furniture – while Daniel sat on her knee, and she folded her hands carefully around his plump little belly to keep him safe.

Once there was a little boy, she wanted to say. But she kept her words firmly inside her head, incarcerated behind her too large false teeth. She talked nonsense instead. 'Horsey-worsey. Puddy tat. Birdie-wirdie. Widdle piggy-wiggy crying wee-wee-wee-wee, all the way home.'

[T*hirteen*]

7 November

Dear Iris

I'm still stuck in bed, Nat hovering like some obsequious handmaiden, plying me with segmented oranges (just like I used to put in Hugo's lunchbox), sandwiches with the crusts cut off, rattling, perspiring glasses of lemonade. Something has happened to the inside of my mouth. Food tastes like wood. My groaning emptiness is sated within two bites, and the discomfort of over-indulgence takes its place. God knows the state of my kitchen. It's been hard enough to drag myself to the bathroom. Same again there, only in reverse. A bladder fit to burst, and all I can manage is a pathetic trickle. You probably don't want to know this, Iris. *Too much information*, Nat would say. He has brought the television in too, and we watched a documentary the other night. *Diet or Die*. A forty-stone woman described the bursting of an abscess on her buttock, and Nat rolled around the floor in agony at the deadpan account of the resultant gore. 'Too much information,' he said, blocking his ears. Too much information. Don't we just suffer from that in our lives?

The society met in my bedroom this week, the first time in years it's been anywhere other than Marjorie's front room. Can you imagine what she must have gone through in making the decision? She must have felt the reins falling from her fists. I shouldn't be unkind. Marjorie is a dear friend. I heard her voice the moment they arrived, bellowing down the hall, ordering Nat here and there, demanding the dragging of dining chairs into my bedroom and their arrangement around my bed. The girls organised themselves around me while Nat went off in the car in relief, and Marjorie clattered about in the kitchen, determined to be hostess regardless. I was going through my own crisis. What would she think of Nat's idea of kitchen hygiene? What if she used the wrong mugs, or the gumboot tea instead of the Lady Grey? When finally she bustled in, she was too excited about the fact that one of her far-off daughters had mentioned the same male acquaintance in two consecutive letters, to notice my white-faced fear. Two consecutive letters. Which must mean imminent marriage. And grandchildren.

'Lindsay?' Serena said thoughtfully. She had placed herself on my right, her unnaturally auburn hair catching the last light from the sun through the window. 'It might not even be a man. It *is* one of those either-or names.'

'Of course it's a man,' Barbara said, before Marjorie's look of horror had time to cement foundations. 'Why else would she mention it? She's putting her toe in the water, that's all. Sounding you out.'

Marjorie, mollified, poured and distributed tea, and arranged her quilt across her knees. She began embroidering the eyes on a sheep, then looked for a moment straight at me. 'Am I supposed to respond in some way? About this Lindsay chap? Communicate approval somehow? Only how can I do that without meeting the bloke?'

'You're right there,' Serena said. 'I mean, for all we know he might be an axe murderer.'

'For God's sake,' Bernie said, glowering across the bed at Serena, her quilt sinking to fill the positive and negative spaces comprising her lap as her hands fell in despair.

Serena giggled. 'Or an accountant.'

'She doesn't mean it, Marj.' Bernie again, the silk flying from her needle like the ribbon from a rhythmic gymnast as she waved her arm.

'It was only a thought.' Serena's needle is sword-like, threaded with jute string, but as weapons go, her tongue has its moments.

'Keep your thoughts to yourself in future.' Bernie looked around, but couldn't catch eye contact with any of us. We were all too interested in our work all of a sudden, too fascinated by seams and clashes of colour. There's so seldom been friction between us that we didn't know how to cope with it. More often than not, our society is an oasis, a green floating space unconnected to time or kitchen benches or marriages that have gone on too long. We are everything to each other, a unit. I bit my lip and felt my shoulder tighten. At last, from the corner of my eye, I saw Bernie take up her work again. 'Think of poor Marjorie,' she said. 'It's bad enough with children living on the other side of the damn world, without clowns planting seeds of ideas.'

'I'm a clown, am I?' Serena began.

'Speaking of seeds,' Suzanne said, diverting her.

'Not again,' Serena gasped. 'Not another baby!'

Suzanne screwed her eyes tight shut. She took a breath and began again. 'Does anyone know where I can get some of those echium? The tall ones?'

'You mean pinata,' said Jane, grateful at last to see a clear path for the conversation to follow. 'I've got a great bagful at home.'

Words tumbled onward then. There was almost a gale force wind of relief within the room, the curtains fluttering wildly, the quilt across my knees barely anchored by spools of thread, scissors and thimbles. We were suddenly effusive, clutching at mundane ideas with far more enthusiasm than they deserved, while the rigid triangle within the room began to yield.

I wondered as I worked why Marjorie should consider me an authority on dealing with adult children. Hugo has never once consulted me on his choice of partner. Two of his weddings might as well have been elopements, they were so sudden and secret. The third, to Amelia, was the opposite. I came to prefer the idea of elopements, after the painstaking decision-making Amelia tried to draw me into. At least once a week she arrived with fabric samples or full colour brochures, which opened like fans, covering at least half of my oak table and displaying wedding venues in all their glory, the gardens at November's peak of blowsy perfection. We discussed combinations for bouquets, styles of shoes, height of heels, colours for bridesmaids' dresses that may or may not date. Wines, beers, spirits, suits, hats, buttonholes, hairstyles, make-up, going-away outfits, and honeymoon destinations. Poor Amelia, intent despite my increasingly glazed expression, so determined to make the third time for Hugo the one that really counted. It must have been daunting to have two very-much-alive ex-wives hovering like dastardly silhouettes. The knowing pouts of those lipsticked mouths. The willingness to exchange glances of disbelief at Amelia's tactics. And worse, the knowledge that they had both tried Hugo first, and discarded him.

Amelia was a wreck by the time the day arrived. She could hardly stand up, from exhaustion. A tropical storm swept in from the north-east, almost liberating the marquee from its stays. And her great-uncle Albie became over-excited, dancing with the matron of honour, and collapsed and died before Amelia had even had the chance to throw the bouquet.

Wedding became wake. The ambulance got stuck on the lawn, showering the guests with mud as the wheels spun. Amelia's brother, whose tow-truck was conveniently in the carpark (his cellphone switched on too), pulled the ambulance free, but not without damaging the door of a nearby BMW.

Amelia retired to a portaloo, refusing to come out until all the guests had gone. I stayed, for her sake rather than Hugo's, making sure the leftovers were distributed fairly, the unopened wine boxed up and returned for a refund, the wedding gifts recorded unobtrusively on the backs of the cards so that when it was time for Amelia to write the thank-you notes, there would be a minimum of confusion.

Charmayne, the matron of honour, seemed hardly aware as she tucked the wedding cards inside vases and casseroles and beribboned sets of manchester and linen, that she had a hand in the wedding's demise.

'If today is symbolic of their lives together,' she said, 'Hugo might as well quit while he's ahead.'

Hugo was gazing at the ruins through the effervescent gold of his beer glass. He roused himself and raised it. 'I'll drink to that.'

'When your time comes,' I told Nat when my girls had gone and he had come home again, 'we'll put a ladder outside the girl's bedroom window, and the two of you can slip away in the dead of night.'

'You're bloody joking,' he said, old enough at the time of his father's marriage to Amelia to have found it highly amusing. He put a cup of tea on my bedside table and sat down on the edge of the bed. His eyes were red-rimmed and his hair was messed up at the back. A twig hung from the sleeve of his T-shirt. He rubbed the floorboards with his bare toes. 'I'm not going to be sucked into all that fuss.'

'Wise boy.'

'And why are you even talking about it? Do I look like the marrying kind?' He held his arms out, crucifix-style, swivelling towards me, and I had to admit he did not resemble much of a prize. His jeans were suspended mid-buttock, always in danger of falling down, the bottom halves worn away by city asphalt. And his T-shirt rode up at the back, showing a stripe of pig-illustrated satin boxers.

'Not in the least,' I said. 'But then, neither was your father.'

Once I dreamed of planning my own wedding, bridesmaids and bouquets and a rare clear London day, sun angling through the church leadlights, the red from St Thomas's robes falling across the white of my gown as I promised away my life. And when I turned to the groom, there was Billy Brydon. We would kiss without self-consciousness, comfortable in our love for each other.

Our first kiss wasn't quite so blissful.

Have you ever thought yourself a fool, Iris, looking back into the past and wondering what could have possessed you to be so dull, so dim-witted? I was a fool over Billy Brydon, overly influenced by the detail gleaned by proximity. The length of his eyelashes – they were like theatre curtains, so dense and velvety – the flecks of brilliant yellow in his brown eyes, the channel between his nose and mouth, and the perfectly formed cupid's bow of his top lip. And there was more than the visual, because he filled my senses. The smoky scent of his breath, the roughness of his serge uniform against my fingertips, the sheen of his boots which he polished and polished, spit and paper, before his landlady's fire. I breathed him, every aspect. He filled my lungs, and pieces of him fragmented like oxygen into my blood, carried around my body by that young, unscarred, pumping heart.

I was a fool, Iris, to fall so helplessly in love with him. How shortsighted we are when we are young, how easily influenced by fairytales with happy endings. The princess always gets her man. Good things come to those who wait. The meek shall inherit the earth. All around was misery: sandbags, bleak grey skies like counterpanes of lumpy rotting kapok, down-turned lips, loss, grief, thankless back-breaking work. And I dreamed of a far-away life with my soldier boy: beaches and children and a kitchen full of butter, eggs, and sunlight.

And he was fool enough to ask me out. I strapped my gorgeous ankles into impractical high heels and tripped off along the cobbles beside him. I drank and laughed, throwing my head back with such abandon. In the powder room I gazed at my perfect hair, my perfect face, and painted my mouth red with a lipstick as sharp as a bayonet. I danced until I thought I would fall down, the mirrorball dangling below the ceiling, turning and casting splinters of brilliance across us all. It's a wonder those soldier boys didn't dive for cover, reminded of flying shrapnel. But they danced on, somehow able to switch between their two worlds.

I had no concept of that other world. I was young. That in itself should explain all, a single word to end all argument. A word that, when spoken, prompts the raising of eyebrows, the nodding of heads in sympathy and understanding. 'Ah, yes. She was *young*.'

Those boys of ours, so irresistible, had so recently been mud-caked, nerve-shattered, unshaved, half-starved, lice-ridden. Those boys had crawled through shit, eaten mush out of cans, watched their mates die, and killed boys hardly old enough to leave their mothers.

In England we danced. And when Billy walked me home all the dark places, doorways and alleys, were filled with lovers, like strange secretive animals with unsociable habits.

I was so different then, unkissed, untried, and Billy was such a gentleman. More than that. A pet. He was my treasure from a far off land. My prize. We held hands in those dark London streets, swinging our arms, talking nonsense, as sweethearts do.

Our first kiss was in the shadow of our porch, a fumbled mismatched exchange where his wet mouth came over mine, and I kept my lips firmly closed, because I didn't know there was any more to it. I heard Ma's steps in the hallway, the rattle of the lock. Our chance was over to try again, to meet in a middle ground of offering and taking. As we sat across Ma's table while she poured tea, I stared at the drawn threadwork of the tablecloth, realising too late my mistake, ashamed at my innocence, my ignorance, my awkwardness. I was afraid to look at him, and afraid he'd leave and never come back.

I lay awake all night, the squirrels somewhere outside in the darkness, curled in sleep. I replayed the kiss, Billy's disappointment growing with each re-enactment, my own lips clamped more and more tightly together until I was convinced I had lockjaw. Even a cold chisel wouldn't prise them apart.

So that was my first kiss, Iris. I know about yours, and I'm not ready to write about that yet. Do you ever think about it, I wonder? Do you ever think about me?

Love
Lily

[*Fourteen*]

11 November

Dearest Iris

At last I'm well enough to get up and walk around the garden. It hasn't stood up very well to the spring, which isn't, by the way, my favourite season at all. Not only are the lambs halfway to the slaughterhouse, the calves long since collected from the little cages by farmers' letter boxes, the daffodils and jonquils shrivelled and lying like rotting seaweed across the pansy seedlings, but there is worse. Spring is full of promises it can't keep, sunshine that yields no warmth, relentless westerly gales, hail, thunder. An unfaithful lover buying flowers and offering up lies before rushing off to a mistress. Autumn, now there's a season.

Mutabilis was flattened, cistus petals frayed into limpid tentacles, bearded irises with stems as tortuous as garden hoses. A truck arrived, grinding gears up the hill road, reversing towards the shed with a blinking electronic screech. Nat, of course, was at the bottom of it, standing on the driveway, all importance, giving signals which meant nothing to an obviously experienced driver. When I came around the side of the house, he frowned at my gumboots, the secateurs which had so recently been dead-heading Jayne Austin.

'It's nothing to worry about, Lily,' he called. 'Something I ordered, that's all.'

'Have you thought about how you're going to pay for it?' I tried not to sound negative. The boy had found himself a project. God – if there is one – be praised.

The driver flashed a look of uncertainty. Was he wise to unload when there was doubt regarding payment?

'C.O.D,' Nat called, waving a handful of twenty-dollar notes. 'No problem.'

Reassured, the driver began to unload a stack of timber, and when he'd gone Nat smiled. 'I'm going to build you something,' he said. 'For your birthday.'

'My birthday's not for months.'

'It'll take me months to build it.'

'Do I have any say in what it's to be?'

'None at all.' Nat grinned, running his hands over the pale clean timber, the arrised edges, feeling the rough end grain and the smooth sides. 'You're going to love it.'

'And what if I don't?'

He left the timber and draped an arm around my shoulders. 'Gran,' he said. 'Lily.' As though I was a child whose behaviour left something to be desired. 'Come with me.' He led me to the verandah and urged me to sit. The sun was warm through the fabric of my dress, a small delight after so many days in bed. Sparrows were bathing in the dust of the driveway and far off, over Fred's sloping paddocks, a magpie was dive-bombing a hawk. They tumbled, mid-flight, wings churning, then separated, the hawk rising and spiralling serenely away, the magpie climbing steeply to regain the advantage.

Nat returned from inside with a book of Italian architecture, a page marked with a slip of torn newspaper. Classified advertisements. Computers for sale. 'I want to build you this,' he said, opening the book onto the hardwood table to display a photograph of a fine Florentine cupola.

'I don't need my own Sistine chapel.' I tried not to sound ungrateful.

'As if,' he said. I hate the way they do that, the young. Truncate sentences. Change the time-honoured rules of grammar to suit themselves. 'It'd be like your pohutukawa tree,' he said, inspired again, his irises so pale in the sunlight I could almost see into his brain. Like the chickens. Only in Nat's case there was more chance of there being a brain.

'Like my pohutukawa?'

'You know how you say quilting has changed from the traditional. I mean, a bloody Mennonite would freak if she saw what Serena's doing with a bit of sack and baling twine. And calling it a quilt. Well, see this.' His fingertip stabbed the book, then traced the curves of the cupola, outlined against a dizzy Florentine sky. I could almost feel the clamour from the streets, the dust rising, settling between my teeth and their own architectural flying buttresses.

'Yes,' I said. 'I see it.'

'I want to build one in your garden. But I don't have scaffolding, or a zillion bloody dispensable peasants as cheap labour. And I don't have sandstone, or gifted stonemasons, or bloody gold leaf to bang around the outside. But I've got this.' He tapped the side of his head. A flake or two of dandruff tumbled onto the shoulder seam of his T-shirt.

'And ...?'

'And I'll do what you're doing with your quilt. I'll bloody *contemporise* it. You know what I'm saying, Gran-Lily?'

For some reason my eyes set about leaking, and I nodded, reaching for the tissue tucked into my bra strap in order to pass it off as an inconvenient allergy. An allergy to the sensation of receiving affection, to finding, so late in life, a kindred spirit. 'Yes, yes,' I said. 'I know what you're saying. But there is a difference. If my designs don't work, nothing's lost, apart from a bag of scraps of material. But you've paid for all that timber now. You can't send it back at the end for a refund and say it didn't work.'

'You're always thinking about how much things cost. That doesn't worry me.'

'Well, it should.'

He looked at me pityingly. 'Dad'll cough up. Don't you see? If the first one doesn't work out, Dad'll fork out for more wood.'

'Shouldn't you be aiming towards financial independence, Nat?' I didn't understand how he could be so blasé. Hugo was always offering to pay my bills, but I couldn't stand the idea of being beholden to anyone, especially not my own son. And I didn't want to give him the satisfaction of thinking he only had to write a cheque and his filial duties were fulfilled.

'There's plenty of time for that,' Nat said.

'You should at least have a design.'

'I'll come up with something. Just give me a few days.'

'Hooray for that, at least.'

'Don't you want it, Gran?' His lips pursed as he spoke, as though trying to disguise excessive emotion.

I could have kicked myself. Too long living alone, I suspect. Out of touch with the sensibilities of human company. 'Come here,' I said, drawing him to me. His long hair, despite the dandruff, was scrupulously clean, the dull brown strands picking up highlights in the sunlight. Copper. Bronze. Gold. His arms went around my shoulders, linking behind my neck.

'You daft beggar,' I said. 'I've never wanted anything so much in my life.'

Is there any such thing as sincerity, Iris? Statements like that make me wonder. Or is sincerity a quality we all pretend to have, while layering on silken shrouds of deceit? Nat seemed sincere enough then, and later, browsing through the photographs his grandfather collected in a lifetime. But am I?

There was no mystery in the box for me, and not much in the way of nostalgia. Some relationships are just enough to whet the appetite, a few too-brief meetings, an intervention of some kind, fate or circumstance. Then separation. Others drag on too long, familiarity like a poison, afflicting the vision, the emotions. Eddie and I began so well, Iris, but we came to know that poison. It tainted our tastebuds for each other. We lived for forty years within arm's length. For thirty of those we hardly bothered to reach out.

Nat knows his grandfather in the opposite way. The very word – grandfather – conjures a fascination within him. The images titillate him, of khaki-clad young men striding down Cairo's streets, cigarettes clasped between unstained fingers, laughter always a mere inch away from sensuous, unwrinkled lips. A grandfather, never met, can be anything. A pillar of perfection. An idol.

'How did you meet him?' he asked.

I was reluctant to answer. Memory is so subjective, and my images of Eddie as a young man revolve more around an afternoon in his mother's front room, the sun as hard as cardboard cutouts against the wall. There was a sense, as I opened to him, that it was the last chance for both of us. He was fierce, insistent, as though he had no right to pleasure when so many were dead. (I'm sorry, Iris, but you wouldn't have been able to cope.) And there was me, passed by, not only by life, but by the soldiers who had returned, taken up residence in their mothers' front bedrooms, and set about building, stone by stone, a new existence with no reference to the previous one, heads down, hoping to never again be noticed. The honeymoon lasted five years. Our love was terrifying in its physicality. Hardly the memories a grandson wants to be a party to. But words came from somewhere inside me, like toy wooden blocks constructing an image between us of a rake, a cove – urbane, cynical, and irresistible.

Nat's forehead is broad, like his father's. It shone as his head moved from photo to grandmother, and back again. He has no reason to doubt my stories. Why would he not believe an old woman like me? What could I possibly have to hide? (Sincerity again.) I looked for it in his forehead, the hair tucked neatly behind his ears, the eyes staring into some faraway place where his grandfather was still alive.

Or was his interest a subtle persuasion? How to get what you want from your wacky, stubborn grandmother. Pretend to be interested in her life.

The french doors were open – a warm night at last – and the room inhaled the cool freshness which drifts up from the pasture after rain: the tang of cow manure, a sour bovine perfume, and the sweetness of star jasmine, clambering up the verandah poles and tumbling from the lengths of number eight wire Eddie hung up years ago to contain it. The curtains tried to deter hopeful mosquitoes, but were unequal to the task. A squadron circled in the air above my head, whining like the distant motorbikes of city children come to the country for the weekend.

'Bloody things,' Nat said, slapping himself on the calf, but otherwise not looking up from his rummaging. His calves seemed out of proportion: solid, hairy, the tops of his feet kissed pink by the sun, with white stripes where his roman sandals buckled. Perhaps it was the angle. Donatello, the father of perspective, might have been studying his own son, or grandson, sprawled across the floor, when it occurred to him that it might be possible to represent depth on the page.

I studied Nat's feet – the curled toes, the yellow, horny untrimmed nails – thinking how like Hugo's they were.

'Where was he stationed during the war?' he asked, unaware of my scrutiny.

For a moment I was tricked into thinking that Eddie was in North

Africa. But that was Billy Brydon. Time was working the memories into a new design. Only those I have stitched already have found form. They can't be changed now. They have structure and symmetry, tangibility. 'He was in the infantry,' I said. 'He was on the boats on D-day. They laughed and joked all the way across the Channel, woke up at the crack of dawn, and within an hour or two, his best friends were gone. So many didn't even make it out of the water, you know. And the ones who made it to the beach weren't allowed to pull them out, to save them. Best friends. Brothers. Your grandfather lost three brothers. Not on D-day, but in the war. He was the youngest of the four, and suddenly he was the only one left. No wonder he didn't want to come back home to England once it was all over. There was too much space, too much silence. Three spaces, three beds, which should have been occupied. At least over this side of the world he could do his best to forget.'

'Shit,' Nat said, the word a eulogy. Nat tucked his hair carefully behind each ear, a ritual that gives him time to think. 'Is that what you meant about him being a war bride?'

I laughed. 'He made friends. That's all. Fred and your grandfather were good mates. He came out here because of Fred's tales of paradise.'

Nat seemed sincere, a line developing between his brows as he studied the ageing photographs, his hair escaping and falling, strand by strand, across his forehead, across his face. Anyone looking at him would have believed in his sincerity. But then people might think the same of me, a harmless old lady, product of a blameless life. Mother, grandmother, friend. Mentor, adviser, superannuitant, each role decreasing the possibility that I should be the possessor of secrets.

Which just goes to show, doesn't it, Iris?

'Was he ever shot at? Wounded? Did he kill Germans? Did he hate them? Did he wish the war would go on and on and on?'

'If you want to know about the war, Fred's the one you should ask.'

'I don't want to know about the war so much. Mostly about Grandad. What was he like?'

'He was a good man.'

'Yeah, well, that tells me a lot. What was he *like*? I mean, well, was he like *Dad*?'

'Yes,' I said. 'I suppose he was.'

Nat cleared his throat. His camera, on its tripod in the corner, whirred away, focusing coolly on the room, observant but non-judgemental.

'Do we have to have that thing on?'

'Forget about it. Just pretend it isn't there.'

Likely, with its hooded eye. Its steady cold-hearted purr.

'Hey, wow. Who's this?' He held up a photo. 'What a babe.'

'That's me, idiot. I told you I was gorgeous once. Of course you knew best.'

'Shit.' The same eulogy. A relief to know a living grandmother can score somewhere near the awe a dead grandfather warrants. 'You were a doll. And who's this? Some cousin or something?'

I hardly needed to look. I could tell by the laughter in our faces, the wrought iron railings of the front steps, by the mass of wild hair, tamed only by the faded monochrome tones of the photograph. 'My sister,' I said, studying my hands as they worked strips together, gold, ochre, charcoal, bronze, olive green, beige, brown, the pohutukawa trunk, solid and imposing, which would rise like a silhouette on the left-hand side of the quilt. The slivers of cloth slid and the pins conspired to stab my fingers.

'What happened to those genes, I wonder. No offence, Lily, but I could do with a bit of her style. I'd have girls coming out my ears.'

'Quiet, for God's sake, Nat,' I said. 'I need to concentrate. I've already had to unpick this seam three times because of your babbling.' He recoiled, stung, shuffling obsessively through the photographs. I could have cut out my tongue, seeing the hurt, when it had taken so long to build up his trust. I never spoke to Hugo with such sharpness. Once when he was about four years old I was so neglectful, burbling away to Maisie about recipes and moss stitch and cables that he grabbed the knitting from my hands and threw it into the fire, needles and all. Maisie's mouth opened like a tunnel preparing to receive a train, and Eddie, just coming in the door for a cup of tea before milking, was livid. He wanted to slap Hugo halfway into space.

I knew it wasn't his fault, but my own. I held him so tightly the breath went out of him, until Maisie strode home, and Eddie saw the cows waddling up the hill on their own. When he was gone Hugo and I made ginger gems, his favourite, and he was tucked safely in bed by the time Eddie came back.

Nat would not be so presumptuous. Nor would he get the same reaction. I was too soft with Hugo. Too yielding. Trying too hard to protect him from a world which would find him anyway. Throwing my knitting into the fire, I know now, was an act of hooliganism.

Time passed while I stitched, and I willed the tension between Nat and I to filter upwards and dissipate. His lips were tight as he searched the box, trying to find information I could so easily have given. Apologising, Eddie always said, was not my strongest point. In fact he used graphic metaphors to describe my post-battle silences. I have never really seen the need to apologise. Time passes. The trivia of living takes over. Sooner or later Eddie would want a shirt ironed.

'Your grand-dad's mother and I were friends,' I told Nat. A snippet. A peace offering. A tantalising beginning. He looked up as though I had just presented him with a banana and chocolate chip muffin.

Beef goulash, flavoured with paprika, garlic, bay leaves, vinegar, sugar, and Worcestershire sauce. My own tomatoes, bottled late in the summer, simmered for two-and-a-half hours with the meat. Sour cream and chopped parsley stirred through at the last minute. Fluffy white rice.

Half an hour later Nat made himself a doorstop sandwich with leftovers and asked, through a mouthful, 'What's for pudding?'

Ah, to be young again, eh, Iris?

Love Lily

Fifteen

20 November

Dear Iris

Drunkard's Path is a deceptively simple design, although I'm not sure you're ready for it yet. It has a curved seam, and takes an experienced sewer to carry it off. There are only two pieces. Imagine a square divided into three-quarters and one-quarter. Now imagine that the line dividing them is a curve. The secret to the Drunkard's Path's diversity is the number of ways the blocks can be arranged, making different designs. I suggest you don't try it yet, not until you've shown you have the perseverance to complete a simpler project. Otherwise it will end up folded away in a cupboard somewhere, another beginning with no end.

That's what I'm starting to think about this thing with Nat, that he is going to stay. The crisis time has passed, and he's still here, more settled than ever. Last night he was stretched across the hearthrug with ruler, pencil, and reference book, trying to design a structure which would not collapse in the first gentle breeze. I knew what he was thinking about, but he could hardly begin to suspect what goes on in my mind at night as I stitch. The old have a right to keep secrets, although sometimes I would like to share mine. Perhaps that's what all these letters are about, Iris. Wanting to salve a conscience.

I loved a man once, I could say to Nat, *who wasn't your grandfather.* Billy Brydon, who undid me. Billy Brydon, who transformed me from girl to woman in so many ways. Taught me love. Broke me, cleanly, in half. Stole my chance of filling my life with children, and never even knew it.

But grandchildren need their beaver dams. Imparting a single fact, like Billy Brydon's existence, could cause a foundation branch to dislodge and, with the current of water, the entire dam could wash away. Grandchildren can acknowledge no other man than their grandfather, as is written in history, as floods their veins, their DNA. No other man exists and if he did, a grandmother would have been far too involved, too well behaved to notice. For well behaved, read sexless. A grandmother is the most sexless of creatures. Warm, loving, accepting, healing, forgiving. A grandmother is designed to adore, and to give comfort, to have no past other than what is apparent, and never to feel sexual urges.

This is what grandchildren should write on greeting cards. *I love you, Gran, as long as you conform to my grandmother image.*

'Any progress?' I asked Nat as he measured and ruled.

'These freaking footings are supposed to be three hundred freaking square, by three freaking hundred deep. That's a lot of sodding digging. Oh, get it? I'm a bloody pun-master. And hundred-by-hundred uprights, hundred-and-fifty-by-fifty bearers, and hundred-by-fifty rafters.'

'You're speaking another language,' I said, fondling a piece of indigo silk between my fingertips. 'Don't blind me with science. I only wanted to know if there was any progress.'

'I suppose, well, I suppose, yeah. Sweet, in fact. Peachy.'

The kid leather suitcases are done now, huddling within a circlet of Double Wedding Ring in shades of blue and lilac, cut from old dresses which have hung in the wardrobe, unworn for decades, hope finally surrendered of one day fitting into them again. Now that I do they are too old, dated, and carry too much of what was happening at the time. My life has come back to me as I cut each piece. Once I was married to Eddie I became frantic for a baby. My friends all had them, parading up and down the streets with gargantuan prams, comparing notes at the park while pieces of their own flesh slept on, pulling irresistible faces and exhaling barely audible sighs. The babies had grown into fat toddlers and school children, the prams refilled numerous times while I cleaned and baked and invited Ma for afternoon tea and wondered what was wrong with me, with the curse appearing, unwelcomed, month after month. How could I bear to wear those dresses again, the fabrics so heavy with despair? Then came the dresses I wore when there was hope after all. They seem too precious to subject to the trivial tasks that fill my days now. Later came the long sea voyage with Eddie and our wee baby, our early days in New Zealand, moving on to Fred's farm as sharemilkers, the homestead with the chicken-pecked putty. Trips to town, Eddie unfolding the pram from the boot of the car with pride while Hugo slept in my arms. Making friends with other Plunket mothers, comparing notes as my England friends had so many years earlier. Bowel motions, nappy rashes, sleeping patterns, milestones. I would sit on the padded benches in the Plunket waiting room, holding the narrow Plunket book in my hands, knowing that on the middle page was a chart to graph progress, a red line for average and a yellow band indicating the range considered normal. Hugo was off the scale.

On his first day of school I wore an indigo satin blouse. The teacher, Miss Green (barely out of her teens), took his hand and led him away to the classroom. His fingers lay obediently within her grasp, and his legs trit-trotted along, but his head was turned towards me as he went. 'Mummy,' he said. 'Mummy.' Louder and louder. Even after he was gone from sight, down the corridor and into the classroom, I could still hear him. It was the first time in my life I hadn't been able to rescue him. My eyes spilled gallons, which poured onto the indigo satin, bruising it the purple of thunderclouds.

Eddie rolled his eyes as I walked towards the car, hardly able to contain the sobs which welled from my wounded womb, and shuddered up through me, choking out of me. I sounded, Iris, just like a sick cow.

'Get in,' Eddie said. 'I've got those bloody heifers to move yet. And I've got to be in town by eleven.'

It was as though the stain of my tears was still in the fabric as I arranged the blouse on the table with the scissors hovering. I never wore it again. It joined the ranks of garments too reminiscent. Eddie disappeared to the back of the farm, and I was left all alone for the first time in years. I cleaned the house, but that hardly took two hours, even though I dawdled over Hugo's room, the arrangement of his Matchbox cars on his windowsill, his crayons and coloured pencils in their tins on his desk. I lined his shoes up in his cupboard, sniffing the leather, the Hugo-smell that hinted at the pale softness of the soles of his feet.

Eddie went off to town with Fred, and I had lunch alone. In the afternoon I put my feet up for an hour, reading *Woman's Own*. Then I baked a banana cake, honey snap biscuits from the *Edmonds* book Maisie had given me as a welcome gift, and pikelets for Hugo's afternoon tea.

Still there was half an hour until he was delivered at the bottom of the hill by the school bus, so I yielded to temptation and cried.

The blouse has hung in the wardrobe ever since. Eddie was always on about my wardrobe, the way you could hardly get your hands between the garments. But there's no one to be troubled by it now. No one who cares enough. If Eddie were alive I'd be having the last laugh. There's not much that hasn't been cut up and given a second chance at life. And the indigo satin blouse's turn has come.

Near the hem I placed my iris petal template, tracing around it in pencil, adding a seam allowance as I cut. I pinned the pieces in place inside the curve of the second wedding ring, rearranging them until I was happy with the design. It was hardly cut before Nat interrupted.

'Just press this button,' he said in the garden, 'and look into this screen here. Watch.' He walked away, appearing suddenly in the box, and making a face. An emergency trip to town had been made to purchase a tripod, which had suddenly become vital to proceedings. Another cheque had arrived from Hugo, confirming Nat's theory that as long as only money was required, Hugo was the world's best father. This time Nat gave me half, in cash.

His foray into the interior of the second-hand shop netted the tripod, seen just days before on a fact-finding mission.

'Which button?' I asked. 'This little silver one on top?'

'That's the one. It says R-E-C. That's short for record.'

'I could probably have worked that out for myself.'

His image on the screen smiled and gave an exaggerated wink. 'When I say *Action*, push the button and keep an eye on the screen to make sure I'm there. If you need to move the camera, just use the lever on the right.'

Nat had set up a kitchen chair for me to sit on, and an umbrella overhead as protection from the sun. He removed his T-shirt, draping it over a nearby lavender bush, and took up Eddie's old spade.

'Why are you wearing those horrible old woollen shorts?' I called, wondering where he'd found anything so hideous.

'Don't worry about those.'

'They look like something out of the Ark.'

'It's just an idea I've got, all right? Now can we get on with it? Come to think of it, Gran, can you tilt it down a bit, so you don't get my head in the frame.'

'No head?'

'Just, you know, shoulders down.'

'You want me to film you without your head?'

'Just use the lever to tilt the camera down a bit.'

I moved the lever. One inch and all I had were his feet, in their craggy old boots. I eased it up again. Sky.

'Action,' he called.

'I'm not ready.' I pulled the lever again. Nat bounced into view.

'Just my body. Not my head.'

'I got that bit. It's sensitive, that's all.'

'Ready?'

'Got it.'

'Action,' he called, and he began to dig. Despite my efforts to feed him, his ribs were prominent. Prime rib roast with skin, and body, still attached. His shoulders were narrow, and he'd already shown me a trick he could do, bending forwards and tensing his muscles and holding his breath, which caused his stomach to meet his backbone. In this era of plenty, of fresh fruit and vegetables and labour saving devices, he looked like a prisoner of war. I watched his image on the screen as he dug, carving out a square of earth first, which he had measured and marked on the ground with a fluorescent spray can, then transferring the loose soil to the wheelbarrow.

'Should we ask Fred's boy to help?' I asked.

'No, Gran. I'll be fine.'

'What about sunburn? Shouldn't you have sunblock on?'

'Later, Gran. I'll be sweet.'

'Sweet chilli peppers, I would say.'

He grunted and groaned as he shifted earth.

'Have I filmed enough yet?'

'No, Gran. I need the whole thing.'

'But there are three to go after this one.'

'Don't remind me.'

'What's so interesting about a man digging a hole? Especially four times over.'

'There is a plan. Wait and see. Don't you remember that book you used to read me, about wait and see?'

I watched for a while, trying not to disturb him, aware that talking made his task all the harder. 'This is like Chinese water torture.'

'What d'you think it's like for me?' He paused to mop the sweat running into his eyes.

'Shall I cut that bit out?' Not that I would have known how.

'Nah, nah. I need it all. Just keep it going. Let me know when it gets to the end of the tape.'

'How will I know that?'

'It will say. *End of tape.* Up in the corner of the screen. And it'll click.'

'Are you sure you want to build this, Nat? It seems an awful lot of effort, to me.'

'I'm not as sure as I was,' he said.

'You *can* stop, you know.'

'Yeah, yeah. I know.'

But he didn't. I watched his tiny screen image dig four holes, pausing only to drink from a water bottle, and to change the tape, the end of which was signalled clearly enough even for me.

Pork chops with apple sauce and brown sugar – the chops wrapped in foil and baked in a slow oven to keep in the juices, the rinds grilled into melt-in-the-mouth crackling. Scalloped potatoes steeped in cheese and sour cream. Fresh steamed asparagus drizzled with melted butter, and cauliflower from the garden, boiled just long enough to soften. Creme caramels afterwards, baked in the cooling oven as we ate.

'Do you want those potatoes, Lily?' Nat asked, fork poised, swooping as I shook my head, eating my leftovers before they had time to cool.

'Didn't have room,' I said, laughing. Really it was the wooden thing. They turned solid as soon as I began to chew. Each mouthful was a challenge. How had I done it for so many years – eaten? 'Eyes bigger than my stomach,' I said. 'That's my problem.'

He could have made a joke here. I realised, too late, how open I'd left myself. But he laughed with me, devouring the relics of creamy potatoes, glancing across at the cooling dessert.

After his bath I smoothed aloe vera onto the skin of his back while he tried not to flinch. 'Grandmothers know some things,' I said, feeling the heat of his sunburn seep into my cool fingers.

'No need to rub it in,' he said, and we both laughed out loud at the pun-master.

I told you he's a clever boy.

Lily

[Sixteen]

The Fat Boy

Jimmy Dodd says, 'I bet you can't jump off the bridge.'

The others do it, backs as oily as seals as they clamber from the creek and up the bank, rats' tails of murky water spiralling from the hems of their shorts as they trek back across the baking concrete, towards the centre of the bridge, over the rail, ready to jump again.

The fat boy clasps the coins in his hand. He has always been afraid of throwing them off the bridge, of some uncontrollable urge that would rise within him, forcing his fingers to open, the money tumbling into the water below while he watched in horror. He is wearing his best pants and his best white shirt. It feels as though his mother's iron is still pressed against the fabric at his back. The cicadas in the poplars at the sides of the road are deafening – squealing, shrieking, taunting. Their rhythm spells out Jimmy Dodd's words. 'I bet you can't – click, click – jump off the bridge.'

The water is green and ducks hover in the weeds near the banks and peck at overhanging branches. One opens its beak and laughs at him. His buttoned cuffs are carving into his sweaty wrists.

'Bet you can't,' says Jimmy Dodd. Water drips from his fringe onto his nose. The freckles on his arms are so close together they almost join up. He is a living dot-to-dot. He throws himself, laughing, from the bridge. The fat boy hears the splash, watches the hair splay under the water like seaweed, the limbs flagellate, the body transform into a torpedo. Jimmy Dodd's head breaks the surface. 'Chicken,' he says, laughing. 'I dare you. I dare you.'

'Yeah, Fats,' says another of the boys, Murray Spinks. 'It's more fun than Sunday School.'

'Christ, anything's more fun than bloody Sunday School,' says Peter Boyle. 'What a ponce, eh? What a freak. Doing what mummy says, eh?

Lily's Cupola 91

She'll never know, Dumbo. Put your clothes over there, behind the tree. We won't tell, will we, boys?'

Jimmy Dodd appears on the bridge again, dripping water. 'I will,' he says. 'I'll tell his old man he's a fucking queer. I'll tell him I saw him jerking off behind the bike sheds. And guess who was watching? Only *Sir*!' The boys roar with laughter. A duck joins in.

'Sir likes boys,' says Peter Boyle. 'At least, that's what I've heard.'

The fat boy tightens his fingers around his money. His sweat mingles with the sweat of innumerable other hands that have clutched the same coins. He knows the earthy smell that will rise from his palm as he drops his offering into the felt-lined offertory plate. The organ will wheeze another chord, and Mrs Hamilton's nostrils will twitch in distaste, and he will feel disappointment that he has not saved some to buy lollies at the dairy on the way home. God would know. He would be watching. The fat boy wonders if He's watching now. He takes a step backwards.

'Sir's Dumbo's boyfriend, Sir's Dumbo's boyfriend,' chants Jimmy Dodd into the fat boy's face. Stagnant water from his fringe splatters across the Splendour-apple cheeks. The fat boy takes another step backwards. 'I seen ya,' whispers Jimmy Dodd.

Sometimes the fat boy stays in the classroom at lunchtime, pretending to work. And sometimes Sir leans over his shoulder, pointing out an error, which the fat boy rubs with his finger until the page threatens to disintegrate. Sir's breath tickles his neck like a feather.

'Use an eraser,' Sir says.

'Can't, Sir.'

'Why not?'

'I don't have one, Sir.'

Jimmy Dodd's desk is like a nest, full of colourful treasures, pencils, erasers, stamps, Weetbix cards, and tight balls of waxed paper which once held home baking.

'You had a new one just the other day.'

'I know, Sir.'

'Where is it then?'

'Lost, Sir.'

'How can it be lost? There's no such thing as lost. Items made from matter – which I assure you, boy, an eraser is – don't simply cease to exist.'

'I know, Sir.'
'Then where is it?'
'I can't say, Sir.'
'Can't? Or won't?'
'Can't, Sir. Sorry, Sir.'

'I dare you to jump,' says Jimmy Dodd. 'I bet you can't. I bet you your lunch for a whole month that you can't jump off the bridge.'

The fat boy takes another step backwards. The coins are hot against his palm. Hot and rancid. He holds out his hand, opens his fingers. A shilling and a sixpence, stuck together with his sweat. The tui on the sixpence eyes him suspiciously.

'Poofter,' says Jimmy Dodd, scooping the coins up and dashing away. The fat boy turns and runs until he reaches the church. The organ grinds from within, and the congregation is already inside. Behind the Sunday School Hall is an oak tree with branches low enough to climb.

On the way home the bridge is empty. His finger delves inside the hole in his best pants where they caught on the bark as he climbed down.

'What happened here,' asks his mother, a mountain of cheese scones steaming on the table behind her.

'The pew had a splinter,' he says. 'They ripped when I stood up.'

'Never mind,' she says. 'But you'd better get them off before your father sees. Then we can have some lunch.'

[Seventeen]

3 December

Dearest Iris

Isn't it astounding how one day can seem like any other, then suddenly someone says something that will change things irredeemably. It was Marjorie, at society night, potential sons-in-law and grandchildren forgotten, even if only temporarily. 'Girls, girls,' she cried before we even opened our quilts across our knees. 'We've been invited to submit work for an international exhibition. In London! Wouldn't that be something?'

We were all ignited by her words, imagining our quilts hanging in a London gallery, studied and commented on by thousands, perhaps hundreds of thousands. A far cry from the Hill Masonic Hall, amongst the leftover paraphernalia of a secret society which has now moved to new premises above the New World car park. We sometimes get an audience of fifty – one hundred if we tie it in with the new vineyard's open weekend, or the school gala day. And all of them critical of anything not strictly traditional. Serena is the one most harshly criticised, with her galloping home stitches and bits of string hanging off, her feathers and twigs and acorns and shells. 'I wouldn't want to go to bed if I had to face that every night,' they say. And, 'What's she on?' Suzanne, of course, is the most popular, with her ditzy prints, her pastel shades, her Friendship Spool and English Ivy designs. Although Marjorie once made a big hit with a Drunkard's Path.

Drunkard's Path. I have yet to make one, despite the scope of the design. The very idea reminds me too much of Eddie. Eddie liked his glasses slim-waisted. Like his women. I didn't know, when I married him, just how much. A cool seven-ounce with a head like sea foam was perfection to him. Condensation frosting the sides, effervescence forming from nowhere, tearing away from its roots, irresistibly rising. He graduated, of course, to a twelve-ounce. Tall and shapely, with a lip as thin as fine china and a solid inch of glass at the bottom through which, if watched, the world distorts.

A Drunkard's Path quilt can have the same effect, depending on the choice of colours. It can be like the two faces with a vase between, a psychedelic design of spirals and checks, an optical illusion. I'm reminded, always, of Eddie making his way every night to bed. A headlong stumble. Nothing so civilised as a wash. Just a gargantuan pee, and collapse.

'The only problem,' Marjorie continued, 'is the deadline. The beginning of February. They want to open the exhibition in the middle of March. Well, girls, what do you think?'

Bernie is working on blocks eighteen inches square. She has hand-dyed the background colour so that it varies from the richest delphinium indigo to a mauve so pale it is almost white. On to these blocks she is appliquéing white daisies, green leaves, and yellow fleur-de-lys. She needs twelve blocks to complete the quilt. 'I'm only on to number seven,' she said. 'If I stopped eating and sleeping I might get it done in time. I'll give it a go, though.'

'What about your last one? Ribbons and Roses. That's glorious.'

'I sold it,' Bernie said. 'Blast it. I wanted to give it to my sister, but I got a good offer at the exhibition in Auckland. A collector. Otherwise I could borrow it back.'

'I can have something ready,' Serena said, holding up her latest project, which resembles a shipwreck. If it weren't finished you wouldn't notice. It has frayed edges and a collection of toothbrushes dangling from the bottom corner. The sort of work which is selected on novelty value alone, though none of us would ever say so. 'We must have this,' I can imagine a selector saying. 'No one will have ever seen anything like it.'

'Jane?' Marjorie asked, determined to do the rounds before settling the focus on herself.

'You've got to be joking. I don't even want my kids to look at mine yet. Half the bits don't even hold together.'

'I'm sure that's not true. I simply love the colours you're using.' Marjorie stroked back a strand of hair, Autumn Russet, her latest attempt to enjoy being grandchildless. 'What about you, Barbara? ... Lily?'

Barbara's quilt shimmered and fluttered as she shook it out, a visible version of the Emperor's New Clothes. Gold and silver thread, strands of cirrus cloud and thunderstorms, bruises and irises and butterfly wings. There are pieces of my own indigo blouse in there too. Hugo's-first-day-at-school blouse. 'I have one corner to finish,' Barbara said. 'And a Flying Geese border with purple velvet and black. I could have it done.'

'Hoorah,' said Marjorie, unrolling her own quilt, its yellow ducks, red trains and blue boats dashing back and forth as it fluttered. 'Me too,' she said. 'There are just the fish. Two rows of fish. Then the border. And the quilting itself, of course. The quilting. But I'm going to machine-quilt this one. It shouldn't take long. What about you, Lily?'

I'd been delving into my wardrobe again, drawing out dresses in shades of blue, and up late at night with my cutting wheel and board, designing gentle curves so the pieces, once sewn, would lie flat. The dress I bought myself the day Hugo got his third-form school report has succumbed. Three As, the clever sausage. The blouse I wore to his last prize-giving. A prize for Home Economics. He was the first boy ever to have taken it at Hill College. The skirt I wore when we drove him through to Auckland, settled him into a strange bedroom in a student hostel, and drove back home without him. It stuck to the back of my legs in the heat, and I could never face wearing it again. But now it has been reinvented. 'The sea,' I explained, spreading the block on the occasional table beside my chair. That huge ocean on which our ship tossed like a walnut shell. The ocean which connects New Zealand to England. The same one which laps at the beach where we spent every summer day, underneath the pohutukawa tree. There is a silhouette on the right-hand side, reaching fingers across the top of the block. A mirror image of the tree which will snake its way up the entire left-hand border of the finished quilt. The pohutukawa. 'I don't have many more blocks to make, but I have to work them all together yet. And I'm going to hand-quilt, so that'll take me a while.'

'Get that grandson of yours to help a bit around the place,' Marjorie said.

'Oh, he does, he does.' In fact it worries me how much Nat helps. Not for his sake, but for mine. The more he does, the more I let him do; the less I do, the less I feel I can ever do again. And one day he'll announce that he's leaving, up and off back to the city, just as suddenly as he came. And where will I be then?

'I think you could do it,' Marjorie said. 'We could all help with the quilting, if it came to it. Let's all set ourselves a target. Let's move heaven and earth to get these quilts done.'

Serena cheered like a wild thing, and Barbara said, 'Hear, hear.'

'Any more news on the Lindsay front?' Suzanne asked once we had settled.

'Not a word,' said Marjorie sourly. 'She's never mentioned him again. How's a person supposed to get grandchildren, for God's sake? Still, I suppose there's some point in sewing together a hundred fishies if there's a chance this might be hanging on a wall in a London gallery.'

The next morning the transparent arrangement, with its neon coils and circuitry, announced that Amelia was coming to visit. 'Fed up with the rat race,' she said. 'Vincent and I need a day in the country. Just thought I'd better check that you're going to be home.'

I rushed to the kitchen. Scones, to be eaten with home-made plum jam and whipped cream. Pumpkin and spinach frittata. Ham sandwiches for Vincent. Red jelly for his pudding. And clementine cake to have afterwards with a cup of tea.

Amelia brought a rose in a black polythene bag. 'Mary Rose,' she said by way of greeting. 'When I saw it I thought of you.'

Sweet girl. Nat's mother, if she'd brought a rose at all, would have chosen Fire Engine or Tequila Sunrise, something modern and flashy, something high-health and disease resistant which would never grow out of control. A stiff pruning in July and a jet of spray every other week, and, hey-ho, blooms till June. Amelia always had more sensitivity than the others. Vanity aside, I've always thought her a bit like me, preferring the wild and unmanageable, the unerringly decadent. Mary Rose. Will she rise like the ship after four hundred years? I hope so.

Amelia insisted on a walk through the tangle of my garden, the too-long-unpruned Fritz Nobis suspending limbs at eye-height across the path, dazzling us with perfect pink blooms and grabbing our sleeves as our attention wandered. Mutabilis splayed like an old woman cast, flat on her back with flailing limbs, her frock woven from magnificent floral fabric, flirtatious blooms in apricot and pink, and every shade in between, on a background of burgundy foliage. Achillea drooping with bees. Poppies and cosmos and shasta daisies four feet high, all out of control. Vincent tore off ahead, discarding luminous blue gumboots as he went, which Amelia stooped to collect. We paused to admire Nat's four perfect holes. 'What's going to happen in there?' Amelia asked.

'Concrete,' he said. 'Gallons of it, but it's all right. I'm going to mix it in the barrow. The builders' mix is getting delivered later on today.'

'I want to be able to grow things right next to the poles,' I said. 'I don't want concrete sticking up above the ground, and all rough and mountainous.'

'I'll only fill up to here.' He indicated a level two-thirds of the way up the side of one hole. 'Then, when it's dry, I'll fill it over with topsoil. You could grow the best bloody pansies in the world there. Bit of compost, and you're away laughing.'

'Ooh, a hole,' said Vincent, arriving, curious.

'You keep away from those holes,' Amelia warned. 'You don't want to go falling into them.'

Vincent went aeroplaning off and returned, swooping dangerously close to the edge of one.

'Watch it,' Amelia called as he dashed off again, taking another path through the garden and reappearing beside Nat. Vincent stared up into Nat's face, took his hand, and swung on his arm.

'Come on,' he said. 'I want to look, but I don't want to go head first into a shallow hole.'

We all laughed, and he looked up, hurt.

'Where did he get that from?' Nat asked. Amelia shrugged.

'Next time you come, there'll be this beautiful thing here,' Nat told him, 'with a curving roof that looks like an onion.' Vincent frowned.

'How are you going to get the roof to curve?' Amelia asked, sipping lemonade on the back verandah, nibbling at the edge of her slab of clementine cake. 'All those bits of wood, well, I couldn't help noticing they're straight. If you want a Taj Mahal effect you'll have to use steel, surely.'

Nat laughed. 'I have thought of that. I might actually only be at the hole stage, but I have thought it through, you know. The whole process.'

'That's not answering my question.'

'Have you ever heard of lamination? Yeah, lamination. Well, it's kind of sticking bits of wood together so they're, you know, real thick. Only you bend them first. Use bits of two-by-one. Stick them on one at a time and clamp them till the glue sets. Next thing, you've got a curved bit of wood. The glue's expensive. Two-pot stuff. But that's no problem.'

Vincent, lying on the verandah in the sun, pressed his perfect cheek against the painted wooden planks, his fingers – pinky uppermost, like a fop holding a champagne glass – giving life to a Matchbox car which he watched with concentration. And I in turn watched Vincent. His skin against the wood. His eyelashes against his cheek like a frayed edge of brown silk. His fingers dented by suggestions of knuckles. So like Hugo as a child.

'I thought you were out of a job,' Amelia said. 'Who's bankrolling the whole project? Not Lily, surely? You're not living off Lily, are you? Expecting her to pay for your brainchildren?'

'Nah, nah, nah,' Nat said. 'Dad's paying.'

Amelia threw her head back and her laughter caught amongst the rafters and corrugated iron of the verandah roof, bouncing back at us until we joined in. Vincent looked up, momentarily alarmed, then went back to his car. His left hand arrived with a tow-truck.

'Hello,' he mimicked in a high American voice. 'Hello. Where are you going? ... Er ... Auckland. What did you have for breakfast? ... Oh, I had ... er ... rice bubbles ...'

'I wanted to talk to you,' Amelia said when Nat had gone down onto the driveway to meet the delivery truck. 'About Hugo.'

I suspected as much. 'What about Hugo?'

Amelia collected the condensation from the sides of her glass, then stroked her damp fingertips down her smooth plump neck to cool herself. 'He's been so good, well, about money. I have to say that first. I have no gripes with him at all in that respect. And he's never spent so much time with Vincent as he has since we separated. Five o'clock on a Friday night, there he is on the doorstep. Five o'clock Saturday night, back again, both of them glowing. Too many icecreams and the like, but there are worse fathers.'

I waited. Diane came once in a fit of rage. Drove all the way from Auckland at ten o'clock at night just to show me the black eye Hugo had given her. I could hardly speak. Hugo was many things, but I'd never thought violent was one. It turned out to be an accident – one of those things with two people, one on each side of a door, one pushing, the other pulling. And bang. After the separation it was constant, a diatribe of Hugo's wrongdoing, everything from extravagance to toenail trimming. I despaired of the sight of that red Datsun clambering up the driveway, Diane, the same enraged hue, at the wheel. At least Nat's mother had the good sense to flee to her own family. No doubt they tired of Hugo's faults as quickly as I did, but at least there was no blame attached.

'He's been generous, letting me keep the house,' Amelia said. 'And he still pays for Monica to clean.'

I wasn't fool enough to ask her to get to the point. I knew she would, soon enough.

'It's Joanna,' she said at last.

'Ah, Joanna.' It was almost a relief.

'Have you met her?'

'Not yet.'

'Has Nat?'

'Apparently so.'

'What does he think?'

'I gather he doesn't approve. But it might be jealousy more than anything. He and Hugo now communicate only by bank balance. Poor Hugo. He must be supporting a large proportion of the world by now.'

Amelia's hand dropped to her lap. She turned away to watch Nat as he chatted with the truck driver.

'I don't approve either,' she said at last. 'And it's not just because I used to be married to him. She's a stick insect, Lily. And about as intelligent. She's a coat hanger, and guess who supplies the clothes. He's got her working as hostess in the restaurant so she's never out of his sight. But she'll get tired of it. He'll get hurt. And apart from that he's making such a fool of himself. All his friends are concerned.'

'They're probably jealous too. A twenty-something stick insect. Who wouldn't be?'

'Me, for one. She's just so grasping, Lily. She's obviously after his money.'

'As long as she realises there are prior claims on that.' At least he had the good sense to space his children out. Otherwise he'd be bankrupt. Bree is old enough now to support herself. And Nat. Officially, at least. But Vincent will need support for another twelve years yet. Or more. And Hugo's old mother? An emotional and financial drain, whose whim requires an elaborate cupola, and God knows what next? A new bathroom? Full-time live-in care?

'What happened between you?' I asked, breaking my own rule of non-interference. The curve of Amelia's cheek seemed so vulnerable. I like her. She and Hugo were so good together. And Vincent deserves a father who lives with him.

She watched Vincent as Nat lifted him into the cab of the truck, as he swung the wheel wildly back and forth. Then her head went down, her glossy burgundy hair falling forward across her face. 'I don't know, Lily,' she said. 'Perhaps it was the arrival of the stick insect. Although Hugo says not. It was something to do with domesticity, with motherhood. No offence, Lily, but he told me once that he had a fear of his lover turning into his mother. Once he caught me in a pair of pink fluffy slippers, and he almost had a fit. I thought he was going to keel over there and then. He's got hang-ups, Lily. None of it's down to you.'

Nat lifted Vincent down from the cab to watch the tray tip, the builders' mix slide with a metallic roar onto a tarpaulin at the edge of the driveway. His face was round and perfect next to Nat's, his plump finger pointing as he babbled away in Nat's ear.

'I'm not stupid,' I told Amelia when the tray had once again descended, and the driver had hoisted himself into the cab and driven away. She turned towards me alarmed, and away again. 'I made mistakes. I didn't see it, at the time.'

'You were a wonderful mother,' Amelia said to the sky. 'No one could hope for a mother more devoted than you.'

After a moment I laughed. 'You're kind. And you're right in some ways. There was never a child more loved than Hugo. Except, perhaps, for Vincent.'.

Amelia frowned, uncomfortable with the comparison.

'All I'm saying is don't make the mistakes I did. Don't love him too much.'

'I don't think you can love a child too much,' Amelia said, still gazing across the circular driveway to where Vincent had climbed to the top of the builders' mix and settled himself with his cars. 'And I don't think you should blame yourself for anything. Hugo is a grown man. He's nearly fifty, for God's sake. If he can't take full responsibility for the person he is by now, he never will.'

But as she drove off, Vincent's thumb making for his mouth as he waved goodbye, his head already beginning to nod against the side of his carseat, I knew she was wrong. And I believed that she knew it too. Everything Hugo does is somehow down to me.

So there you have it, Iris. A catalogue of my undoing. You can have the last laugh.

Lily

[Eighteen]

Floss

Sixteen weeks, Floss writes, *and one day.* It is morning, but there is no sun as she writes at her tiny table, no shadow as her pen meanders through the words. *Too cold to go to the market. Frozen peas for three nights in a row.*

She winds the cap carefully onto her pen, turns away from the book with its meagre entries, and draws her ankles together, watching her slippers with their bunion elbows, their fluffy asteroids through which peep her big toes, nails too long, unreachable. Then she turns suddenly back to the book.

I don't know what to do, she writes. *I couldn't keep my mouth shut, and now I've made trouble.* Her hand shakes, giving the letters bulges and deformities. *I had to go and say something, didn't I?* She stops, terrified by those words. Just what Reggie used to say. 'You had to go and say something, didn't you? Why can't you ever keep your mouth shut?'

He was right, all those years ago. Reggie knew she couldn't be trusted. She was young then, and stupid with it. Her problem now, she knows, is the solitude. Too many hours alone each day. And when at last there's someone to talk to, it all spills out, layers and layers of words, tumbling indiscriminately outwards and downwards, spreading across the floor until they are ankle deep, seeping over the tops of her shoes. And then comes the realisation that it has happened again. And the remorse. But it's too late. She is forced to wade through the words, leaving them to be scooped up, cleared away, by someone else.

In the park, while Julie pushed Daniel on the swing, Floss had been careless. 'My soldier,' she said, and spoke of his arms, his charm, his teasing humour.

'Sounds lovely,' Julie said wistfully, as though she could do with a soldier of her own. Then, 'He got medals, din'e? You said one other time.'

Floss felt an eel of fear slither through her. Julie thought her soldier was Reggie, and Floss couldn't think how to put her straight.

'How old was y' then, when y' got wed?'

'Twenty-five,' Floss had said, knowing already that her chance had gone.

The clock on the wall grows cranky as the long hand approaches the hour, the pendulum swinging wildly in time with Floss's heartbeat. Then, a groan, a croak. Bong, bong, bong. Ten bongs. She counts each. The sound echoes inside her head. In between each is an eternity of solitude, of memory, of remorse.

Her soldier was married, of course, and it was years after the war, but that's how she has always thought of him. Her soldier. He had a vegetable patch at the back of the garden, and she used to watch him from her bedroom window while she sat at her desk pretending to write letters. When he got hot he would peel off his shirt and singlet and take up the spade again to dig. She turned to paraffin at the sight of him, liquid and burning. Every night she daydreamed herself to sleep, thinking of running her fingertips over the ridges and curves of his arms and back, seeing the whiteness of her fingers against his olive-brown skin, imagining the scent of his breath, the taste of his tongue in her mouth. Once or twice he caught sight of her through the window and winked while the blood rushed to her cheeks.

His wife, Lou, was old and fat, but she was always kind to Flossie. They would bake together and sew together, and chat and laugh over all the neighbourhood gossip. They would play cards and have afternoon tea, and all the while Flossie was dreaming about her soldier, about how to take him away from his wife.

Reggie was right. She was born to deceive. She would have made the perfect spy, the perfect secret agent. Her entire being was a double-edged sword.

She hoped, in a way, that her passion would pass. But years went by, and still she stared from her bedroom window. Still she watched him work in his garden. Sometimes he gave her strawberries over the fence, which she sucked with delight, or a cabbage for her mother. Once she took him a glass of lemonade. It was so hot and Lou was baking sponge cakes in the kitchen. She sat with him on the steps, and he drank it in one go. A trickle escaped from the corner of his mouth, running down his chin, and dripping off onto the hot bricks. She mopped his face, laughing, with her handkerchief.

She finished school and went to work in a drapery in the High Street. She spent all her wages on fabrics, and all her weekends sewing them into irresistible dresses with full skirts and tight waists. Her mother began to make noises about suitable boys for marriage. Her regret at the circumstances of her own life only stretched so far. Flossie should not be let off, if agony was to be had. Flossie looked, but she couldn't find a single boy who interested her. They were all too lanky, too spotty, too adolescent. She went to dances and accepted every invitation, but it was as though her soldier had emblazoned an image across her consciousness and no boy she met could fill that silhouette.

[Nineteen]

Floss

Fifteen weeks, Floss writes, *and two days. Cold with drizzle.* She goes into the kitchen to make tea. One spoonful for each person, and one for the pot. Just two these days, now that Reggie is gone. The gas ring hisses, the kettle sings, the aroma leaps up at her as she pours on the boiling water.

It was tea that brought them together in the end, she and her soldier. She wonders now if it really happened, or is it something she has fabricated with her lonely old lady mind, something she has wished so much that now she believes it. But it's no dream. Her life would have been so different if she had merely dreamed it.

She let herself into Lou's house, like any other day, but it was silent. There was no sound of Lou singing in the kitchen, or the old treadle sewing machine rattling away upstairs. Flossie's soldier was smoking at the kitchen table. He looked up as she entered.

'She's out,' he said. 'Your Auntie Pat's poorly.'

'Oh,' Flossie said. Her confidence from that day on the step had gone. She couldn't imagine what had possessed her to wipe his cheek with her handkerchief. Perhaps it was knowing Lou was in the kitchen, her own mother over the back fence, that allowed her to lead a man on and pass it off as the innocence of childhood. Now she was seventeen, alone in a house with a married man, and all she could think of was getting out that front door. She turned to go, but he caught her by the sleeve of her cardigan.

'Not so fast. Make a man a brew, will you?'

The gas ring hissed, the kettle sang, and the aroma leapt up at her as she poured on the boiling water.

How many times has she made tea in her life since then? Five times a day for more than fifty years. Five times three hundred and sixty-five, times fifty. A lot of times. And every time she has thought of that afternoon, the way his arm snaked around her waist, the way she turned to him without a thought for Lou, for the morals her parents had bred into her. She opened her mouth to his kisses, pulled him to her so tightly he could hardly breathe. The tea went cold as he took her upstairs, into the spare room, as he unbuttoned her cardigan, unzipped the carefully sewn dress which had been cut out in the kitchen below, by his wife. She watched, terrified, as he undressed in front of her, showed her the body she had tried to conjure so often, the penis she had not known how to imagine. Her daydream images had always had a marble Renaissance mystique about them, a strategically placed fig leaf, because of her innocence. Now the shattered fragments of stone whispered against the carpet as they fell.

'I love you,' she said as he forced his way in.

'I know that,' he said, running his hands over her waist, her thighs, over her breasts, her neck, the curve of her chin. She had never imagined anything so exquisite, so ghastly. It seemed to go on forever, but she wanted it to, because once it was over it might never happen again.

They lay on the bed for hours, until it got dark. He drifted in and out of sleep, but she was afraid to in case she missed a minute of being with him, or the sound of Lou's key in the lock. Eventually the telephone rang, and he pulled on his trousers and went downstairs. His voice wound its way up two flights to her ears.

'No, no,' he said. 'Stay with her, love. I think you should ... Flossie's here. She'll cook me some supper. Do you think – well, I mean, how bad is Pat? Flossie won't want to be in the house by herself. Do you think she should stay here the night?'

And so they played happy families for the evening, Flossie at the stove while he read the newspaper. Afterwards she washed the dishes and put them away while he listened to the radio. She went upstairs at ten o'clock, sleeping in the bed they had romped on, pulling the sheet up over her chin and smelling Lou's soap, Lou's steaming iron against the embroidered edging. Through the wall Flossie's soldier slept in the big bed alone. She heard the creak of the wirewove as he lowered himself into the hollow his body had made over the years. She heard him cough and sigh and roll about, and then snore softly as his body succumbed to sleep.

She stared, wide awake, at the grey space which in the daytime would have been the ceiling. There was too much blood, suddenly, in her veins and her heart pounded frantically, trying to circulate it through distended arteries. The fizzing in her ears was so loud she worried it would wake the neighbours or, worse than that, her soldier. She tried to rid her mind of the image of him coming towards her, the sculptural quality of his body. And what it did. But the image lurked inside her eyelids, springing forth as soon as she allowed them to close, a stark red silhouette of his bronzed shoulders, flat belly, muscled thighs, hiding in their shadows that secret place.

She rose in the dark and crept down two flights of stairs. She lifted the latch on the back door and crossed the cold brick path to the lavatory. The light snapped on with a crack like a whip, and there it was in all its whiteness, the porcelain bowl, scrubbed each morning by Lou, glowing under the harsh bare bulb. Flossie swayed and pressed one palm against the wall. She leaned over the bowl and spat into it. She wanted so much to be sick, and thought of all the worst things she could imagine: maggots, intestinal worms, junket, bacon fat. The sense of betrayal Lou would feel if she knew about the statue and the spare bed, the girl lying with her knees apart, stealing the essence out of someone else's husband.

Flossie spat strings of bubble-edged saliva, but nothing else came, no violent chunky suffocating rush of shame, no cleansing elimination of any kind.

She climbed back up two flights, a hand on the wall all the way so she would not have to turn on the light, stroking Lou's floral wallpaper, her fingers delving into the corners of each landing. She came to Lou's bedroom door, feeling the coolness, the smoothly mocking finish of the gloss enamel paint applied, years ago, by Flossie's soldier. She placed an ear against its surface but there was no sound, not even the soft snoring of earlier. She wrapped her fingers around the door handle, hollow brass with a toothed ridge around its circumference. But she could not turn it. What if Lou had come home while Flossie swayed over the lav? What if Lou was lying now beside her husband, tired from ministering to the sick, grateful for the warmth of his body beside her, the softness of her pillow, jolting awake just as she began to drift at the sound of the handle turning, watching with sudden understanding as

Flossie floated towards the bed in her borrowed nightgown?

Flossie moved past the door into the spare room, climbing into the bed, cold where she had left the covers turned back. She shivered momentarily, then began to breathe more deeply and doze. Her dreams were of over-ripe strawberries, of her dead father who had taken a bomb in the war, of others she had known in childhood, of severe, disapproving stares from passers-by. She dreamed a hand onto her cheek, its fingers weaving amongst her curls.

'Lonely?' he asked.

Of course she was lonely. She would be lonely forever now, because she knew what it was like to be with him.

'Move over,' he said, and he slid in beside her and did it all again, only slowly. Afterwards she cried.

'You'd better go back,' she said towards dawn, 'to your bed. Lou might come home.'

'Forget about Lou.'

'But she might ...'

'Forget it.'

She woke up alone, and when she went downstairs she found Lou making tea in the kitchen. 'Sit down, love,' Lou said. 'I've got something to tell you.'

[Twenty]

6 December

Dearest darling Iris

Double Wedding Ring is another difficult quilt, because of its complex design and curved pieces. It symbolises the bond of marriage and the rings exchanged at the altar, husband and wife performing the ultimate act of trust. It's an old design, first produced halfway through the nineteenth century and peaking in popularity early in the twentieth. You're not ready for it, Iris. You wouldn't even be able to complete a single circle. Better to stick with something simple, until your skills improve.

My Double Wedding Rings are complete now, rolled away in the corner of a pillow case until I'm ready for them again. They are the least of my worries. I am in trouble with Nat. 'What do you call this?' he demanded as I came in the other day from the garden. He was curled on the floor in front of the television with his ever trusty camcorder attached by wires. 'Sit down,' he said, 'and tell me what this is all about.'

I don't like to sit in armchairs early in the day. It is too easy to stay. My quilt in progress or a book is likely to leap into my hands, and my day is gone.

'What are you on about?' I moved his latest pile of books about architecture from the chair.

'This,' he said, indicating the television screen, largely filled with my floral-draped behind as I stooped over the china cabinet. It showed me removing items: cup, saucer and plate sets, vases, ornate platters. Holding them up to the light. Studying them as though I'd never seen them before. They were almost forgotten, although they've been with me forever, with Ma before that, and Olivia earlier still. But stored away behind leadlight they lose their familiarity, seeming like jewels when retrieved after time. Fine china has always appealed to me, its translucence, its crisp edges and glorious designs. The colours, the delicate clink as the pieces kiss.

On the screen I turned over each object and placed a sticker underneath. Once everything was done I filled the china cabinet again, arranging each set on the green baize with care, locking the door so Nat would never know.

'What do you call that, then?' he asked.

'I call it unauthorised surveillance.' I was suddenly angry at the silver box, whirring away constantly in corners, taking in everything through its fish-eye, invading any privacy I might have had left.

'You don't need to jump down my throat,' he said, frowning. 'You don't like being caught out, do you?'

'Caught out? What I do in my own home is surely my own business, Nat.'

He took a long slow breath. 'I just want to know what you're doing. That's all.'

'Don't play the innocent. It doesn't suit you. You know exactly what I was doing. Because you've been through the cabinet yourself, haven't you? You've turned every one of those plates and cups over to see whose name is on the bottom. And you're upset, because none of them says Nat.'

'I'm not bloody interested in your stuff after you die. The others can fight it out between them for all I care.'

'Well you should care! You should. That china is part of me, Nat, part of my life. It came across the world with me, and in some ways it's the only tangible thing that ties me to my home, my childhood. It would make me feel a lot better to know someone cared.'

He coughed three times, flattened his palms across his face so I couldn't see his expression, drawing them down finally across the curve of his chin and onto his neck. 'Okay, so I screwed that one up. It wasn't meant to come out like that. What I meant was, why do you suddenly decide you have to label everything? Why now? Why this week? Has something happened that I don't know about?'

'How could anything happen without you knowing about it? With that bloody thing always watching me?'

He picked up the remote control and paused the frame on the screen, capturing an image of my back as I arranged cups back inside the cabinet. The bevel-edged glass in the door caught a ray of sunlight, casting prisms onto the wall above my head. 'It can't film what you're thinking,' he said.

'Can't it?' It might as well have gone straight inside my head, spelt everything out in large letters. But Nat seemed vulnerable. 'It doesn't hurt to think about the future.'

'And you think the future is death?' He looked up, his eyebrows forming the hypotenuse of two back-to-back triangles.

'Nat,' I said, trying to sound gentle. 'I'm eighty-three.'

'That doesn't mean you have to give up.'

'I'm not giving up. I'm just trying to be ... well, sensible. I've seen the fights when people die. Maisie next door. Her sisters swooped in like vultures. They scratched through that house with their claws until there was nothing of hers left. Poor Fred was too stricken to stop them. They scrapped over her coats and her shoes and her trinkets. God knows, she didn't have anything valuable – all the money went back into the farm. Two of the sisters still aren't speaking to each other. I just can't bear the thought of that happening here. All those wives of your father's. And he'd just stand there and watch.'

Perhaps I was flattering myself. I couldn't imagine Nat's mother stooping to the depths my wardrobe contains. 'It's not that I've got much worth taking,' I said. 'But some things are special. Some things I would like to gift. They can do what they like with the rest. It doesn't mean I'm going to die.'

'Doesn't it?' he said, cynical. 'The mind has power, you know. As soon as you let something like the possibility into your consciousness, that's it. You're a goner.'

'I've got far too much to do for that,' I said.

He stopped the tape and rewound it. He labelled it and filed it on the shelf with all the others. I wanted to hug him, for caring, but I felt too old and too tired, and he was too awkward, too burdened by his mother's reserve. He stood by the french doors, looking out. 'I'll make you a cup of tea,' he said. 'Why don't you do a bit more on the quilt?'

'Because if I do I won't get another thing done today.'

'Is that so bad?' He winked as he went off towards the kitchen. I was determined not to pick up the ocean block of my quilt, the silhouette pohutukawa onto which I'd decided to embroider chocolate-brown chain stitches to imitate bark. But it was only an arm's length away, on the occasional table beside my chair, folded neatly with embroidery cotton attached, the needle woven through the fabric. A look wouldn't hurt, to see if I was on the right track. Then it was spread across my lap, and the next thing I had taken up the needle.

When Nat returned with our mugs he laughed. 'Cyril's been,' he said, brandishing the mail, which he tucked between my box of cotton reels and my scissors.

'It's your fault if I don't do another thing today,' I said.

'Don't hit me, please!' He cowered, slopping his tea and laughing again. He drank what was left in audible gulps, three and it was gone. Most times he is up and away before I've even taken a sip. Today he was conciliatory, arranging himself on the floor at my feet, running a finger over the fabrics which made up the ocean block.

'Tell me about it,' he said.

'It's the sea,' I told him. 'This is the block that separates the two halves of my life. The journey from London to the sticks of New Zealand. By sea.' And as I spoke I recognised the true symmetry for perhaps the first time. That my life has been divided into two not-quite-equal halves, into northern and southern hemispheres, urban and rural, childlessness and motherhood.

When his interest had waned and he'd gone back into the shed to laminate his precious bits of Taj Mahal, and when I had finished my last mouthful of tea, I picked up the pile of letters. A telephone bill. Three glossy circulars. An airmail envelope with an English stamp.

Summer left me instantly. The pain in my shoulder returned. My hands shook too much for stitching chocolate-brown chains of pohutukawa bark. I was terrified, Iris. I thought it was a letter from you.

I heaved myself out of my chair, tucked the envelope behind a vase on the mantelpiece and walked out into my garden. I needed to be filled with the scent of roses and to discover the joys of things that had sprouted while I wasn't looking.

But even so, my head was filled with England. The first time real bombs fell while we huddled in the Anderson shelter was terrifying. We'd had our Phoney War, and now there was no doubt it was the real thing. The All Clear didn't sound till morning, and we stumbled out into the daylight with our bedding, and hardly a wink of sleep between us. Ma's china plates had fallen from the dresser and smashed on the floor. Our precious ration of sugar, too, had fallen in its cannister and spilled amongst the shards of porcelain. We spent an hour on our knees – sweeping up every fragment, washing the floors – then rushed out the door for work. It wasn't until evening that we had time to cry. Ma subsided over dinner, the stew so watery you couldn't tell the gravy from the tears. 'Never mind,' I said. And, 'It'll be over soon.' All those clichés no one is ever qualified to say. I was plotting ways already of replacing the broken china. But it turned out she was crying for the sugar, the thought of a fortnight without it.

After that it was kept in a tin with a firmly fitting lid, and we wrapped the remaining china and stored it in boxes under the stairs. Except the chipped pieces which we used every day. And we didn't get it out again until it was all over. I will never forget the shock of that first post-bomb morning, but more than anything now the china reminds me of Ma's post-war afternoon teas where her friends cried at the kitchen table from the shock of living with strange men masquerading as husbands, while I boiled water for tea. Then they repainted their lips, straightened their hair, rushed back to the pretence of normal life. A pound of stewing steak for his tea, and jam roly-poly for afters.

But I'm getting ahead of myself, Iris. The war can't be wiped out just like that. History has put a date on the end, but for us there was no counting down. *Only two years to go. Only five months to go.* It felt as though it would go on forever. There was a war, and there was Billy Brydon. You'll be wondering about him. He can't simply evaporate, not where I left him, wondering if he would ever kiss me again, if I would ever return a fragment of the affection he had offered that night on our dark porch.

He did come back. He took me dancing, and home to Mrs Lusk. Her garden backed onto ours. She had empty bedrooms, and let them out to soldiers on leave. The kid gloves, the ones I cut up to make suitcases for my quilt, were the same ones I wore when I was with him. My gloved hand was tiny inside his. His fingers curled over mine, his scars and calluses catching on the leather. Inside Mrs Lusk's, I left them on the dresser in the hall. We hung our coats on a row of hooks and hurried into the warmth of the living room. She looked up from her knitting, not bothering to smile.

'If you want cocoa, you can get it yourselves. I've only just sat down.' We shook our heads, too exhilarated from dancing to be concerned about anything as concrete as sustenance. Billy's eyes were bright, expectant. I followed him across the room, sat on a corner of the sofa, my knees and ankles decorously together, the toes of my shoes lined up. Billy sat beside me, his thigh pressing against mine. I could feel his hot breath on my neck, each exhalation so exquisite the whole room went out of focus. I could smell the wool of his uniform, the malt on his breath from the beer he had drunk. He planted his hands firmly on his knees, his arms like architectural buttresses, and studied the fire, Mrs Lusk's twitching knitting needles, the old floral design on the carpet. He lit a cigarette and blew the smoke at the ceiling. He put an arm around my shoulders, pulling me closer and kissing my neck. 'I want to take you back with me,' he whispered while I stroked the red velvet arm of the sofa. Mrs Lusk pretended not to hear as she knitted socks for her four sons at the front. She leaned closer to the wireless as Churchill's voice spilled into every corner of the room, sticking in the folds of the blackout curtains, falling into the space between her collar and the back of her neck, sliding underneath the old rolled-arm chairs, and into the weave of the threadbare carpet.

'Would you come with me?' Billy whispered, and I waited, in case it wasn't really happening. 'Would you cross the ocean with me, Lily? Would you leave everyone you know, to start a new life? Would you be mine?'

Still he hadn't said the word, the crucial word that Ma had taught me to wait for. The word that opened a girl's heart, like a key. (Her legs too, so I learned.)

'Be moine,' he said in his quaint accent, running his rough fingertip across the palm of my hand. The scars glowed on his knuckles, across the back of his hands, places where the dark hair didn't grow. From farm work, he had told me, detailing each one, which tool was to blame, where he was on the farm when it happened, how many stitches it had taken to stem the flow of blood. It was nothing for him to have ridden his horse two hours across the farm and lonely gravel roads, to get help.

And always there was a sense of wickedness as he told his tales, at laughing when I knew it could have been so serious. If he hadn't made it he wouldn't have been there on Mrs Lusk's couch, whispering to me.

His palms were callused from digging in. He didn't talk about that, though. He didn't volunteer a word about that other life, the one that could take him at a moment's notice back across the Channel, and into the path of death. And I never asked. I wanted to pretend that the war wasn't real. That it would all stop tomorrow, and Billy and I could sail across those vast blue oceans to our new life.

And in a way it did all stop the next day. For me at least. Billy was called back and I was left with a chasm which had to be filled with dreams. Every night I tried until it hurt, but I couldn't recapture the fabric to make him seem real. Months passed without word from him, and I was trying to convince myself I'd done the right thing in not giving myself over without constraint. He was a long way from home, after all. And lonely. How could I even begin to imagine his loneliness, secure as I was in the family home, with all the routines I'd grown up with? I hounded poor Mrs Lusk, asking every day if she'd heard from him. Of course she hadn't. Why would a young soldier bother to write to an old widow with rooms to rent?

I was still stitching when Fred came in the afternoon, and we drank tea on the verandah, watching Nat construct profiles to hold his poles in place while the concrete set. He used a string-line, measuring tape and level. He drove boards into the earth amongst my lavender and penstemons, trampling the faces of pansies beneath his steel-capped boots. The silver box stood on its tripod, aimed and focused, set in motion without my help.

'He'll never get them plumb,' Fred said through a mouthful of biscuit. 'I'll send the boy over when I get home.'

'Would you?' I have faith in Nat, of course, but he doesn't know when he's out of his depth. 'He'll go at it for weeks, until he gets it right. A bit of help might save us all a lot of time.'

'Ah, bugger it,' Fred said, hauling himself out of his chair. 'I'll ring the young bugger. He's got one of these yuppie phone things. Give him the shock of his life if it actually rang.' He went into the hall and negotiated with my neon arrangement. 'Christ, the numbers are big enough,' he called.

'Hugo's idea,' I said. 'I might have trouble seeing numbers of normal size.'

Fred laughed. *He, he, he.* Then I heard his voice, dry on the edges, shouting down the phone. 'Drop everything, lad. You're needed over here.' Laughing again as he hung up. *He, he, he, he.*

We watched the two of them setting up the profiles, driving in the nails, tensioning the string-line, measuring the diagonal, making adjustments, remeasuring.

'He hasn't shot through yet,' Fred said.

'Not yet.'

'Might hang around a while after all.'

'He just might do that. But I can't think why. God knows, there's not much to hang around here for.'

'Little gold mine, this place. A few more years they'll put a motorway through. They'll be selling pocket handkerchiefs of your hillside there for a million bucks.'

'Yours too,' I said.

'Mine too.'

'Only I hope I'm dead before it gets to that.'

Fred laughed. He reached over and took my hand. His was leathery, scarred, rough on the palm. Mine has grown soft and pink since Nat's arrival. Fred's eyes were bright blue, brighter than the sky, and mischievous as always. 'If you were a few years younger, Lily,' he said, lascivious.

'Oh yes?' I laughed. 'I'm sure you're well beyond anything you're imagining right now.'

'Don't be too sure. I'll take you on anytime you want. Just say the word.'

We both laughed then. We can joke about it now that so much time has passed.

When he'd gone home the boys mixed concrete and poured it into the holes. They worked the ends of the poles into the mixture, then tacked them into place. Fred's boy went home and Nat found himself a beer and drank it on the verandah steps.

'What will you do if your quilt is picked?' he asked me, evaluating the angle of the poles against each other and against the sky.

'I have to finish it first.'

'I know, I know. But assuming that happens ...'

'I don't know. Perhaps I'll go to England with it.'

'Would you want to do that?' he asked, surprised. 'I thought you didn't want to go back there.'

'To be honest, I don't know.'

'What if I came with you? What if you showed me round, took me to where you used to live, all that stuff. The stuff you reckon your kids and grand-kids should care about.'

'Would you do that?'

'Hell, yeah. If Dad pays. There's no one else in the world that knows how much work you've put into that quilt. I'd be so proud of you if they chose it.'

'Would you, Nat?'

'Hell, yeah. We could jet off together, Gran. Just you and I. Stay in hotels and let someone else do all the cooking for once. Would you like that?'

The thought terrified me. Could I stand being constrained in an airline seat? Could I cope with seeing London again? Would it be too different, or too much the same?

Nat's grin was suddenly conspiratorial. 'Just you and I, Gran. That'd be so peachy. We could stride into that exhibition hall as though we owned it. Can you imagine? And you'd be famous as hell. Everyone would want you to sign autographs. And someone would come along and offer you fifty thousand bucks for it. Hey, I'll tell you what. I could have my film showing alongside the quilt. It could have its own story, Gran. From old dresses and stuff to the finished product. What do you say?'

I said nothing, Iris. What could I say? The young are so carried away by impossibilities. Which is more than I can say for Nat when I served his dinner.

'What's this?' Not a thought for manners or any display of gratitude.

'Vegetable curry.'

'Sweet,' he said. 'I think.'

'I felt like a change. It's good for you to skip meat occasionally.'

'Fine by me.' He tore a bread roll in half and dipped it into his curry. 'Are you having any?'

'I might have some later.'

The truth was, Iris, the thought of going back to England had taken my appetite right away. Perhaps I wouldn't have to try so hard to look after my heart, if I lived over there. I would just fade away to nothing.

All my love,
Lily

[Twenty-one]

9 December

Dear Iris

The Tree of Life is an ancient design, from back in the seventeenth century. It symbolises the basics of survival, the necessities – logs, wood, for homes, furniture, interiors, and firewood for cooking and heat. Did you ever stop and think of the value of wood? The design is made up of isosceles triangles for the branches, a rectangle for the trunk, and a larger triangle for the roots. It has a lot of variations, and a lot of names: Christmas Tree, Temperance Tree, Tree of Paradise, Tree of Temptation.

Despite all those symbols, and the Tree of Life cushion in my own living room, Paddy has been denied his. Life, that is. I found him dead in his kennel when I went down this morning to let him off. He was curled in sleep, or would have been, if he were a younger dog. Arranged might be a better word, his nose trying to reach his stiffened back paws, trying to warm them, trying to complete the circle. Shock passed through me in a physical wave, stinging my neck and spine and lingering in my fingers and toes. Death still has the power to do that, even after so many years and so many encounters with it. Finality frightens me, and the unfathomable transformation of a live body into simply a body. Yesterday I patted him, fondled the warm drooping ears. Today I was terrified by the rigid set of his bones, the blankness of his gaze. Paddy was gone, and there on the baked dirt in front of the kennel door were the three Tux biscuits I gave him last night when I tied him up, accusing me of negligence. Sniffed, perhaps, but not touched. Shouldn't I have sensed something, known he was on the edge? Did I ignore a pleading frightened look as I scattered his biscuits? Did he have any premonition? At least Eddie had seen his son, had known his family was near, our voices rolling like dust bunnies down the hall as he felt himself slipping away. Paddy had no such consolation. What kind of friend is solitude when you're dying?

I forced myself to lean down, to stroke the top of his head, the still-soft brown ears, wondering what kind of life I had given him, tied there every night, a bit of old sacking to sleep on, a few Tux thrown at him by way of nourishment. What was there in the way of love? And yet he was prepared to give such loyalty.

Nat had gone to town for coach bolts, and I was glad. He wouldn't have let me bury Paddy, and yet it was the only thing left I could do for him. And I wanted to do it.

I took the shovel from the garage and wandered down through the garden, past the four towering spikes of Nat's half-baked cupola, past the reclining Mutabilis and the possessive Fritz Nobis to a bald patch where a large cistus died from wet feet in the winter, which I never bothered to replace. In amongst the achillea and buds of shasta daisies I started to dig. A breeze came across the hills, tasting of salt and baking grass. It filtered through my nostrils and settled on the back of my tongue. What if it brought with it fragments of the lives it had caressed on its journey so far? A molecule of panic as a lone yachtsman miles from the coast went about. An atom of sweetness from a couple on the beach whose first kiss was shared in the night. All trepidation was gone, and familiarity, ownership, had crept into their movements. Anger from a sixteen-year-old daughter of a family in the valley, who stormed out after breakfast after an argument over a boy. Fear from a wife whose husband had come home past midnight three nights in a row. What if it all settled here, on my tongue, compounding with every breath I took? And with it, the jumble of my own life. The exhaustion, my fears for Nat, my regret that Hugo had to grow up.

I kicked the dirt with my gumbooted toe. In my mind's eye the hole was dug already, a few effortless shovels of soil tossed carelessly to one side. But the reality was harsher. The ground was hard, crying out for compost and aeration, for a tireless gardener's ministrations. The shovel swivelled and tipped, losing half of every load, and the wooden handle, polished from years between Eddie's palms, rubbed my soft quilters' hands into blisters. Why did I have such a big dog? Why not a bird-like chihuahua or a royalty-endorsed corgi?

The hole grew, and I paused more and more frequently to draw breath. The sun was climbing, the shadow of the house drawing back, exposing me to the stinging heat, the humidity so dense I could hardly breathe the air. Sweat formed on my lip and in the creases of my body, beginning to trickle like streams in the crinkles of a mountainside. It dissolved into the cotton of my dress and the fabric clung to me. I wanted to give up. It would have been so easy to collapse onto the step, to wait for Nat to return, and watch his face warp with sympathy as I bemoaned my situation. He'd have had it done in half an hour, a cinch after those four holes for the cupola.

Then I thought of Paddy, and picked up the shovel again.

It was done before noon, Paddy wrapped in an old grey blanket and stowed with care inside the earth, overplanted with Mary Rose, freed from her polythene bag at last and watered excessively, because only mad gardeners plant roses in December.

Afterwards I could hardly climb the steps, and left the shovel propped against the verandah pole. I lowered myself onto the couch and glanced up at the clock. Seven minutes to twelve. Nat had been gone so long, too long for a handful of coach bolts. Six minutes to twelve. Would I get his lunch, or could I stay where I was, gasping for air, holding my chest so my heart wouldn't leap out, balancing on the edge of something too awful to contemplate. The silver fish-eye, the airmail letter, Paddy in his grave. Nat, gone for too long.

I wanted to cry. But just when I had given myself permission, ensured the silver box was not humming, calmed my heart, allowed the loss to flood through me, there was the sound of tyres on the loose gravel of the driveway. Nat was home.

He brought a paper bag, and inside was a rainbow of fabric arranged from violet to red, and freshly ironed with crisp creases. 'Bernie hand-dyed it for me,' I explained. 'For the next block.' The one I've mulled over for so long, trying to locate a symbol for my life since crossing the ocean. Motherhood. What does it mean? More than nappies flapping on a line held up by teatree sticks, white against green hills and a blue, blue sky. More than booties and knitted matinee jackets and first days at school and steaming hot ginger gems and helping with homework and kissing goodbye. A single symbol to encapsulate so much, the tears and fears and overwhelming love.

So many symbols have occurred to me over the months. A stylised madonna and child, like those ebony sculptures carved in third-world countries. A scaled-down version of my first quilt, with the hillside and cows and the glitter of distant ocean. In the end it had to be flowers, a tangle of blooms appliquéd on a hand-dyed background. A daisy, a lily, a pansy, and an iris. One for each corner. The garden has been my solace for so long. It filled my days once Hugo had gone to school, rewarding me with growth and blooms and sweetness. It was mine alone, perhaps the only thing – apart from Hugo – I had ever truly possessed. No part belonged to Eddie, or to my parents. I will be there, amongst my four favourite blooms. And so will you, my sweet.

Since making the decision I have sought out photographs in gardening books, drawn and simplified and drawn again. Traced my designs, each leaf, each petal and stalk, onto acetone and then onto two-sided iron-on webbing. The pieces would be pressed onto the back of the rainbow colours, cut out with care, pressed onto the block, and appliquéd into place, the stalks and leaves overlapping, pulling the design into a circle, like poor Paddy. What more can be said about nurturing?

I couldn't wait to begin, and dragged the ironing board from its cupboard in the kitchen. The leg screeched and clicked into place, and the iron began to warm the already steamy air.

'Hang on, hang on,' Nat said, drawing travel brochures from a plastic bag and spreading them across the ironing board. He turned the pages, revealing special deals to London via Los Angeles, Singapore or Kuala Lumpur. Stopovers, accommodation packages, rental cars, coach tours. Photographs of the Tower of London with ravens and beefeaters. And Tower Bridge, the Globe Theatre, and a terrifying construction called the London Eye. 'What about that, Lily, eh? Can you see yourself in that, looking down over London? Wouldn't that be something?'

'Is this where you've been so long? Wasting Helen's time down there at the travel agent's? Dreaming about something that can't ever happen?'

He scratched his head vigorously. 'Is that what you think? That it can't ever happen? Why the hell shouldn't it? Tell me that.'

'Because I'm too old, Nat. It's just a dream, that's all. I'll never get back to England now. I don't even know if I'd want to go back. It was a different life. I was just a girl when I left, you know. It'd be too much like turning the clock backwards. And nothing good ever comes from trying to do that.'

'You're not too old. That's just a cop-out. D'you know what I read about a few weeks ago? This woman, right, a hundred years old, and leaving England to start a new life in bloody Australia, to be near her son.'

'Mad.'

'Not mad. Brave. And I've never met anyone braver than you, Lily. So don't let that dame put you to shame. If she can do it, then you can get to London, and jitterbug on top of Big Ben.' His eyes were bluer than Hugo's as he stared at me, and far more defiant than Hugo's ever were.

'I'm tired, Nat. I can't even face thinking about it at the moment, let alone going.'

'Oh no, not this putting-names-on-china stuff again. You know how I feel about that.'

'It's not that at all.'

'Go and have a sleep. You'll feel heaps better afterwards.'

'I don't want to sleep. I want to get started on this.' I stroked the pieces of mottled blue and mauve, the curves of webbing waiting to be ironed on, to become the petals of an iris.

'And anyway, what about your lunch?'

'I'll tell you what, I'll get my own lunch. How's that for radical? Then you can have a sleep.'

'Good grief. What kind of concoction are you likely to come up with?'

'You might be surprised. I'm not exactly useless in the kitchen.'

I laughed. 'Aren't you? How would I be able to sleep, anyway, worrying that the house might burn down any minute.'

'Ye of little froth,' he said, narrowing his eyes at me.

'Anyway, I've got Maree coming this afternoon, to do my feet.'

He sighed exaggeratedly. 'Did I say brave? I meant stubborn. Steamrollers are easier to move than you are. Now, what do you want on your sandwich?'

It wasn't until later that he noticed Paddy's absence. 'That bloody dog's run away,' he said, coming up the steps onto the verandah, tugging off his T-shirt to reveal his peeling shoulders. The hair on his arms is thick and fair, and stops abruptly halfway up his biceps. He rubbed a hand across the back of his neck and skin flaked away.

'No he hasn't.' I'd brought lemonade for both of us, two tall irresistible glasses. And florentines, with almonds and toasted coconut, chocolate which melted on our fingers before we had time to eat it.

'Then where the hell is he? I've looked everywhere I can think of. He's not after that bitch of Fred's again, is he? Speaking of dreamers.'

'He won't be going after her again.' As I sipped my lemonade Nat turned.

'Christ. What have you done with him?'

'I buried him, Nat. I buried him.'

Just then the neon contraption rang, drawing me inside. The orders for Christmas. Nat and I are to report to Hugo's restaurant for lunch. A table for four, one chair for Joanna and the last one for Hugo, in case he might have time to join us. 'I'll send a taxi,' he said.

'There's no need for that.' A taxi, for an hour each way. Typical of Hugo and his money, throwing it in the general direction of things but seldom hitting the mark. And I've always disapproved of unwarranted expense. 'Nat'll drive me.'

'You'd get into a car with him at the wheel? Do you have any idea what his driving's like?'

'It's improved, actually. A lot. All he needed were a few pointers.'

Silence. 'Well, if you're sure.'

'So I'll get to meet Joanna at last, will I?'

'I haven't been keeping her away deliberately.'

'Oh, I know that,' crossing my fingers against another rundown of his busy schedule. 'What shall we bring?'

'Mum! You don't have to *bring* anything. Just yourselves.'

'It's because he hasn't got time to come out here,' Nat said when I told him, back in the cool shade of the verandah roof. 'This way he can squeeze us in between other appointments without any effort.'

'I don't think that's very fair ...'

'Nor do I. But typical of him.'

'I don't mean that. I mean *you're* not being very fair. And what are you going to do if Joanna's there? You can't ignore her the whole time. It'll be far too obvious with only four of us.'

'Ah shit. Hadn't thought of that. Maybe I'll chat her up. Try to steal her off the old guy. Shouldn't be too hard. I mean, look at me.' He flexed his muscles. I laughed. 'Better still, I'll film her. *You don't mind if I film the meal, do you, Joanna?* Then we'll be able to laugh about it when we get home, watching her showing off her best side all the time, peeling the shell off her prawns with her pinkies sticking out. Good for a laugh.'

I tried to show disapproval, but the image was too clear in my head. The beautiful Joanna with matching lips and nails, an immaculate finish on her foundation, aspiring to be caught on film and discovered. 'That's not fair, Nat. I don't want to walk in there with preconceptions about the girl. I want to keep an open mind, accept her for who she is. Not the bimbo you've built her up to be.'

'Why not?' He snorted. 'You don't actually think she's going to be deep, do you? Mature? Concerned about the state of the environment? Shit, no. She's shallow as. Only after him for his money.'

'Aren't you guilty of that?'

His head snapped around. 'Oooh, Gran. Below the belt. True, though, I suppose. There's not much else to be had from him.'

'He was such a lovely little boy,' I said, and it was true. 'So sweet. So imaginative. Sensitive, too. He was never the sort to make a mess, or run round in the mud.'

'Like me, you mean? Chasing those bloody steers through the gate. I can't see Dad doing that for you.'

We both started to laugh, imagining Hugo in his chef's hat, chasing steers. We laughed until we could hardly stand up. The image died away slowly. We looked out over the garden, the paddocks, anywhere but at each other, in case it all started up again.

'S'pose we'll have to buy him a present,' Nat said finally.

'Oh, don't remind me.'

'What do you buy a guy with everything? Something kitsch that he'll hide away in a cupboard? Something useless?'

'Something useless sounds good.'

And so the next morning we began our hunt for something useless for a man with everything. He loves kitchen appliances, but he has them all, and far more expensive models than we could afford. Chocolate and special trays of nuts and dried fruit are out, when he can buy them wholesale. Cologne, aftershave - only top of the range will do. Magazines? Would he have time to read them? And what titles would interest him? Travel, perhaps, although he hardly ever goes away.

Nat took an interest in a book about travelling around Asia on a shoestring. He stood in the aisle of the newsagent's with it open between his palms while I tried to argue its unsuitability. Marjorie's daughter Waverley was behind the counter, giggling at the faces Nat was pulling.

'We've had this discussion,' he said, loud enough for her to overhear. He winked at her, and I tried to work out what was happening. Was he *flirting?* 'What's the use of *trying* to buy something useful? You know, actually thinking about it, agonising over it. Anything we get'll be just as useless to him as if we deliberately try to get something he doesn't need. So let's have some fun here.'

We bought him the BBC version of *Pride and Prejudice* on video in the hope that he would lend it back to us. And for Joanna, violet-scented body wash. Waverley wrapped the book about Asia for me while we were in the chemist's, and I slipped it into the boot of the car while Nat pretended not to notice, and I looked the other way while he smuggled on board a chemist-wrapped package with a red bow on top.

Stroganoff made from grilled bacon, sauteed onions and mushrooms, the sour cream stirred through at the last minute, served on a bed of white rice, with hard-boiled eggs sliced into quarters. Fresh fruit salad with plums and peaches from the orchard, watermelon, apples, and strawberries. Home-made icecream.

'To Paddy,' Nat said, raising his glass of light beer.

I pushed my plate away and took up my cup of tea. It must still have been the thought of England at the back of my mind, because I left most of both courses. 'Ah yes,' I said. 'To Paddy.'

Goodnight, now.
Lily

[Twenty-two]

Floss

Twelve weeks, Floss writes, *and three days. How can I ever wait that long? A nice cabbage and a bit of bacon.* She screws the cap on her pen and counts the coins in her purse. Reggie always counted his money at the end of every day, last thing before bed, and wrote what he'd spent in the back of his diary. Milk, bread, cigarettes. Sometimes a beer in the corner pub, a shandy for Floss. If the two amounts didn't tally, he couldn't go to sleep. She would lie on her side of the bed, turned away, measuring her breath – in, out, even and slow – pretending to sleep, knowing what was to come, the accusation that she had helped herself from his wallet. She did sometimes, just a penny here and there. She saved them up amongst her stockings until she had enough for something nice. An ice-cream cone or a nice cake at the tearooms while he was out at his model train enthusiasts' meetings. Hardly enough for him to bother about, but he always did.

'Once there was a little boy,' she says to Julie in the train on the way to Richmond Hill. The words have become real at last, forcing her lips to make possible their escape.

'Yeah?' Julie asks, as though it's nothing. Her eyes remain fixed on the window opposite, her head nodding as the carriage encounters inconsistencies in the track. 'I wondered,' she says. 'Only I ain't never seen him. Is he dead?'

'No, no.' Floss searches for something in the bottom of her bag, something non-specific, like a memory. *You've been and gone and done it now,* Reggie used to say. 'No,' she says. 'Not dead.'

'Bastard,' Julie says, through teeth as rigid as the bars on a cage. 'Never comes to see y', does 'e? Y'know, that's what really scares me about being a muvver. All this stuff y' do, wiping shit and going without sleep, what's it all for? Soon as they're old enough, they piss

128 *Lily's Cupola*

off. Don't even remember yer birfday.'

Floss tries to say it's not like that, but Julie doesn't hear. She goes on and on about the unfairness of it all, the imbalance between being a mother, giving, giving, giving, and being a child, receiving. All the while stroking Daniel's fair hair back from his perfect forehead.

They have a picnic on a bench overlooking the river. Floss shares her Thermos of tea and the scones she made this morning, and Julie opens a bag of crisps and a couple of chocolate bars without taking off her gloves. Daniel toddles about nearby, his layers of clothing making walking difficult.

'Tell me about your boy, then,' Julie asks as she watches him.

But there is nothing to tell. What can Floss say, apart from *once there was a boy*? That's all. The beginning and the end. Once there was a boy.

She changes the subject. They talk about Reggie instead, the way he gave up his travelling salesman job, how he bought a little shop on the Isle of Wight, how they lived in a council house in Oaklyn Gardens in Shanklin.

'It's bloody nice down there, I've 'eard,' Julie says. 'It must've been like living in paradise.'

'Oh, it was,' Floss says. 'Just like paradise. And Reggie, so sweet.'

'And your little boy ...'

'Yes, yes. And our little boy.'

Only Reggie never knew about the little boy. What would he have said? She was going to tell him, in the beginning, but decided it would be best to wait until after they were married. They lived with her mother for two years before Reggie gave up the job. He was away all week, and it seemed a shame to spoil a weekend when they went by so quickly. By the time they had moved south to the Isle of Wight and into their own house she knew it was too late. Reggie was anxious for children, and she knew when that happened there would be no need.

Daniel falls asleep in the train on the way home and Floss is forced to manoeuvre the pushchair out through the doors onto the platform while Julie struggles with the weight of the sleeping child. Floss manages at last to unfold the contraption, and Julie arranges Daniel inside. They laugh, walking home from the station, but Floss's laughter is false. Her jaw is clenched in an animal grimace and she doesn't know how she's going to climb five flights of stairs. All she wants is to be home, even if home is a stained square of carpet inside a council box.

She is too tired to cook. She makes tea and toast, spreading marmalade thinly, to save money, the way Reggie showed her, even though he's been dead for years. 'Putting it away,' he always said, 'for a rainy day.' Only she never found out where he put it. When he died there was nothing, just his bank book and his pension due to be paid in the next day. There was no nest egg, no investment that he'd been on about for years, his eyes sparkling as though it would grow simply by being mentioned. 'You don't need to worry about a thing,' he always said. 'That's what I'm here for. To look after you, and to do all your worrying for you.'

The rainy days have come now, she thinks as she carries her toast to her chair, as she stabs at the remote control and fills the flat with sound. The rainy days have come and there's nothing put aside, and she went without for the whole of their marriage just so there would be something left over at the end.

She watches the faces of the actors on the television. She loves their voices, their wonderful accentless speech, the way they have become familiar over the years, like friends, turning up in this or that drama, coming into her own home and being with her in the evenings. But tonight she can't seem to stay focused on them. Her thoughts keep drifting, back to that morning when she came down the stairs and found Lou in the kitchen.

It was obvious she'd had no sleep.

'Auntie Pat,' Lou said. 'She died in the night.'

In the night? In the night? Was it when Flossie was giving herself, was gasping like a whore? Was that when Lou had watched life withdraw, had watched a face turn from living to dead? Flossie put a hand out and touched the edge of the kitchen bench. It grew taller and taller and, though she tried to grip it, her fingers slid ineffectually down the face of the cupboard door. She pressed her cheek against the cold floor and watched Lou's fat ankles as they dithered. Her soldier was there too, his polished black shoes and immaculate pleats down the front of his best trousers, his wedding and funeral trousers.

'Help me,' Lou said, trying to lift Flossie, and Flossie tried, but her bones were gone. She was nothing but soft yielding flesh, so formless she was like liquid trying to find the lowest point.

'Leave her,' her soldier said. 'She's just being self-indulgent.'

'Self-indulgent! She's just a kid, for God's sake. She's grief-stricken. Now give me a hand.'

Flossie's soldier's arms scooped her from the floor, but there was a reluctance about them, a rigidity. She opened her eyes as he carried her to the front room and saw that his face was remote, closed off to her. He was worried she would give away their secret. She wanted to tell him not to be, that it was far too precious to ever form into banal words. But there was no opportunity. Lou was there, fussing, clucking, taking Flossie's hand and patting it.

'It'll be all right, our kid,' she said. 'Pat had no pain. She just drifted off when the time came. Just drifted off. Peaceful as you like.'

Flossie lay on the sofa for half an hour while Lou stroked and patted. 'It's all right, love. It's all right.' She didn't know what she was saying. It wasn't all right. It would never again be all right.

Finally Flossie pulled herself upright and forced herself to sip tea. And then duty took over. Word spread up and down the street, and her mother needed her. Flossie spent the rest of the day in her mother's kitchen making sandwiches and tea for the still-living sisters, for the stream of neighbours who came to express sympathy. The kitchen table was lost beneath the garden produce, the pies, tasteless grey biscuits which were offered up with as much generosity as rationing would allow, with such willingness, because words were so hard at such a time.

That night she slept in her own bed again, missing the smell of her soldier on the sheets as she stared at the wall thinking about death.

She endured the funeral, the hours, days of distant relatives huddling in the darkened front room murmuring anecdotes about Auntie Pat, uttering tight little fists of fond laughter, as though the separation of death made criticism into a form of kindness, of affection. Flossie saw in her mother's face the shadows of grief, of regret. The sisters had fought sometimes, had competed with their cooking, their clothes, their children. And now when Pat had been so ill, her own children too far away, too busy with work or family, too tight with money to come, it was

Lou who had been with her. Yet there was no point to be won at this late stage. There was not even acknowledgement that Lou was a daughter to be proud of. Pat was the star of the day. Pat's name was the one spoken.

Flossie kept the kettle on, the teapot filled, the scones buttered. She cooked cauldrons of bland vegetable soup for anyone around at meal times. She washed endless cups and saucers and plates. And ached.

A week later life took over again. Flossie's mother rose at dawn and started cleaning the house. Flossie's soldier was back in his garden, and Flossie went back to work.

[Twenty-three]

Floss

Life, like a tide, swept in from each side and erased any evidence that her auntie Pat had ever existed. The sisters swooped in and cleared out the wardrobe, the china cabinet. The children, Flossie's cousins, sorted through the furniture, selling some, keeping some. The kitchen cupboards were emptied, bowls and utensils claimed by anyone in the family with an appropriate lack. Then new tenants moved into the house, planted new vegetables in the garden, hung different curtains at the windows, and set different beds in the bedrooms.

Flossie tried to keep away from Lou's, but she couldn't. There was always a stinging snake's tongue of hope within her, lashing her insides with its forked end. She and Lou crocheted doilies, they darned her soldier's socks, they patched his worn gardening trousers. She crossed the days off her calendar. She counted the weeks. Her mother's grief was withdrawing into the cupboard where she had kept it when Flossie's father died. Summer was arching across the weeks towards its conclusion, that first official day of autumn. The vegetables were coming into Lou's kitchen in boxes. Flossie's soldier worked every day with the soil. He sweated in the heat, and harvested in the cool of the evening. His vegetables fattened – climbing beans, carrots as thick as Flossie's wrists, tomatoes lined up along the kitchen windowsill to ripen. Everything he touched blossomed and burgeoned and fruited, and Flossie was no exception. Finally she could think of nothing but the coarse pencil crosses on her calendar. Her hands shook as she sat opposite Lou at the kitchen table, guiding the fine china cup to her lips. 'I'm late,' she said into the tea. Lou's finger stopped halfway around the outline of an iris, embroidered onto the tablecloth. But she didn't say a word. 'I'm late,' Flossie said again, the words that had echoed over and over in her mind at night when she tried to sleep. The only two she'd been able to think for weeks. Ever since the date on her calendar had come and gone, and she hadn't been able to write the monthly C for curse. Late seemed so much milder than pregnant. Late made it feel as though there was a chance it would come after all. Like a train. Late didn't mean cancelled. Not even postponed. It meant there was still hope.

But that hope drained away as she looked into Lou's face. There was such wild accusation that she must surely have been hiding in the wardrobe that afternoon as they romped on the spare bed.

'Are you sure?' she asked at last.

Flossie nodded. Her eyes stung. She dared not blink in case the world began to spill out of them. 'I didn't know who else to tell.'

'Oh my God.'

'Mum'll kill me. Worse.' Death would be bad enough. But her mother's reaction would be unimaginable.

'How late?'

'Four weeks.'

'Four weeks.' As though calculating. As though pinpointing the moment of ovulation and placing Flossie's soldier's penis right where it was as Lou sat at her dying aunt's bedside. 'I didn't know you had a boyfriend.'

'I haven't. It was just ...'

'Did he force himself?'

'... after a dance. In an alley. And ... yes.' She put her cup down feeling her cheeks flaming, Lou's intellect cutting away the lies.

Lou reached across the garden of embroidery and clasped Flossie's hands. 'What are you going to do?'

Flossie had thought, of all the people in the world, Lou would have an answer. She turned away, blinking at last, feeling the tears fall hot against the cotton of her summer dress. She stared out the window, at the back garden rising behind the house, the brick steps that had started it all, the vegetables at the far end signalling to her in the wind. 'I don't know,' she said.

'He's due in from work any minute,' Lou said. 'You'd better get off home.'

Flossie stayed in bed for three days, her mother drawing back strands of her hair with worry, and fussing about the curtains and the covers and the hot water bottle, bringing endless cups of tea and sandwiches Flossie couldn't eat. Flossie wondered if it was concern, or part of grieving. Her mother had spent so many hours since the funeral just staring into space.

At last Lou came. She sat down beside the bed and took Flossie's hand. 'I found some lemons at the market,' she said. 'They're full of vitamins, and you can't let yourself get run down at a time like this. A hot lemon drink's what you need.' They heard the kettle whistling in the kitchen below, the tinkle of a spoon against the side of a china cup.

Flossie stared at the ceiling. She clenched her teeth, but couldn't stop her chin from wobbling. How would lemons help? What she needed was gin, a crochet hook.

Her mother came in with a tray.

'I think she needs a change of air,' Lou said. 'She's been pale for a good long while now. I don't know what you think of this, Flossie, but I've a friend in Devon who's looking for a companion. I wouldn't even mention it if she was old and cranky. But she's the sweetest person you'll ever meet. Recovering from illness. Needs someone to read to her, amuse her. Are you keen?'

So she was to be sent away. She knew she should have been grateful, but all she could feel was despair. A tear rolled out the side of one eye.

'It's not that she's ungrateful,' her mother said. 'She's just been like this lately. It sounds better than that dusty old shop. Just give her a couple of days.'

Her suitcases were packed and she and Lou struggled under their weight to The Angel. But instead of getting onto the tube, they sat on the platform. A dozen trains or more came and went.

'What time's my train?' Flossie asked bitterly. She could hardly bear to look at Lou. The deceit seemed to cling to her in a thick red cloud, clogging Flossie's nostrils and making her sick to the stomach.

'We're not catching a train,' Lou said, playing with the wedding ring on her finger. 'I've got a better idea.'

[Twenty-four]

27 December

Dearest Iris

Another Christmas is over. What was it like for you? I suppose your children came with their families, loaded with food and presents. I suppose you drank sherry and were fussed over and given beautiful things. I still miss an English Christmas, the smell of the turkey roasting while the aunties vied for the seat nearest Grandma Olivia's fire, and the uncles told stories that grew wilder each time their glasses were refilled.

Ours was quiet. Nat drove me to Hugo's restaurant, as ordered. It was jammed with pathetic souls like ourselves busy pretending they wouldn't rather be seated at a trestle table under a tree somewhere, with twelve chairs, babies crying, toddlers tumbling on the grass, and salads covered in plastic wrap. Jammed with those who've failed at families, whose bloodlines have dwindled to almost nothing, who are intent on smiling rigidly and seeming to enjoy themselves no matter what.

Picture this. Brick red restaurant walls, rough-plastered, with huge rustic timber beams criss-crossing the ceiling. Olive green carpet, expensive. A wall of glass bricks separating us from the street. A candle burning at each table, beside a sprig of specially imported holly with berries.

Nat and I perched self-consciously at a too-small table, watching Joanna while she watched us. Sometimes age is not much of a consolation. She was beautiful, with a perfect straight nose and auburn hair brushed back from a high round forehead. Her eyebrows were immaculately plucked, and her tan slid like golden syrup down the front of her little white dress. One strap slipped from her shoulder, and she retrieved it with an absent movement, the painted nails of her thumb and forefinger coming together like a clasp.

'I've been so looking forward to meeting you,' she said in a harsh young-person voice. 'Hugo's told me so much.'

A simple well-meant statement which terrified me.

'You should never listen to what middle-aged men say about their mothers,' Nat said, fiddling with his camera. He slid his chair back, taking the tripod from its case and beginning to set it up. Other patrons watched from the sides of their eyes, glancing at us again and again in case our fame had escaped their notice. 'They've all got hang-ups,' Nat said. 'Hell, I'm not even middle-aged, and I don't think I'd give a very balanced view about *my* mother. Lily's the best. Doesn't matter what Dad says.'

I tried to silence him with a look, but he was too intent on tightening levers and bolts. I was grateful for his support, but subtlety is a skill he has yet to acquire. Why not simply pick up a vase and hit her over the head with it?

Joanna's smile did not waver. 'Amelia said you were hard case.'

Nat's head snapped around. 'You know Amelia?'

'Oh yes. Amelia and I are like sisters.'

I feigned fascination, remembering Amelia's visit, her discomfort at Joanna's very existence. What does it mean, anyway, *like sisters*? As though sisters have the closest bond of all. Our record, Iris, isn't so good. It's almost fifty years since we last spoke. But who's counting?

'Oh, Amelia and I have known each other for years,' Joanna said. 'I used to babysit for her when Vincent was just born.' She blushed suddenly, hinting at the beginnings of a relationship with Hugo I would never have considered otherwise. The two of them alone in his Jaguar late at night, Amelia brushing her teeth, donning flannellette pyjamas, secure in the knowledge that Hugo was running the babysitter home.

Nat pushed a button and the camera whirred into life. A waiter brought our entrées. Nat devoured his garlic mussels, Joanna swallowed oysters *au naturel*, and I chased eight pieces of deep fried camembert around my plate. I've always hated eating in public. I've told you, Iris, I'm not so big any more, but I can't shake the hangover of when I was. Others take such interest. As though large people have no right to eat when out. Or that they will give away the secrets of maintaining their size by what they choose from the menu.

'Hugo says you make quilts,' Joanna said, nasal, studying the curve of her professionally shaped cuticles.

I nodded, giving up on the camembert, sliding my fork in amongst the frill of lettuce leaves.

'My auntie made one once. Took her seven years. All these little stars, only I think they were called compass points, or something like that. You know, made out of skinny diamonds. She made the whole thing out of her husband's business shirts.'

'Lovely.' I pushed my plate away. A waiter swooped in with an anxious look.

'Is everything all right with madam?'

'Everything's fine with madam,' I assured him. But even so Hugo appeared within moments from the kitchen, causing a stir as he strode across the dining room. His hat was starched, leaning slightly to one side, and his white jacket was the size of a spinnaker. The sideways glances began again. We must have been famous if the chef left his kitchen to speak to us.

'Was there a problem, Mum?' he asked.

'Of course not. It was delicious.'

'How do you know? You didn't even taste it.'

'Of course I tasted it.'

'I counted the pieces. Eight. Not even a nibble out of one.'

You've got to eat, my own voice says, slicing down through the years, Hugo's Splendour-apple cheeks wet with tears. *You haven't taken a single bite, and I'm not leaving this room until you eat every last thing on your plate.*

'You've got to eat, Mum,' Hugo said.

Nat, delighted at the drama, glanced at the camera. Joanna replaced the errant strap again, sipped her wine.

'Just send me something light,' I said. 'A chicken salad. That's all I feel like today. I'm tired, that's all.'

'A salad? I can do a salad easily enough. Do you want mayonnaise? Hollandaise? Dijonnaise? Croutons?'

'No, darling. I'm sure they're delicious. But a salad's all I want.'

Hugo rolled his eyes in despair at Joanna before trudging back to the kitchen.

'You should come and visit some time,' Nat said. 'Come for a weekend when Dad's tied up. Oh, I suppose that's every weekend. Anyway, Lily and I'd love to have you, wouldn't we, Lily? We could get to know each other better.' His eyebrows flew up and down suggestively. I watched the family at the next table, who seemed to be as uncomfortable as we were. An elderly couple and their daughter. Then the man and younger woman exchanged a kiss, and the relationships altered. They became a couple and a mother-in-law.

'You wouldn't know the meaning of articulate,' the mother-in-law said, glaring.

The man withdrew his hand from where it lay across his wife's forearm, interweaving his fingers neatly. 'No,' he said, downcast. 'Probably not.'

'I used to think I'd be bored in the country at night,' Nat said. 'But I could teach you a thing or two.'

'Do you think so?' Joanna's look was challenging. 'I very much doubt it.'

Our main courses arrived, my salad exquisite with its mesclun mix and rocket, its carrot rosebuds and fan of moist chicken breast. Joanna had a small indeterminate tower, and Nat's schnapper fillet hardly left room for vegetables. I listened to his flirtatious chatter, Joanna's stony silence, and wished for the meal to be over. But there was dessert. Steamed pudding with toffee sauce for Nat, a sundae out of all proportion for Joanna, and I chose an apricot-drizzled meringue.

'I wouldn't expect you to understand,' said the mother-in-law, finishing another glass of wine. The son-in-law refilled it.

'Of course not,' he said.

'I wish you wouldn't,' said the daughter, glancing across with embarrassment and catching my eye. I looked away, back at Joanna, who seemed almost orgasmic at the home-made ice-cream and fruity sauce.

'He can cook, your father,' she said to Nat.

'He's rich too,' Nat replied. 'Have you noticed?'

Afterwards, when most of the guests had gone, we exchanged presents. Nat's chemist-wrapped gift for me had grown into a box – inside, a trug and four smaller gifts spelling out my name. Lily-of-the-

valley hand cream. Insect repellent. Low-calorie chocolates. And Yves
St Laurent perfume. I tried out the hand cream, laughing at his
ingenuity, feeling outdone as he opened the book about Asia and kissed
me. Hugo had bought Joanna a diamond on a chain, and she was so
enamoured she hardly noticed our carefully selected body wash. Hugo's
pretence at delight at his set of videos was so blatant I was forced to
avoid Nat's eye in case we lost control. Hugo had bought me a new
kitchen mixer, and Nat a cordless drill. Then only one box remained,
from Nat to his father. Hugo opened it with care, peeling each strip of
Sellotape away from the foil wrap. He peered inside and looked back at
Nat with rage.

The traffic was heavier on the way home, cars emerging from the
privacy of their garages to make the pilgrimage from one set of in-laws
to the other. In the back seats children were in a gift-opening frenzy.
No amount would be enough. In the front, wives nursed pavlovas or
exotic carrot and beetroot salads and husbands drove in silence. I looked
into the emptier cars with empathy. The father wondering how to make
his allotted two hours with his children into a childhood memory worth
treasuring. The singles wondering how they were going to endure twelve
hours of family tension, smiling brilliantly and gulping down their words
of choice with too much wine.

Nat followed the car in front, mesmerised. 'It went quite well, I
thought,' he said after a while.

'Don't be daft. Take me to the beach,' I said. I needed to be embraced
by my pohutukawa.

We walked down on to the sand and into its scattered shade. Nat
spread himself full length at the high-tide mark and I found a low curving
branch and arranged myself side-saddle. How many hours had I spent
here with Hugo? It seemed the setting for his entire childhood. The
beach and my kitchen.

I took a deep breath, the air seeming less contaminated than by the
time it reached my hillside, with only an ocean between me and South
America.

'You really are despicable,' I said, staring out across the flat sea, into
nothingness. A few people were swimming, heads bobbing like balls on

the surface. Voices carried across the water, the laughter of children. A young boy, five or six, ran towards the edge of the waves with a mobile phone.

'Coil [Kyle],' called the mother in her foghorn voice. Her shoulders were Barbie pink against the black Spandex of her bathing suit. 'You come here with that, Coil.'

The boy giggled delightedly.

'Coil,' called the mother.

'Coil,' called the father, an octave or two lower. Coil dug a hole in the sand and put the cellphone in.

'Coil!' called the father, his voice rising. He unfolded himself a limb at a time from his blanket beside the car, a scrawny specimen hardly taller than five feet. 'Come here and get a hoiding.'

Coil looked around, seeing his father in his terrifying pose, a crazed chimpanzee with arms almost to his knees. Coil dug up the phone and returned obediently for his hiding.

I turned away. Nat was laughing silently and hysterically. I wondered if our voices would travel as far. 'I can't believe you did that,' I said.

Nat wiped his eyes with the palms of his hands, trying to gain control. 'I'll never forget it. There've been some moments at Christmas. But this?' My voice cracked and dried and drifted away in pieces on that South American breeze.

'Sorry.' The word squeezed out from between tight, trying-not-to-giggle lips. He didn't mean it. He would never come to regret something he enjoyed so much. The realisation on Hugo's face. His determined closing of the wrapping, and Joanna's insistence that he show her what was so provocative. Until then we could almost have saved the occasion, continued feigning festivity, pulling crackers and sipping wine. She pleaded and put on the puppy eyes, which must so often have worked. She stroked his arms and his neck, his cheek and his earlobe. She pouted and whined, and finally resorted to a rugby-style dive, exposing acres of tanned leg, the straps of her dress slipping off both shoulders, its only hold in the end a minimalist structure of curved underwire. She fell upon the parcel, ripping it open in short-lived glee. Nat laughed aloud, Hugo performed a chameleon impression, merging seamlessly with the wall behind him, and Joanna transformed from coaxing siren to raging street-walker.

'It had your name on,' Nat said. 'See, on the top of the box. *The Joanna Doll*.'

Joanna left the restaurant without a word, dropping the box onto the carpet. Hugo rushed out after her, and Nat and I were left with the detritus of Christmas dinner and the box with its grinning blow-up doll face and lettering. *Three authentic life-like orifices.*

All the way home I couldn't help wondering what the third one was.

I know now that I am almost as innocent as the day I was born, and plainly not conversant with the language of sex toys. I know too that there was never any chance of being friends with Hugo, not just because of who we are, or over-mothering, or any of the issues he's taken from his childhood, but because of when we were born. My generation lived through the war, and there was something about us that wanted our children to know about suffering. We had lived in fear and terror for years on end in a sandbagged city where no light shone at night. We had eaten greasy colourless meals day after day, month after month, year after year. We lost friends, fathers, neighbours. We lost whole streets, neighbourhoods. And though we so wanted to forget it all, we never could.

We were jealous of our children, who grew up careless. They wasted food and took up frivolous pursuits. Our hardship bored them, and our efforts to inflict it vicariously upon them. They didn't want to know anything about how we had survived.

Hugo despised Eddie for his drunken ranting, his predictable complaints about how the world was going to the dogs, that no one knew respect any more. And fear? They didn't know what fear was. I sensed a desperation in Hugo, to be gone as soon as he was old enough, away from the cloying misery of it all, the memories which were so vivid they were almost viral. As though if he stayed too long he would be dragged backwards in time and forced to relive his parents' experiences.

His rebellion was mild, compared with what goes on today. A simple announcement over dinner. 'I'm going to be a chef.'

It was the perfect revenge for all the years of belittlement. Eddie's knife hacked at the meat on his plate. The cooked muscle, with its striations, became indistinguishable from Eddie's weathered cheeks. 'You're bloody not,' Eddie spat. 'Only a pansy wants to spend his life in a kitchen. Is that what you are, a bloody pansy, sniffing around other men's arseholes?'

The only sound after that was the scratching of our cutlery against my new Crown Lynn dinner set. A month later Hugo attended his first class in food hygiene.

Hugo rang before dark. 'Tell him that's the end of the money. I'm not forking out another cent for someone so insensitive.'

'You were young once,' I said, remembering episodes of cruelty down through the years, the worst of which might be his busyness, his endless excuses for why he can't spend time with his mother. Or perhaps the silences when he does.

'I thought you'd take his side.'

'I'm not taking anyone's side. Anyway, it's no way of punishing him, cutting off the money. It's me who has to feed him.'

Hugo exasperation was like a serpent slithering through the receiver and into the tortuous canal of my ear. 'What else can I do? Joanna's really upset. She can hardly bear to look at me. Vindictive, that's what I call it.'

'It was only meant as a bit of fun.'

Nat hovered at the hall door. I hoped he was wishing I didn't need to be intermediary. Plainly he lacked the courage to take on his father twice in one day.

'Fun? That's a joke. I'm probably going to have to take the weekend off to take Joanna away somewhere.'

'It'll do you good to get away.'

'Mum, in case you haven't noticed, it's Christmas. The restaurant is booked solid for months.'

'Look,' I said before he had a chance to get started. 'I'll speak to him, all right. He knows he should never have done it. But cutting yourself off from him is the last thing he needs. Give him another chance, will you?'

'Why should I?'

'Because he's your son.'

'Don't remind me.'

'Hugo!'

'All right, all right. But I'll need at least two weeks to cool down. And I'm not forking out for wood any more, or cameras, or anything but essentials. He can join the real world and get a job. That might help him to grow up.'

Why the rush, I wondered as I hung up.

Nat and I watched the scene again and again, Hugo with his painstaking peeling of the Sellotape, Joanna with her persuasion tactics. Every time the outcome was the same, and yet we laughed, cringing all the while at the wickedness.

Fred rang to say he'd survived a day with his daughter, and Nat brought me a cup of tea. 'Happy Christmas,' he said. We were so full from lunch we didn't worry about dinner. I began tacking ivy leaves into place on my motherhood panel and the television chortled in the corner, reruns and safe family-rated comedies to reassure us there was no sudden rush of suicides or family violence at Christmas. I was content to be lulled.

Nat downed his tea and slipped out. A minute later I heard the car start up and drive out through the gates and down the hill, while I prepared for a late night viewing of *Pride and Prejudice*.

That's enough for tonight, my dear. Midnight has come and gone, and I have chosen this letter instead of *Pride and Prejudice*. Nat is still out and about. It's no longer Christmas. The stress and worry can be put aside for another year. Where are you now, I wonder? Somewhere happy, I hope. I always thought you would rise in your life.

Goodnight, sweet girl.

Lily

[Twenty-five]

The Fat Boy

'Why doesn't Jimmy come home with us for the afternoon?' the fat boy's mother asks. Jimmy Dodd grins, his eyes narrow, his freckles standing out against the pallor of his skin. 'He gets sick of his old mother sometimes. It'll do him good to have another boy around the place for a while.'

'I don't know why they don't play together more often,' Jimmy Dodd's mother says.

The fat boy climbs into the back seat of the car. His thighs press against the cracked red leather. He holds his knees together so they don't spread. Two lumps of lard, his father calls them.

Jimmy Dodd's knees are bony and his grey school shorts are baggy. His skin smells hot from running. He won ten races, collecting a red card each time from the parents at the finish line.

Boys under twelve, fifty yards, called Sir through the megaphone. When he turned his head away the sound rattled and muffled, and when he turned back it was clear again. *Boys under twelve, fifty yards.* The fat boy put his bare toes on the starting line. Each blade of grass was glossy in the sunlight. When the wind blew they tossed about like hair. *On your marks.* The fat boy clenched his fists. He imagined himself running like Superman, dust flying up behind his feet, the crowd cheering. *Get set.* He pressed his toes into the grass, arranged himself in readiness. The starting pistol sounded. He wasn't ready. The others leapt into motion, and he forced his body belatedly forward. He gritted his teeth and began to knife the air with the heels of his hands. His legs pumped, left, then right, left, then right. He kicked them up at the back, the way his father had taught him. 'Fast runners you know, boy, they always bring their feet up high at the back.' They pounded against the back of his thighs.

Jimmy Dodd was already across the finish line, collecting his red card with a careless grin, sauntering over to one side of the track with the ribbon still caught on his chest. The fat boy ran harder, harder. He ran the best he had ever run. He crossed the line last, the volunteer parents already winding the tape for the next race, a single lonely clap coming from where his mother stood.

Jimmy Dodd's knees jiggle against the leather as the motor starts up.

'Have you had a nice day?' the fat boy's mother asks. Jimmy Dodd nods, shuffling his red cards. There are blue too, and yellow, and at prizegiving there will be a silver cup. More than one. 'I've got some nice pikelets at home,' says the fat boy's mother. 'You must be so hungry after all that hard work.'

Jimmy Dodd eats ten pikelets, one for each red card. The fat boy counts them as they disappear between the grinning lips. He eats four. Outside they stare at each other.

'Got any matches?' Jimmy Dodd asks. The boy nods and creeps inside to retrieve them from the mantelpiece. They gather twigs and leaves and creep under the house to light a fire. Jimmy Dodd takes a pen-knife from his pocket and cuts the fat boy's mother's hydrangea prunings into pieces. 'You can smoke these,' he says dipping one end into the fire. The fat boy imagines the flames licking upwards, tasting the rough-sawn joists and the floorboards. Dirty cobwebs, abandoned years ago, dangle against his head, and he worries that his father will smell the fire. It would eat his bedroom first, melting the model planes pinned to the ceiling with fishing line. The wings would twist backwards, the cockpits with their hero pilots collapsing and falling in silver drops like mercury onto his eiderdown. Jimmy Dodd lies back on his elbows, grinning, smoking. He tosses more twigs onto the fire. The fat boy takes up a hydrangea pruning and tries to draw the smoke into his lungs. It catches in his throat and he coughs until his eyes water. Jimmy Dodd laughs. 'You're a twit,' he says. 'Do you know what a twit is? You're a homo. You're a mother-fucker.'

He scrambles out from under the house and squats down to look back in at the fat boy. His knees and the seat of his pants are covered in orange clay dust. 'Yeah, d'ya know that. You're a mother-fucker.'

The fat boy watches as the skinny legs walk around the house.

'Are you going now Jimmy?' calls the fat boy's mother.

'Yeah. I gotta help with the milking.' The legs walk out of sight.

The boy bashes the fire with one of his roman sandals. He imagines the fire is Jimmy Dodd, and beats it until it is dead. Inside his head his strokes carve out a rhythm. *Mother-fucker, mother-fucker, mother-fucker.*

[Twenty-six]

31 December

Darling Iris

Have I told you about the Triple Irish Chain? It's a little like the one-patch, or the Trip Around the World. You use the same size pieces, but fewer colours. The effect is created with a band of squares, five wide, which cross the face of the quilt on the diagonal. Grandma Olivia's was a Single Irish Chain, the yellow cross that kept me safe at night. This one's simple, Iris. Even you could try it.

Mine is coming along. I keep sewing while Nat amuses himself at night. He is tired of the photographs now. He has shuffled through them so many times he knows them by heart. He has moved on to the pile of seventy-eight records from the hall cupboard. My stereo is an early model with a three-speed turntable, a hand-me-down from Hugo, and Nat has it spinning, cranking out sounds I haven't heard for decades. The sounds of my youth: the brass, the strings, the rhythms. The clubs of London are conjured up about me as I listen, the smell of cigarette smoke whirling in a cloud above us, of liquor and perfume. The whisper of off-the-shoulder dresses, high-heel shoes against the parquet. The feel of hot skin against the night. I am with Billy Brydon again. I am young.

A letter came from him, finally, in case you were wondering. There had been others, but the boat had been torpedoed and the mail lost. He had been to Egypt and North Africa, although because of the censor he could not include details. Would I never write back, he asked. And so I did, and our affair developed with words and paper instead of kisses and caresses. I would take his OHMS envelopes upstairs to my room and experience his letters as though he was in the room with me, as though I could hear his voice and feel his hands on my skin.

On his next leave there was a moment of hesitation as I opened the red door, and he stood on the step in the afternoon sunlight. As though our pens had run away of their own accord, creating reckless curves and strokes. As though we had said far more than we should have, and now suddenly here we were, face to face, inhibited by the flesh. His chin was shadowed with stubble. His eyebrows were thicker than I remembered, with whorls at the bridge of his nose.

'Aren't you going to invite me in?' His accent enchanted me again. I had forgotten it through our ink and paper courtship, his inside-out inflections and the tone of his voice.

'Of course.' I stepped back into the dim hall, and as soon as the red door closed behind him his arms were around me. His scent was too subtle to be emulated by cosmetic companies, and may not have had the desired effect without his proximity, but it caused me to momentarily forget my nice-girl morals. But it was all right, because Ma arrived from the kitchen to see who had come.

Billy loved to dance, Iris. How he could dance. Hearing the old tunes even now can make me cry. The potency of cheap music. Who was it said that? Noel Coward, I think. Billy and I would dance alone sometimes on those polished and powdered dance floors, while the crowds stood back and cheered us on. And then Billy would whisper in the musicians' ears and pull me onto the stage, and I would take up the microphone and sing. I loved to sing in those days. What a voice I had, soaring above the crowds, swimming its way through the clouds of cigarette smoke, drifting and somersaulting while the bandsmen offered harmonies. And the crowds would cheer until they were hoarse, and I would sing again. I would bow and smile, and Billy would come to the stage and take my hand, and lead me in the next dance. Then we were famous, basking in the reverence of the faces all around us, swinging and swirling, twisting and twirling, shuffling and jitterbugging as though there was no world beyond the club walls, no war, or violent en-masse death, or prisoner-of-war camps. We would dance until those old brassy wartime bands began to pack away their instruments. The bandsmen were all old, Iris, because the young ones were enlisted. They didn't have the stamina. But even so Billy would shake each one by the hand before we left to walk home. The streets were dark, with the blackout, but alive with sweethearts like us, meandering home with no thought for the morning. I had to get up for my work in the War Office typing pool. Sometimes after a night with Billy my fingers could hardly remember how the alphabet was arranged. Mistakes had to be re-typed. Some days I re-typed so many pages my tray filled faster than I could empty it. At lunchtime the girls talked about their sweethearts, but I didn't say much about Billy, the feeling too precious to put into words.

Here, after all these years, I have gone some way towards recreating the life we had. But when I read back over it the words seem only to scratch the surface. There is so much more beneath that I haven't managed to portray. I am beginning to understand what Dad was striving for, the tones of chiaroscuro here in my letters, so that you might understand a little of what happened.

Billy and I, at least for a while, were having a good war.

The sirens began to wail one night as we walked home. We ran down the street and up the steps to Mrs Lusk's front door. She came out, grimacing, from her kitchen. 'They don't give you a minute's peace.' She pulled on her gloves and reached her coat down from its hook, gathered her knitting and the air raid kit she kept by the door, with a candle, a Thermos, and a pack of cards. It was the real war by then, and Mrs Lusk had never had an Anderson installed. She hurried off to The Angel, to descend the stairs in a rush with the rest. I was amazed the first time I went down. It was a home away from home for some, with permanent bunk allocations, and cooking and ablution facilities. Some folks never spent a night in their homes. They headed off to The Angel whether the siren sounded or not. It was like a community, the neighbourhood transported below ground. Everyone knew each other. There were card games and families eating dinner.

'Are you coming, you two?' Mrs Lusk asked on her way out the door.

'We'll be right behind you. Wait there,' Billy told me, touching my elbow, galloping up the stairs.

Mrs Lusk was long gone when he came back down, and I was growing anxious. He kissed me. 'Come into the living room and sit down,' he said. 'Do you mind? Will you risk it?'

We felt the ground shake, heard the roar of a bomb exploding, but it seemed distant. 'Somewhere in the South End, I'd say.' Billy ran a fingertip down my cheek.

I thought of Mrs Lusk, safe in The Angel, surrounded by cheerful families trying to make the terror into an adventure. In a way I envied her, with romance far behind her and no difficult choices to make.

'Will you stay here?' Billy asked. 'With me? I want to be alone with you. There's something I've been wanting to ask you.'

It was the word Ma had taught me to wait for. The marriage word. I forgot all about the sirens, and the planes overhead, the bombs falling. The chaos only added to the excitement. Billy Brydon loved me.

We crept upstairs as though Mrs Lusk might hear us, although we both knew she wouldn't be back until after the All Clear.

I loved Billy Brydon, and I'm glad, even all these years on, that we shared those few stolen hours. Within two days he was back with his battalion, and I never saw him again. Typical, you might think, of a man. But Billy had his reasons.

Last night Nat played my records, end to end: Vera Lynn, Hogie Carmichael, Hutch, Glenn Miller. He played them all, frowning as he listened, and I stitched and sang along. I have forgotten most of the words, and my voice isn't strong as it was. It is wavering now, an old-woman-singing-hymns voice.

'What the dickens?' Nat said when he packed away the last one. He picked up the airmail letter from the mantelpiece. 'What's this? Aren't you going to open it?'

It took me a moment to shuffle back into the room, to cast off the last chiffon threads of the music. I looked up at the letter dangling between his thumb and forefinger. 'As it happens, no.'

'And you call me hard. Someone's sent you a letter and you're not even going to open it.'

'I don't want a letter from England, Nat.' I picked up the ocean block, the blue fabrics graduated from palest to deepest, discarded when the rainbow of hand-dyed fabrics arrived. There are tiny florals woven in amongst the plains, the lines almost horizontal, flowing like waves.

'Who's it from?'

'I have no idea.'

'Don't you want to know?'

'I don't, actually. There's no one left in England I even vaguely want to hear from.' (Don't take offence, Iris.)

'What if it's to say your quilt's been accepted for the London exhibition?'

I took a breath. 'Nat, I haven't even finished the quilt. Try to think things through, will you?'

'They might have seen some of your others. They might know you by reputation.'

'Hardly.'

He picked up the envelope, holding it up to the light. Inside, the pages held their secrets. 'Aren't you just a little bit curious?'

'No. I told you. I don't want to know.'

'It might be from the Queen.'

'I'm not a hundred yet, so it's not likely to be.'

'Can I open it?'

'No, you can't. Now put it back, and forget about it.'

'You must want to know, secretly, or you would've put it in the rubbish instead of leaving it here.'

'Oh, is that right, Mr Freud?'

He began to slit the envelope with its treacherous red and blue stripes.

'Leave it. Leave it, Nat.' My hands were shaking. (See how frightened I am, Iris, of hearing from you.)

Why hadn't I thrown it out on sight? Was he right, perhaps? Was there a tiny duct of hope remaining that things could be worked out?

The envelope yawned. Nat's fingers delved inside. I closed my eyes. I heard the paper scrape against the envelope. Then silence.

Nat laughed. 'It's Bree,' he said. 'It's from Bree.'

'Bree?' My thin wafer of a granddaughter, on the other side of the world, having flown across the oceans of the fabric block in my hands? My little Bree, with her piercings and anger, her militant tendencies? Save our earth. Stop animal testing. Cut back on CO2 emissions. Underneath she was as vulnerable as Nat. But now she had retraced my journey, and I didn't even know.

'She's been over there for six months, would you believe, Gran?' Nat said. 'In Cornwall. Listen to this. *Been living in an old place on the coast, but we've moved to be closer to our jobs. The new place is much more modern, only a hundred years old.'*

'What?' I said. 'Pass it here and let me see.'

He handed the first page of the letter over. 'Who did you think it was from?'

'No one. I already said there's no one left in England I want to hear from.'

'Except Bree.'

'I didn't know she was there.'

'Who did you think it was from?' Nat asked again.

'Oh, never mind about that now,' I said. 'Listen to this, will you? It's only been raining for a hundred days straight.'

We both read and reread the letter, and I took up the ocean block again. It seemed to have taken so long to finish. I ran a finger over the bark of the pohutukawa, its trunk curving up the right edge of the block, its branches forming a canopy across the top. All that remained was the embroidery of the flowers, blood red against a silvery-green background, little explosions of Christmas colour. I stitched frantically, anxious to finish so I could begin piecing the whole quilt together.

Nat's carefully laminated rafters have gone up now. He has nailed joists between the tops of the poles to hold them in place, and battens onto the rafters. He insists there is just the roof – wooden shingles he's been staining in the shed. But it's New Year's Eve and he's gone off in the car, my warnings chasing him down the driveway. 'Don't drink if you're driving. Sleep over somewhere if you're too tired to drive. But ring me. Ring me to let me know you won't be home, so I won't worry. Don't link up with anyone you don't know. Remember what happened in the Sounds.'

He rolled his eyes on the way out the door.

'It's just that ...'

'Yeah, yeah. Leave it will you, Lily. It's all a bit much.'

'I just want you ...'

He slammed the car door, started the engine, accelerated sedately through the gate.

' ... to be safe.'

It's like going back so many years, to when Hugo was young, to when Hugo was going into town and I could hardly bear to let him out of my sight. I need not have worried. The danger, for Hugo, did not involve ending up in some roadside ditch.

Are you relieved, Iris, to know he has made it almost to fifty, that no childhood disease carried him off, or rugby accident, or grisly teenage murder? I can give you this, Iris. Reassurance. Let it be my Christmas gift to you. My late Christmas gift.

Love Lily

[Twenty-seven]

Floss

Eleven weeks and five days to go. How miserable leeks are, with their suggestive name and their crispness and their pallor. How they squeak against the plastic of false teeth, and spin you back through the years to things you shouldn't remember. Floss's hands are as cold and pale as the vegetable they write about. Her letters are shaky on the page, each stroke apologetic. The last sentence mocks her. It has no right to be there. Her journal is supposed to be in code, meant only for her, since she doesn't know who will sort her belongings once she dies. Some social worker or religious volunteer from the city mission. She doesn't want eyes prying into her secrets. *Once there was a boy ...*

Net curtains, she writes, not so she will remember today, but because she is remembering that other day, the first day of her new life. She looks out on the building opposite, the weak glimmer that passes as winter sunlight. The sun hardly bothers to rise these days, rolling over in its low arc across the southern sky. Could travellers get their bearings from such an unreliable astronomical centrepiece? She wonders herself sometimes which way is east and which way is west.

Net curtains, dense and obscuring like steam, layers and layers between her and the world. And a blackout curtain for after dark. Four brown papered walls, flowers with stems curving in a gentle arc, like the sun's winter path, five flared rose petals with yellow stamens exploding from their heart. The leaves were more like ivy than they should have been, curling back to embrace the flower below. And so the design began again. The grain on the door suggested an old man's bald head, a furrowed brow, bulbous nose, and jowls. There was an owl too with startled eyes, a silent waterfall, and two hands held together in prayer, but they didn't frighten her the way the old man did, his eye always turned towards her in judgement, in pity, in disapproval. He watched her undress for bed, and when she switched on the light in the night, he watched her crying. Flossie was seventeen.

A knock on the door startles her. She screws the cap onto her pen, closes her book. There is only one person who comes now. Julie.

There are bright spots of colour amongst the piercings. Daniel, wrapped in winter layers and balanced on her hip, seems far too big to be her child. His nose is running and mucus has crystallised across one cheek.

'Is this him, then?' Julie asks once inside. She puts Daniel onto the floor and he toddles into the kitchen in the hope of a chocolate biscuit. Floss has taken to buying them in case of such emergencies.

'Yes,' she says. 'That's him. Just a few months old there, and two – ' She turns the photograph over to check the pencil scribble on the back. ' - yes, two-and-a-half in this one. This is his first day at school. Look at his little bag. And I think about eight – yes, eight here in his scout uniform.'

'He looks like you.'

'Do you think so?' Floss purses her lips to disguise the smile that tugs at the corners. She must be modest, the way parents are with children these days, even if they can't believe their luck in having borne a genius, and not only that but perfection in every physical sense as well: ears as soft and curled as a nest of sightless baby mice, cheeks like Michelangelo's Sistine cherubs, opalescent fingernails, skin like camellia petals, eyes to rival delphiniums.

'Got your mouth, innit?' Julie says. 'Can you have Daniel? Only I got a job interview.'

'Of course,' Floss says, still tangled within the faded black and white of the snapshots, hidden for so many years amongst her stockings in the drawers of her upstairs bedroom in Oaklyn Gardens, and now displayed like trophies.

'Careful, my dear,' Reggie said as he steered her up the stairs. And then proceeded to take no care at all.

'I'll only be an hour,' Julie says. 'Or p'raps two. Won't be long at all.'

'What about Daniel's things,' Floss thinks to ask at the last minute, as Julie sprints towards the door. 'Napkins? Bibs?'

'Napkins? I don't think so. There's a disposable in the bag if y'need it.'

Julie jangles out, the door slams, and Floss is alone with Daniel. A chocolate biscuit first, she decides. And a drink of milk, which he sips then places too near the edge of the table so that it falls and breaks. She feels hopelessly unprepared, with no plastic cups, no books or music, no toys of any description. She thinks of her button jar. She used to play with her grandmother's when she was a child, but he puts them in his mouth. She finds a wooden spoon, a spatula, but he is bored within five minutes. She tries to remember nursery rhymes but the last line catches her out.

London's burning, London's burning,
Call the engines, call the engines,
Fire, fire! Fire fire! ...

Daniel, arranging himself on her knee, his two middle fingers placed thoughtfully in his mouth, stares up at her with his perfect eyes. She can see the world in them, the globe with its land masses and oceans, its swirling glaze of cloud.

'Three blind mice,' she sings. Her voice is weak and quavery. 'See how they run.' All the rhymes in her head are ghastly, violent and bloody. Tails cut off with carving knives. Blackbirds baked inside pies. Noses being pecked off. Children whipped before bed, old women – like herself – with bare cupboards. *Atishoo! Atishoo! We all fall down.* Who decided, she wants to know, that they were suitable for children? Oral history in a teacup, the worst moments given jaunty tunes to take away the sting.

Daniel doesn't care. Each time she stops he smiles around his damp finger and says in his sweet voice, 'More.'

She sings until she has remembered all the words. He doesn't care how many times he hears the same tune. Then he falls asleep, draped across her lap with his cheek pressed against the arm of the chair. She watches his chest rise and fall, and thinks she would like to stay like this forever, with the weight of him across her knees, his gentle exhalations purifying the air of her council box, his tongue still curled around his fingers although his lips have surrendered their hold, allowing them to withdraw by degrees.

But she can't stay. Her thighs are buckling under his weight, and there are things she must do. She slithers off the chair, stooping over him breathlessly in case she has disturbed him. A frenzied sucking starts up, but it soon settles and the fingers begin their subtle retreat.

She wishes she could settle as easily. His presence terrifies her and she begins pacing, the way she did so many times in Oaklyn Gardens, a mindless back-and-forth movement to block out the awfulness, the responsibility, of living. Reggie in his High Street hardware shop, smiling at the customers, telling them which paint brush is best, which furniture tacks or crockery or bucket, and Flossie at home descending into a pit.

'Another breakdown,' he told the neighbours over the fence, and their faces formed into expressions of pity. Poor long-suffering Reggie, burdened by an unstable wife. Why didn't she do everyone a favour and pop off? She tried to a few times. 'You can't even do that right,' he said in the hospital. 'You wanted me to find you in time. Otherwise you would have done a proper job.'

She keeps thinking that when Daniel wakes he'll have nothing to do. She can't go through that again, all that singing and remembering. She's fit for nothing but sleep herself.

If she went to the market she could buy a toy or two, a couple of cars for him to whizz about on the floor. But what if he wakes? She studies his face, as though it will tell her how long his sleep will last, how long before consciousness creeps back in and he opens his eyes and needs her. How long before Julie returns with her clodhopper boots and fingerless gloves and fraying cuffs. Will she risk it? Can she bear it if she doesn't?

At the market she finds a set of plastic cups which fit inside each other and some Matchbox toys. She fumbles with her money, dropping coins on to the street. People step over them as she tries to pick them up. Rain starts on the way home, and the lift is broken. She is breathless when she steps onto the last landing, gasping for air, her whole body seeming to pulse with her heartbeats. Julie is not yet waiting outside the flat door. She rushes towards it, key aimed ahead of her like a divination device. Will he be awake, crying? Will he think the whole world is gone and he is all that is left, alone, helpless? She slides the key into the lock and turns it. The door falls open. She closes it behind her, gently, just in case. She hangs up her dripping coat, peels the plastic rain bonnet from her head. She steps through into the living room, creeps around the side of the chair. He hasn't moved. She feels relief, then fear. Is he dead? But at that moment he takes a deep breath and sighs in his sleep.

Floss's knees wobble and she subsides, gasping, onto a dining chair, her bag tumbling over at her feet, spilling its precious cargo, the toys she has risked Daniel's life and her friendship with Julie to secure.

Twenty-eight

31 December – late

My dear sweet Iris

Grandmother's Flower Garden is a design you might have heard of. It's made of tiny hexagons like a beehive. You can include a larger design made of the smaller ones – flowers, for example, made of two or three concentric rows – or you can simply use whatever you have in random order. Grandmother's Flower Garden quilts were popular during the Depression, because every minute scrap of fabric could be used to keep the family warm.

I've created my own version of a flower garden, my motherhood block, finished now, and I have even finished the last few stitches of the ocean block. At last I'm ready to piece the blocks together, to drape the pendulant pohutukawa branches across the top and applique the red and green shards onto them. This afternoon I cleared off the kitchen table, set up the sewing machine and the ironing board, and began to work. The row houses, the explosion, the curling lizard in its red cocoon and the eggs which will spill off the bottom edge of the quilt. The wedding rings, the kid glove suitcases and iris petals. The pohutukawa trunk up the left hand side, its roots curling amongst the bricks of the Islington houses. The ocean block, the motherhood block, the crown of red and green embracing all. Darkness fell as I pinned and sewed. I had missed dinner without noticing, and when I did I couldn't be bothered. I couldn't face an egg or a piece of toast. I switched on the kitchen light, made tea and turned on the radio. Outside, the window spilled light in distorted rectangles on the ground. Fred's own kitchen light winked back at me from down the hill.

The blocks lined up, Iris. A minor miracle. My fingertips pulsed with excitement as I pinned, seeing my plan, after all this time, coming together. My plan, which no amount of description could have ever made real. My life, with its traumas and secrets, spread out before me across the kitchen table. Grandmother Olivia's quilt from those Anderson shelter nights, reincarnated. Every memory I own is there, even fragments from her quilt sewn in, the red door of Number Thirty-two, the washed-out turquoise of those tumbling eggs.

And yet it seemed incomplete, as though something was missing. As I ironed the red and green parallelograms and arranged them to overlap the edges of the ocean and motherhood blocks, I realised what it is. There was nothing of Nat in it, and Nat has come to be so much.

I walked out onto the verandah. The crickets were in full party mode, shrieking like rusty axles. The creases in my body trapped the heat, sweat bubbling out, trickling down into the waistband of my panties, dissolving. The glow of Auckland illuminated the sky behind the hills, casting Nat's cupola into a shadowy silhouette, its skeletal curving rafters black like dinosaur ribs. Nat's cupola.

Music trailed out from inside, rivalling the crickets. My music. Once every five or six weeks the radio plays forties' music in the afternoons, and now too, as night thickened. The programmer must have decided we were the generation most likely to be home, alone, on New Year's Eve. The rich parlay of brass, strands and strands of brass coming together like the strings on a violin's bow, rising and falling, filling the night. Billy Brydon and I were dancing again, dancing and dancing, ruling the dance floor. How we danced.

Billy Brydon was my love, and I was his. Billy Brydon left his legs in North Africa. Where are they, I wonder, as I have always wondered? What use are two legs without a man, and what use, if any, is a man without legs?

I didn't learn of Billy's fate until after I'd had a death of my own. I was not his next of kin. We hadn't even had time to buy a ring. Mrs Lusk heard eventually, from another soldier who lodged with her while on leave. She forced him to tell me. It was Fred, in another incarnation, a young and dashing Fred who sat on the edge of the suite in our best room, rolling the band of his hat between his fingertips while I sobbed into his handkerchief.

Billy was going home, Fred told me, once out of hospital, and I imagined him, truncated, strapped into a stretcher, loaded onto a ship.

Billy, in a wheelchair, smoking casually, as though he was whole. Tossing off stories that made people laugh because he was only half a man, a war hero who wished he had died. A wheelchair, arranged beside the table in the dance hall, while Billy sipped beer and watched other men dancing.

I knew I should ask where he would be, where he would sail from. I knew I should catch a train and flee London in the hope of one last glimpse of Billy. But I went on crying into Fred's handkerchief.

I had an address, the kind nice girls never visited, and I had been there that morning, and while Fred sat on the edge of our chair the pain sliced me in half. I went to bed for a fortnight. They thought it was grief. I burned with fever while my mother mopped my forehead. She was so frightened she even called me Lily.

It was weeks before I had the house to myself long enough to burn the evidence, the nest of rags hidden at the back of the wardrobe, black with the remnants of Billy's baby.

Then, belatedly, I had the urge to rush to him, to nurse him back to health and show that my love was real enough to see past deformity. I discovered he was in a hospital in the south of London, and caught a train the next morning. It burst out finally from the underground tunnels into the grey London air. Houses shrieked past, backyards displayed for inspection, tiny rectangles of vegetable garden, grimy laundry strung between two sticks. I pressed my forehead against the glass, wishing and wishing that the train would rush on forever. My courage had fled just as I had left the house. I played out our reunion again and again in my head, just as I had played out that precious first kiss. Each time I was tongue-tied, trying to explain the delay. Each time Billy's eyes saw through my ceramic façade. It cracked and shattered into slivers, falling in a clatter on the polished floor of some anonymous hospital ward.

The train sped on. I kept wishing. Anything – a bomb or a fatal derailment – would have been better than arriving.

But there was no need for all my worry. Billy Brydon never made it home to New Zealand. By some blissful intervention he was spared the agony of life without legs, of knowing his love, his lover, couldn't love him if he was incomplete. As though his essence was in his legs, and once they were gone there was nothing worth loving. I was left in a hospital corridor, the nurses, hard from all they'd seen, unsympathetic. They could count how many days it had taken me to come.

I've never seen Billy's grave, nor met his family, though once when I was in Hawke's Bay I looked up Brydon in the telephone directory. There were four. His family might never have known that we were engaged. Perhaps his mother had a neighbour's daughter in mind, someone Billy had known since birth, whose parents his own parents approved of, whose genes would pool with Billy's to make perfect barefoot Kiwi children. I was shocked back then that children went barefoot. Were they so poor down there in the South Pacific? Which just goes to show how unsuitable I would have been.

It was years before I married. My father had given up all hope, even before the war had ended. I was thirty, well past the accepted age for spinsterhood. Ma had begun to look on me differently, as her carer rather than her daughter. She had no fears about growing old, as I would be there. The image of herself as a grandparent took longer to fade, and I would sometimes find her half-buried in my hope chest, retrieving tiny garments which had sprung from her knitting needles within moments of Billy Brydon's first visit. There were booties and layettes, helmets and bonnets and shawls. Confrontation would have heightened my sense of failure. So I crept away each time, pretending I knew nothing of her despair.

The church organ rang out as I walked up the aisle. The pews were full of neighbours, aunts and uncles with identical condescending smiles. Wasn't it nice that Lily had found someone at last, prepared to take her on at this late stage?

As we approached, the groom kept his eyes on the front of the church, his hands clasped rigidly behind his back, his shoulders square, his hair freshly cut, short back and sides, or as Hugo called it in deprecation many years later, short top and no sides. As I came alongside, the groom turned, appraising me with his brown eyes. He smiled, and took my hand.

Eddie Lusk.

Fred had visited me every leave after he told me the news about

Billy Brydon. And sometimes Eddie came along. He lost all three brothers before the war was over, so we had common ground in a way, a shared horror, a vast emptiness within, and the understanding of this lack in each other.

After the war Eddie emigrated to New Zealand with all the soldier mates he had managed to keep. It was good sense, I thought, that took him off across the world, where he could pretend none of it had ever happened. He worked in the bush and he worked on farms, sweating out the grief. He had friends there, mates he called them, who took him in when he needed a bed. Who drank with him, or cranked up out-of-tune guitars beside back-country campfires. Whose wives spoiled him with scones smothered in jam and cream, and tried to interest him in their sisters.

Eddie never said, but I'm sure he had his fair share of those sisters, in shearers' huts and the back seats of dangerous beaten-up cars. Just as I had my share of soldiers seeking solace, in alleys and up against walls and sometimes even in a soldier's mother's bed while she was out at Bingo, or helping the woman next door to give birth. I was, after all, unsuitable for marriage. It didn't take much in those days.

And I was Mrs Lusk's only comfort. With an armchair each beside the fire, we would work away with our needles, sharing, without words, better times. She talked sometimes of when her boys were young, dastardly deeds they had dreamed up, times they needed to be stitched together again. These she told with fondness, the gore and panic sanitised by nostalgia. I didn't need to mention Billy Brydon because he was in the room between us as our needles worked.

'Eddie's working on a farm,' she would say. Or, 'Eddie's bought a horse.' Or, 'Eddie's bought a truck, can you believe? I always knew he'd make something of himself.' But even she could see the pointlessness of trying to match-make us, when we lived half a world apart with no chance of meeting again.

When we did I knew straight away what he was thinking. That I was bigger. I knew it was true, and I'd overheard the remarks of neighbours and people on the street. He had come home to bury his mother, and arrived on our doorstep when the ghosts in his mother's house became too outspoken.

I made him tea, and produced cake from a tin. I walked back to the house with him. We climbed the stairs and I put out for him, just as I had for Billy Brydon. Fred too, if truth be known. My spinster status allowed me certain freedoms. I had proved myself uninterested in inappropriate activities. There was no need to worry about the shame of an unwanted pregnancy when it was so long, they thought, since any man had shown interest.

Mrs Lusk's sheets were cold against my skin, but Eddie was warm and full of adoration. He was grateful, that first afternoon, for my experience. He would have thrust a virgin clear into the next world. Afterwards he held me and kissed me and stroked me until there was nothing for it but to begin again. This time more slowly. Afterwards we lay together as the sunlight arced across the room, with the beginning of the realisation that it could mean something.

'I'm going to make a go of it here,' he said. 'For a while, anyway. See how things go.'

Later I washed in his mother's bathroom and we sat in his mother's armchairs and he talked of New Zealand, of Fred, and his farm, of endless wild beaches with no other soul in sight, of bush, silent and holy as a cathedral. And I thought how his mother would like it if I married him. And, as though she was still in the chair opposite, knitting socks for the Red Cross in the absence of fighting sons, I felt her approval. And the next day we buried her.

We were married in the spring and I packed my suitcases and moved into Mrs Lusk's house.

What would my life have been like if Billy had lived? There is no one else left who remembers him. Except Fred. And we never talk of him. The end was too ghastly, too sudden, too marred by my inaction. I wonder still why I didn't go to him earlier, why I waited until it was too late. Did he know that I couldn't make myself do it, that with his legs went every hope of mine for a future with him? Or was the septicaemia too swift? Did he sink into delirium before he had time to notice my absence? I hope so now, that he never suspected my inconstancy.

On my verandah the music played and I dreamed of Billy, the

complete Billy, with legs and wild-man eyebrows which only needed to twitch to send my mother into hysterics.

Old women, you will know, Iris, are allowed to be eccentric. I felt like crying into the hot night, and so I did. Billy is gone. Eddie is gone. Ma and Dad are gone. Paddy is gone. Hugo is as good as gone. And so are you, Iris. If I want to cry, I have permission.

All my love
Lily

[Twenty-nine]

1 January

Dear Iris

I should have known it was too much to expect that I might be able to cry in peace. The neon contraption began to ring inside. Of course. I thought it would be Hugo. He always rings on New Year's Eve, the last vestige of his sense of filial responsibility. Or Nat, deciding after all that he would stay the night somewhere rather than brave the winding road home.

'Lily?' It was Fred. 'Lily, are you there?'

'Yes, I'm here, Fred,' I shouted. 'Happy New Year.'

'It's not that,' he said. 'It's not that, Lily. Will you come? Will you come down?'

I felt a chill despite the heat. 'Of course, Fred. Of course I'll come. Give me a few minutes, and I'll be down.'

I checked that the oven was off, that the iron was off, but I left the kitchen light blazing across the garden, and I left the french doors open to the night air, to the glow of Auckland. I folded a light cardigan into my basket. I put in my angina inhaler and a purse pack of tissues, and headed down the old path across the paddocks, the one I used to take every day when Maisie was alive.

'Fred?' I called, coming into the house. 'Fred?' His bachelors' condiments huddled in the middle of the table: salt, pepper, butter, marmite, jam, tomato sauce. A saucer rested on a cup on the draining board. His newspapers were folded neatly in a corner behind his chair.

'In here,' he called. 'In the bedroom.'

'You haven't lured me here on false pretences, have you?' I asked, ready to laugh. But the sight of his face drained away any humour. It was made ghostly against the pillow by the light of his bedside lamp. 'Fred?'

'It's just, well, a bug, I suppose.'

'Shall I call the doctor?'

'Nah, nah. I've been to the doctor. I've got some stuff. It's just that, well, with it New Year's and all ...' He coughed, a long, wet, exhalation, a paroxysm that it seemed would never stop. Then he lay back on the pillows, exhausted.

'I'll make some tea.' I spent too long in the kitchen, fussing about with his shelves, removing things and wiping underneath, putting them back again. When Maisie died I spent weeks with Fred, teaching him what needed to be done so he could look after himself, explaining that he needed to wash his sheets every week, that he needed to clean the bath and the toilet and wipe out the shelves in the fridge. I taught him how to clean the oven as well, but he wasn't impressed.

'I won't bother with that,' he said, and he's fried everything since. There it was, the pan on the ring, wiped out and ready to do a breakfast. What would my doctor say about the fat? He probably knows already that most of the population over sixty would even fry their weetbix if they could. I am so good with my high calcium milk, even though the watery sight of it turns my stomach. Half a cup of it each morning on my cereal, and just a dash of cream to make it palatable.

At last I took in Fred's tea.

'With it being New Year's and all,' he said, 'I just felt like having you here.'

I dragged a chair over from the corner and sat beside the bed, holding his hand.

'You've been good to me,' he said.

'There's no need for all that.'

'I mean it though, Lily.'

'Well, you haven't been too bad yourself, eh, Fred. We've been through some times, eh?'

'Haven't we just? Haven't we just?' The back of his head was cupped in a bowl of linen, but his eyes clung on to me. His hand felt dry and papery, but his fingers held mine with a firm grip.

'I'm sorry,' he said. 'About Billy.'

'So am I, Fred. I was just thinking about him tonight. Only, well, who knows? It might have ended up just the same, as with Eddie. Who knows?'

'You loved that boy.'

'I loved him. But I was just a slip of a thing. If I turned sideways you couldn't see me.'

He laughed, a tortured sound like screwing up paper.

'You're not thinking of leaving, are you Fred?' I felt suddenly afraid. He was the last one, the last one who knew anything about Billy. And about Lily.

'Would I do that?' he asked. 'Would I, Lily?'

'I bloody hope not. We've got to stick together, you and I, Fred. You're all I've got now.'

'You've got that young boy. He's not so bad, your Nat. I had my doubts, but he's okay.'

'Nice of you to say so.'

'Nah, nah, it's not that, Lily. I'm just tired, you know. Tired. And I fancied a bit of your company. You don't mind, do you?'

'I don't mind.'

It wasn't the first time we had comforted each other. There was a time, years back, after Maisie had gone. Fred lost his son. His only son. He used to come up to the house while Eddie was out on the farm. He hardly knew what to do otherwise. It was enough that he had to learn to wipe out cupboards, to fry his own bacon in the mornings, to hang his underwear out on the clothesline. But to lose a son. To be faced with the prospect of healing when he could hardly understand the depth of the loss. Maisie, he insisted, would have known what to do, but I had my doubts.

Hugo had left home by then, so in a way I was the same, bereft. And I was suddenly afraid that Hugo would die too, and what would be left? What would be left?

Fred and I were good together too, something we'd missed years back, those knee-tremblers against the wall after the clubs shut, after we'd tried to dance away the war and couldn't think of any other way since the dancing hadn't worked. Precious moments of oblivion conjured between us, but we never gave it enough thought to consider making a go of it. It was over in a flash, he was back in the trenches and I was tapping away on the old Imperial. Years later we were better, less distracted. We'd learned a bit about being lovers.

We stopped when Eddie got sick.

All this talk of Billy and Fred. You must be wondering if I ever loved Eddie, the man I married. I've asked myself often over the years. Was there love in my marriage? Although it seems pointless so far down the track, so long after Eddie died, to ponder. Prostrate cancer, as so many of my acquaintances insisted on calling it, and I hadn't the desire or the energy to correct them. All cancer is prostrate by the end. Eddie's certainly was. He hardly made a bump beneath the quilt. (Trip Around the World, each piece a memory my fingertips rediscovered as I sat by his bed, thinking of things I could have done better.) You wouldn't have recognised him from that muscular ex-soldier you stared at for so many hours from your bedroom window, the one who inspired such a deep and longstanding infatuation. The one who turned your life on its head. I wondered as I watched him dying, what he made of it all – of you and I, of the decisions we made on his behalf. The decisions I made, because if I'm honest you didn't get much input, Iris. Surely that melon-hued man eating pureed vegetables from a spoon deserved a giggling bride at some stage of his life. He'd given his youth away without hesitation, for the sake of his country. Just because one man had a dream of taking over the world. He'd gone off to war, tender and compliant. Returned rigid, a fleshy outer casing to shield the world from the horrors within.

He had softened to a degree by the time he got news of his mother's illness, set off on his exhausting journey home, arriving days late. But the landscapes lived on within him. Ruins of trees, sharpened like swords, bayoneting the grey sky of war. Mud, trenches, rubble. Mutilated bodies. They were closer than yesterday, as though he might turn aside from the rebuilt London houses, from verdant antipodean hill country, and find that other world, a hair's breadth away, a shadowy negative behind every one of life's pleasures.

Mothers grieved for sons who had not returned, and for sons who had. Armless, legless, soul-less. Even the most normal were hard, impenetrable.

Husbands came back strangers, impatient to reclaim marital rights – they had thought of little else since victory was declared – to hammer their merciless way towards a state of ecstacy, of forgetfulness. Wives who had written so lovingly, longingly, for years, worried until they were ill with worry, felt brutalised, raped, used. They walked down the streets, aching from the sex, wondering how they would ever knit the family back together, their children terrified of men they had never known, who lashed out with belts or fists at the slightest provocation, and who had taken up residence in the haven which had always belonged to the children, their mother's bed.

Ma was a widow by then. That doodlebug, the one I came to think of as Dad's. It seemed ironic that he had fussed around for so many years, trying to save those intent on endangering themselves, ushering them into shelters as the sirens rang, preventing them from leaving before the All Clear. Yet when his turn came there was no one to protect him. He had no time to ponder his own death. It fell upon him, out of the sky, with no more warning than doodlebugs usually gave – the drone, the silence, the explosion. He was on his way home from a Home Guard meeting in the South End.

Ma coped – as she did with anything by then – with tight-lipped acceptance. Life wasn't much to hold on to with any great tenacity. For Ma, all its pleasures had gone. Meals were grey, tasteless, monotonous, something to be endured rather than enjoyed. We wore the same clothes week in, week out, darning and patching to prolong the lives of garments we could hardly stand the sight of. The streets were bleak, sandbagged, flanked by smouldering rubble. Homes were gone, friends were gone. Billy Brydon, who had introduced a spark into our dull living room, was gone. And then Dad went too.

We weren't the kind to share our grief. Nothing so intimate as holding hands at the funeral. And afterwards neighbours came for an austere cup of tea in our front room, bemoaning the unfairness of it all, the bleakness, the endlessness, of war. When they had gone Ma took off her hat, collapsed into an armchair and downed three sherries. Then she took herself off to bed and the next morning came downstairs intent on carrying on as always.

I rescued Dad's art gallery copies from the spare room wardrobe in case she took a fit and burnt them all. To me they were all that was left of him, precious relics of my childhood Saturdays. He would never talk to me about Goya again. Or Constable, or Canaletto. Everything I could glean from my father was already inside me.

Ma's afternoon tea parties became marginally more elaborate as time passed and sugar rations increased. Her friends, orange-hued from cheap face powder, wore brilliant red lipstick, silk stockings with seams up the back, and folded their gloves neatly in their laps. Widowhood gave Ma an air of superiority. She listened with empathy to their tales of woe. When I came in from work there was always a sense that I had interrupted something. The women became at once formal, conspiratorial. Glances were exchanged, knowledge held close to their wool-encased bosoms, because they were married and I was not, and they were careful not to leak out even a hint of what I could expect in the future. I would sit in their midst, smug in the knowledge that their concern was wasted on me. I thought I already knew more than they ever would. But I played the game.

I didn't know at the time there was more to marriage than sex. There was endurance, year after year of togetherness.

They all took great interest in my wedding, offering advice and practical help: sewing the dress, arranging the flowers, baking for the reception. Afterwards I became one of their number, an ample rump filling one of Ma's front room chairs.

After a few months they grew restless. I pretended not to notice their glances at my waistline, their blatant references to babies. Sometimes now I touch the river of red silk I have appliquéed onto my quilt, the tiny black cave with its curl of fishy-lizard embryo. My fingers – once shapely and feminine, now pudgy and worn from farm work, from gardening, from age – follow the river as it tumbles from the edge of the block, spilling eggs.

I knew why Eddie's sperm could not find purchase in my womb, why they dribbled out of me in the mornings as I cooked his breakfast, sticky on my thighs, chafing into nothing as the day went by. I knew why blood gushed every month, with clots like raw liver. I was womb-wounded, stabbed and gored and scraped into oblivion, a casualty of war, like the men. I knew that I could not conceive a child in the first year of my marriage, despite the raised eyebrows of Ma's friends, counting the months since our wedding night, expecting an announcement any day. And I knew that it would never be any different, that I would never be able to tell Eddie the news he most wanted to hear, broadcast my good fortune by excusing myself from afternoon tea in order to vomit.

What a thought, Iris. What an event to look forward to.

I will never forget their faces when I told them I was pregnant. They had long since given up hope. I was privy to their tales by then, the misery some called marriage. Their enthusiasm towards my pregnancy was unfathomable. It was as though they couldn't bear for another woman to be spared what they, themselves, had been through.

Would Eddie's mother have approved if she saw me at the end, beside his bed while he fed like a baby, the lids on his eyes like shutters, like the blinds at the windows of the rows of state houses on the edges of the Hill township, closed, allowing no access to the inside.

Did the landscapes of his war return to him then, as he lay dying beneath my Trip Around the World quilt? The sights and sounds, the blood and the mutilation? The desolation? Did he dream of our afternoons in that London bedroom, the coming together of two lonely spirits who saw a way out at last? Did he dream of his mother, her arms, her undying and unconditional love? Or did he dream of you, Iris, the young girl who would have given him everything, the sister who would have made him a better wife?

I had no access to his thoughts as I fed him or wiped the clammy sweat from his face and hands.

'Drink,' he said sometimes in those final weeks. 'Hugo,' he said, although he knew his claims to Hugo had never been as great as mine.

'He'll come,' I said, hoping.

And Hugo did come. Amelia stayed in the kitchen, unwilling to face death when she herself was so young and fleshy and obscenely healthy.

Eddie smiled at Hugo, a gummy incomplete flutter of a smile – he hadn't worn his teeth for months – and the shutters opened at last. I have never been religious, but the last image I have of Eddie is looking up to his son, as Jesus looked up to the heavens in all those Renaissance paintings, transfixed, illuminated. Hugo sat by the bed and held his hand for an hour, and there was nothing I could do, standing at the door, fussing over the battalion of medication on the bedside table, wondering whether Eddie was too hot or too cold, whether the window should be open or shut. Would he tell? Would he have the energy? Would the bond between Hugo and I be able to survive if he knew?

Eddie's eyes closed after a while, the look of adoration masked at last, and we withdrew to let him sleep. Amelia had baked a lemon cake in our absence, with a syrup made from juice and sugar poured over while hot. Hugo made tea and we sat at the table and drank the pot dry. We ate every crumb of cake between us too, and when Hugo went to say goodbye he found his father had died.

My withdrawal from the marriage bed seemed cruel then. That I had left Eddie to sleep alone for so many nights, through heatwaves and storms and after late night farm animal crises, and through illness and worse, loneliness. Eddie became married to the farm, and I became married, in my own way, to motherhood.

Hugo was only five or six, and needed a place to nestle through bad dreams or thunderstorms. I was far more in love with his Splendour-apple cheeks, the way his lips pouted in sleep, his soft innocent exhalations, than I had ever been with Eddie. And I wanted to be able to comfort him, to feel his tiny fingers weave between my own, as he drifted towards sleep.

Eddie laughed at first, so sure I'd be back, unable to resist the pull of his sexuality. It had driven me wild at first, the thought of his taut stomach muscles, the soft hair on his thighs, enough to summon butterflies. Not the ordinary kind. Huge tropical creatures as large as birds, flapping and fluttering within me. And through those early years of our marriage, before realisation of my barrenness dawned, we could hardly sit out the requirements of our day – the chaste welcome-home kiss, the meal eaten in titillating proximity to each other, the obligatory fireside needlework and newspaper perusal and wireless listening – before galloping upstairs and throwing off our clothes. (You see, Iris, I did love him once.)

But Eddie underestimated his competition. Hugo was perfect, everything I had ever wanted encapsulated in a single entity. And sex with Eddie had become tiresome. A month went by, sometimes, when we hardly glanced at each other. It's hard to summon passion from a dispassionate position. He stank of mud and cows and shit. He bickered constantly about my treatment of Hugo. He drank too much. He stopped calling me Lily, and started calling me Mum.

To make love with passion you must first feel like a woman, and something I heard recently on radio confirms this. That Friday night's seduction begins on Monday morning. Old women, I know, have no place listening to such speak-easy programmes. (I bet, Iris, *you* never would.) We are supposed to have grown up in total innocence, given ourselves on our wedding nights, and remained faithful for the whole of our married lives. What do we know, or need to know, about seduction?

Still, the statement spoke to me. If Eddie had treated me more like a woman, and less like a farm and household multi-purpose implement, he may not have had to sleep alone so many nights.

So there you have it, Iris. The fate of your dream lover. What do you make of it? Would he have suited you, do you think? Innocence is so slowly lost, and its loss is a lifelong process. Old women are dismissed easily enough by the world at large, but I believe we know a bit. What about you, Iris? Have you learned a thing or two? I'd love to know.

Back to Fred's bedside. That's where I was when I was thinking all this, watching him sleep, the poor man. I decided I would stay the night. I couldn't walk up the hill and home. It was too steep even in daylight. But I couldn't sleep. His breathing was too laboured, seeming to penetrate every corner. I knew he was dying, and I wanted to pace the house, end to end, wall to wall, door to door, a mindless frantic motion to lull my heart, to fool it into believing everything was all right. If Fred went, so much of me would go too. Was that selfish, to fear the loss of so much that has made me real? What about Fred? Was he afraid? Was he ready to go?

He wanted me with him, but what if I wasn't equal to the task? I squirted my puffer onto my tongue. I forced myself to sit by the bed and hold his hand, drawing my breaths to match his. In, out. In, out.

But there were so many questions I wanted to ask him. How could he even think about leaving me, when he had always been there? I watched his chest rise and fall. I lay my head beside him on the bed and listened to his breath rattle in and out. Eventually I drifted off.

When I woke, he was gone. Fred had gone and left only his body. Like Paddy. There was nothing left, nothing to cling on to. The vital part had been spirited away while I was carelessly looking elsewhere. I phoned the doctor and the ambulance. I phoned Fred's daughter in Auckland and his sister in Western Australia. I made arrangements. At dawn I took up my basket and began the walk home.

Halfway up the paddock I stopped to catch my breath, turning to look out to sea. That same wind was coming again from South America, bringing with it fragments of other people's lives. Had it taken a piece of Fred now, for someone on the coast of Australia to breathe in? Or would it be caught in a spiralling weather system, sucked to Antarctica or lured north to the tropics?

As I rested, I thought about my quilt spread across the kitchen table and knew what I must add. I had just the fabric, the last dress from my post-war years to hang in the wardrobe all this time, untouched. Antique cream satin, and worn only once. What an extravagance, especially in those times. And now I knew why I had saved it all these years.

I turned and began again my trek up the hill, gasping for air the moment I lifted my thigh to climb. The grass was lush, each strand shining in the morning sun. Even after so long there was a remnant of the track I used to follow to visit Maisie, kept alive perhaps by the sheep making their way in single file from one gate to another. Even Fred gave up on shanks's pony years ago. He always drove the ute next door.

My scissors were working as I climbed, cutting into the satin, an extravagant half circle, segmented. I would need eight pieces in all, and on top, a button, a finial, a golden gallery to finish.

When I reached the house I climbed the steps onto the verandah and went in through the open french doors, discarding my basket onto an armchair as I passed. I went straight into the bedroom and flung back the wardrobe doors. There it was in its plastic dry-cleaner's sleeve, tainted slightly by naphthalene. I seized it from the rail. There was hardly a thing left hanging now, just my recent floral prints, the ones I wore every day.

Hugo was waiting in the kitchen. The sight of him almost sent me off too, following Fred. I clutched my chest. 'You scared me.'

'For God's sake, where've you been? I had to come because I couldn't get you on the phone. I've been worried sick.'

I pulled out a dining chair and sat down. My quilt had been folded neatly and placed at one end of the table. I looked into his face but found no clues. Had he studied it, panel by panel, recognising the haphazard track of my life? Or was it merely another quilt, another time-consuming project his mother had taken on to fill the empty hours? It mattered to me, because I was not sure that my life was up to Hugo's scrutiny. Perhaps there was something in those mosaic pieces that would tell him more than he needed to know.

I ignored the quilt and looked to the bench for spoor. He had made tea, at least two cups.

'Is Nat here?' I asked.

'No one's here. Just me. Well, you now too, of course. But where the hell were you? I thought you must have collapsed somewhere. I've searched the whole garden. And the paddocks. I nearly rang the police. Everything was on. The lights. The doors, wide open to the general public, inviting every burglar from here to the Bombay Hills. What's going on, Mum?'

I told him about Fred, fondling the satin between my fingers, and he busied himself in the kitchen, making more tea. I was too tired to cry, although it was obvious he expected me to. 'Isn't there anyone you could have rung? Doesn't he have any family?'

'Only his daughter. And a sister. The only family he has left. You know that.'

Just like me, dear Iris. Just like me.

Lily

[Thirty]

The Fat Boy

It was the fat boy who found Jimmy Dodd, hanging from a beam in the shed. They were both twenty-two. The fat boy had changed. He wasn't fat now so much as big. He was a 'big guy' and he had friends and he could have cooked for his country. He had a qualification and a job as sous chef in a top Auckland restaurant. He was home for a Monday and Tuesday, his equivalent of a weekend, and was on some message for his mother – 'Find Fred and ask him if he can help your father to fix the tractor this afternoon' – when he came into the shed, with its high stud and rickety mezzanine floor.

Instead of Fred, the fat boy came face to face with Jimmy Dodd's dangling feet. He tried to scream but it was as though someone had stuffed his mouth full of paper. He grabbed the feet and tried to lift the weight off Jimmy Dodd's neck, but this caused the body to tip sideways, swivelling on its rope axis. He found a ladder, but it was too short to reach the rafters.

Then he ran, out of the shed, past the house and through the back gate, then up the hill, following the track in the paddock his mother had worn over the years. He was choking as he ran, drawing in loud stinging breaths as though his voice would not switch off. And the lenses in his eyes had turned into obscure glass, blurring and distorting everything. When he blinked, two hot tears fell onto his T-shirt, and others followed, burning his cheeks.

He ran headlong into Fred. The man was like a brick wall, tall and solid and unmissable. The fat boy rebounded backwards, falling onto his arse in the middle of the paddock.

'For God's sake, boy. Slow down. What the hell's up with you?'

The fat boy pulled himself onto his elbows and stared up at the man. The sun was behind him, almost blinding, blotted out by the big strong head and the brim of the straw hat. As though Fred was somehow divine, an image so similar to those faded Sunday School prints, hung at random on the pinex walls of the old church hall. A man with soft cow's eyes and a yellow plate balancing on his head.

'What is it, boy?' Fred demanded. 'What've you done now?'

But it wasn't anything the fat boy had done. It was something that had been coming for years. Jimmy Dodd on a collision course with death. Jimmy Dodd, bigger than life, louder than life, more profane than life. Jimmy Dodd, always sleeker, smoother, cleverer, crueller than a boy should be. At Sunday School the fat boy prayed for Jimmy Dodd to fall, for some chip to tumble from his impervious coating. God, like everyone else, ignored the fat boy. Jimmy Dodd went on to play provincial rugby, to date a Miss New Zealand finalist.

'How are things, warthog?' he'd ask the fat boy under his breath when they were both home at weekends. 'Elephant man? Blubber chops?'

'Get up, boy,' Fred said, holding a hand out to him, a hand Jimmy Dodd would have withdrawn at a crucial moment so that the fat boy would have fallen again.

The fat boy sobbed. He squinted up at the shadowy face with its brilliant halo. He had stopped praying for vengeance years ago. It was typical of God to answer now.

[Thirty-one]

Floss

Ten weeks and two days to go. Daniel coming after lunch.

Daniel has been so often now that the terror is not so acute. Julie must be desperate for a job. She is out almost every afternoon looking. Floss has six Matchbox cars now, and a fire engine. She has a few books of nursery rhymes to help her remember the last lines, and some blocks. Conversation between her and Julie seems to have dwindled to arrangements about Daniel, but Floss is relieved. There is too much potential for misunderstanding, and Floss has always had a knack for misunderstanding. She sets out to say one thing, and the harder she tries to explain herself the more she is aware that the picture in her own head differs wildly from the one her words are painting. Julie is a prime example. Thinking Flossie's soldier and Reggie are the same person, and that the boy has grown into a man who doesn't treat his mother well. She had to shut herself inside for the whole of Christmas Day, so Julie would think she was off somewhere with him. Instead she opened a can of soup and ate it with bread and butter. She kept the television low in case the voices drifted through the wall.

When Daniel comes Floss suspects something is wrong. Julie is away out the door in a flash, and Floss focuses more closely on the little boy as he eats his biscuit. His cheeks grow redder by the hour and her initial suspicion turns to panic as she realises he is feverish. She has never dealt with a feverish baby. She has no books to consult, and her doctor is far too busy to give advice over the phone. She cools his forehead with a damp flannel, and it comes away burning each time. She paces up and down the flat as he whimpers and drifts in and out of sleep.

In desperation she goes next door, just in case Julie has come home earlier than expected, just in case she is grabbing more disposables for Daniel or a quick packet of biscuits to share over a cup of tea. Floss rattles the letter slot.

'Julie. Julie, are you there?' She waits, but there is nothing. As she turns to go she thinks she hears a giggle, a high-pitched arrow of sound shooting towards the sky.

Floss creeps back. What if there are intruders, and she has disturbed them in the middle of the act of ransacking? What if they've waited with breath held until they think she's gone, and then burst out laughing with relief? She crouches by the door and opens the letter flap soundlessly. She can see a slot of hallway and a flood of spring sun angling onto a patch of dull brown carpet. The sunlight flickers. Someone is there. She waits, her mouth suddenly dry, her knees cramping under the pressure of maintaining such a precarious pose. Then he comes around the corner from the kitchen.

'I don't remember,' he calls into the bedroom. 'D'ya take sugar?'

'Yeah. Two,' comes Julie's voice.

He disappears, then comes back with two steaming mugs. Floss can't seem to move. He's stark naked, blue-flecked with tattoos of dolphins and dragons, and his family jewels swing from side to side as he walks closer and closer to the letter flap. Floss panics, the flap clanging shut as she struggles upright.

'What the ...'

She doesn't wait around to be discovered, but flies into her own flat and shuts the door without a sound. Daniel's fever has broken in her absence and he's sleeping peacefully now on her armchair. She strokes back a lock of his hair. She makes tea and drinks it scalding hot at her little table. She seems to have been tossed back fifty years, and the smell and the taste of that afternoon in Lou's house is with her again. Is it any different for Julie? Floss can't seem to find a parallel. Her old lady mind protests. There is something obscene about doing it in the afternoon.

Julie aside, Floss knows that Daniel's the sweetest thing that has ever come into her life. It doesn't matter what she tells him. He doesn't judge or misconstrue. He simply stares up at her and offers a string of equally unintelligible articulations in return. Then grins. And he goes off to sleep in her arms when she sings to him, leaving her alone to remember the way things really were.

'I was held prisoner for six months,' she tells him as he sleeps. 'I wasn't even allowed to show my face at the window.' The net curtains were thick as a dowager's petticoats, thick as the cobwebs in an attic. She could just see out if she sat still enough, but no one could see in. She watched her soldier working his garden. Tomatoes clustered on the vines like grapes, the beans like witches' fingers against the teepees. She ate the tomatoes in sandwiches at lunch time, and the beans with her dinner. She shelled the peas between her lonely fingertips, and every night at dusk Lou came in to fix the blackout curtain. Part of her longed to escape. She could easily have done it, walked out the door on the day each week that Lou went to Devon, to post the letter she had helped Flossie to construct. They conjured a parallel world between them, of seafront promenades and afternoon teas and a lapdog called Horace that created mayhem in the household. Every week they came up with some new story, and Flossie wrote the adventure as though she was deliriously happy, ensconced in Devon with Lou's friend. And every week Lou went off on the train so the letter would come back to London with an authentic postmark. So when she left in the morning Flossie knew she would be gone most of the day. Her soldier was off at work, not that he would have tried to stop her. He could hardly look her in the eye, and wouldn't have made a scene.

But there was more to it than that. She had grown. She was sticking out, and it would have been a foolish move. It wasn't just her mother's reaction she feared, but the whole street would have noticed before she reached her mother's front door, and shame would have descended on the household forever and a day. Her whole life would have been tainted by the tongues of idle women, and the only husband she could have hoped to snare would be one who, for whatever reason, was prepared to take on damaged goods. Any motivation was suspect, hinting at a future of humility and abuse – in effect, what Floss ended up with. But she didn't know it then. She still dreamed of princes, soldiers at least. She still dreamed of happily ever after.

So she stayed in the room with the brown roses tangled into infinity, with the bald man frowning on her nakedness, her bulge, her shame.

Lou was attentive as a servant. She brought breakfast every morning while Flossie lay in bed. Tea and toast with marmalade. A boiled egg in a purple ceramic egg cup shaped like an owl. She cracked the top every morning with the back of her spoon and ate the flowing yolk but left the white. There was a mound of salt and a sprinkle of pepper on the edge of her plate. The toast was cut into fingers, into soldiers. She ate the soft middle parts but left the crusts. In the afternoons she knitted for the baby, and in the evenings she read books Lou had brought from the library, romances which ended always with the beautiful heroine in the arms of her lover.

It was a boy. *Once there was a little boy* ... Flossie's soldier watched, calling Lou a bloody idiot.

'What if something goes wrong?' he asked.

'It won't.'

'I mean, have you ever done anything like this before? Have you ever delivered a baby?'

'I've watched. There's not much to it, you know.'

He sucked on his cigarette. Flossie could hear the paper burning as she waited for the pain to descend again. 'Oh yeah? Is that why so many women die?'

'Don't say that in here,' Lou snapped. 'Either help or get out. I can't have that sort of talk in here. She's alive, you know. She doesn't need to hear that sort of talk at a time like this.'

He crushed his cigarette out in an ashtray beside the bed. 'Let me go for the midwife.'

'Don't you dare. If you do this will have all been for nothing. That woman can't keep her mouth shut. The whole street'll know within minutes. And what kind of future does that give our Flossie, eh?' She thrust her face at his. He turned away.

'She's ripping bloody open.'

'Yes, she's ripping bloody open. It's what happens. What do you men think? That we open a few snap fasteners?'

'Jesus.'

'*He didn't have a clue either.*'

'Promise me,' Flossie said, her head rolling on the pillow, her eyes rolling too, as though the irises were adrift in the whites. Her focus wandered from Lou's face to the wallpaper on the other side of the single bed, the brown floral, the fan of petals on a stalk bent back on itself. A forest of brown flowers with broken backs.

Lou wiped the sweat from Flossie's forehead. She could feel each bead, diamonds swept away by the cool cloth, their sharp edges inflicting pain, swept away and springing forth again, instantly, crystallising.

'Promise me,' Flossie said, her eyes clinging to Lou's, 'that whatever happens ...'

Lou wiped away more diamonds. 'You mustn't talk like that. Nothing's going to happen.'

'... that whatever happens, you'll be there.'

Flossie calculated, realising only after she had undergone a series of complicated mathematical equations, that they were unnecessary. That it would be after the turn of the century, an inconceivable time away. Lou was calculating too. 'If I'm alive,' she said, 'I'll be more than eighty. Come to think of it, I'd rather be dead than more than eighty.' She wiped away more diamonds.

'Promise me?' Flossie tried to communicate urgency.

'I promise,' Lou said, full of lies. She must have already had her idea by then.

Another pain came and Flossie clenched her teeth together. She knew she couldn't make a sound which wouldn't spill from the window, alerting Mrs Donaldson next door. She'd had seven of her own and wouldn't be fooled for a minute. Flossie felt herself duplicate, as though one of her had come away, rising from the body on the bed, a weightless white self, hovering towards the ceiling, rising, rising. And then something shifted within her. She was one again without warning. She tried to speak but a sound came out, an animal moan, and she pushed and hot liquid flooded out and then a stinging, burning she couldn't bear.

'It's the head,' Lou shrieked. 'Don't push any more. Don't even breathe. I have to make sure everything's all right.'

But Flossie couldn't help herself.

'Jesus Christ,' her soldier said, turning away.

'It's a boy,' Lou said, crying. Flossie put her head back on the pillows, staring up at the stained ceiling, and sobbed.

[Thirty-two]

2 January

Dear Iris

Do you know about the House Quilt, Iris? The design is more than one hundred and fifty years old, and it symbolises houses, cottages and barns, churches and schools. Sometimes there are variations, including cupolas, steeples, silos, or bell-towers. More often they have simple chimneys. You could try a House Quilt, Iris. There are no curves or difficult seams. You could use all your old dresses. My House Quilt is one of my favourites, the first double quilt I made. Nat has been sleeping under it since he arrived, though not on New Year's Eve. He didn't come home until lunchtime yesterday, insisting he had called, or tried to, but I wasn't home.

'You need an answering machine,' Hugo said, still installed at the end of the dining table, forsaking the role of father in favour of over-possessive son. He rubbed the lip of the table with his thumb and forefinger. 'Then you would've known where he was. Where were you, by the way?' He turned to Nat, who jumped visibly, an unwilling object of the sudden and unprecedented paternal attention.

'I stayed with friends. Lily said I should if I was too tired to drive home. That road's a killer at night.'

The pun-master struck again, although none of us made any sign of acknowledgement. Hugo was too angry, Nat too apologetic, and I was too distracted by the fabric in my hands, imagining the shape of the pieces, the bite of the scissors, the whispered pop of the needle as it penetrated the sheen of the satin, embarking on the curving seams. The look of recognition on Nat's face when he saw that he had been sewn in.

'You won't be able to stay here now, Mum,' Hugo said, leaning on his bare earnest forearms, his fingers interweaving while his thumbs wrangled with each other. 'It's too isolated, with Fred gone.'

'Fred?' Nat asked.

I nodded, and Nat seemed to deflate, to curl his shoulders forward and lower his chin towards his chest.

'You're so predictable,' I told Hugo. 'There are houses all around. And I've got Nat now. I'm not on my own any more.'

'And how reliable is Nat?' Hugo asked, casting a glance across the kitchen. Nat sighed and stooped to retrieve the frying pan from a cupboard under the bench. He took mushrooms and asparagus from the fridge, and cracked open a couple of eggs. He measured ingredients into the Breville and turned it on so we could have fresh bread by five o'clock.

'There's a place on the Hibiscus Coast, Mum,' Hugo said. 'I can pick you up some information. You get your own unit, as much independence as you want.'

'I've got that already. I don't need to move into a matchbox to find it.'

'But there's security too, Mum. No worries about noises in the night. And medical help, if you need it.'

'I've got a good doctor. And I'm way past worrying about noises in the night.'

'Think about it, anyway.'

'I'll think about. Oh, I've thought about it. No, thanks.'

Hugo sighed. He had hair growing out of his ears and his neck was thick, with horizontal stripes where it creased, stubbled too where the hairdresser had shaved it. I almost had to remind myself that he was my son, my little boy. I wondered momentarily whether I should feed him. There were bought biscuits in the cupboard. I could make toast from yesterday's bread. But I was tired, suddenly, of feeding people. Perhaps it was Hugo's turn to feed me.

'I know you mean well,' I said, feeling sorry for him, as though I was being deliberately obstructive when it wasn't my intention. 'But most of all don't you just want me to be happy? Because I am happy here, with Nat, even if once in a blue moon he goes out and does what nineteen-year-olds do. I have a good life,' I said, and it was the truth. My quilters with their octogenarian awe, my home help, my grandson. And, until so recently, my friendship with Fred.

'Of course,' Hugo said, with reluctance. As though the wrangling of his thumbs was also occurring in his mind. Did he really want me to be happy, or did he just want to cleanse his conscience? His eyes seemed suddenly vulnerable, and I saw a spark of that little boy with the Splendour-apple cheeks.

He hugged me before he got into his car to leave, and I inhaled the cool laundered scent of his cotton shirt, a whiff of his tired, applied-twenty-four-hours-ago aftershave. 'How is Joanna?' I asked through the car window.

'I'm not seeing Joanna any more,' he said. 'High maintenance, girls like that. She couldn't come to grips with the fact that I have prior commitments. Perhaps it's for the best.'

'Prior commitments?'

'Oh, you know. Vincent. Amelia. Nat, I suppose.'

I put a hand on his shoulder, distracted for a moment by the fabric of his shirt, wondering how it would look as part of my quilt. But then I reminded myself that it was nearly done. That Hugo was in the quilt already.

When his car had slid between the gates and off down the hill towards town, I felt suddenly leaden. The thought of climbing the verandah steps was daunting. So I waited, my fingers fondling the soft fabric of the dress I had carried with me from the kitchen, as though I couldn't bear to be separated from it. And in a way it was true. I had one more thing to do before I could begin to grieve for Fred. How strange that Hugo didn't pick up on this, that on the loss of my friend I had been hugging my wedding dress like a security blanket.

Nat was asleep on the couch when I came in, his empty plate discarded in the sink, the pan half-full of water on the hob. Instead of cleaning up I lay my dress across the table and took up the scissors. I cut out all the shapes and began stitching with great care, so the curves on the finished piece would lie flat. Then I cut a mirror image for a backing and spread the three layers on the kitchen table – the backing, the wadding, the antique cream half-circle. I pinned all together with safety pins, my tiny quilt, thrown together in a couple of hours, while

Nat slept. Then I began, on the machine, to quilt it – the magic finishing touch, the icing, the polish. My needle bobbed methodically up and down, passing through the fabric at the seams and again beside them, parallel. The satin took on three dimensions. The curves became like the whalebone in a corset, the skeleton of the crowning glory of my quilt. In between I stitched a criss-cross pattern for the shingles, a hit and miss design. Hit and miss.

Like so much of life.

Lily

[Thirty-three]

Floss

They left in the dead of night. She writes it in her diary. *They left in the dead of night.* Why was it called 'the dead' of night, when there were plainly many signs of life, creakings and stirrings, secrecy, hypocrisy and deceit? She slept blissfully. She had pushed the baby out into the world. The pain was behind her now, and the fear of discovery. Lou had pretended she was pregnant. She was so big no one would ever be able to tell. She was the sort of woman who could have a baby one day and show no change in dimensions. All that remained was for Flossie to recover, to write a letter to say she was coming home, to creep out to the station at night, and to arrive. The letter had been posted a week before. She was healing well, staying in bed at Lou's insistence, the baby whisked away and cared for out of sight. She couldn't wait to get up, to walk barefoot through the house, to skip up and down the stairs as though she was a sprite, weightless after what she had been, a blob, a blimp, a zeppelin on legs.

She lay in bed late that morning, that awful morning, waiting for her breakfast tray. She had slept so well she hadn't even heard the baby wake, or Lou's clucking as she fed him. It was after ten when Flossie ventured down two flights to the kitchen. No one was home. Worse still the cupboards were empty, not just of food, but of everything. There was no kettle, no frying pan, not even a knife. The table was still there, the old brown suite in the front room, the beds and dressing tables and wardrobes. But the bedding was gone, the clothes, the embroidered doilies and antimacassars. There wasn't even a cup so she could drink water from the tap.

She dressed and packed her bag. After dark she crept from the house. She spent the night in a doorway near the station, and at first light descended to the platform where she would have arrived. An hour or two later she emerged into the daylight and walked home.

'They've emigrated,' her mother said. 'To New Zealand. Well, I always thought he'd go back. You know what he was like, always on about it – the hills, the space, the beaches. What a shame you've missed them, and the baby too. Barely a week old. I don't know how they could take him so far. What if something happened? That's what I said to her. "What if something happens? What if he gets sick and there's no doctor on that ship you're on?" But, well, your sister wouldn't listen. "It's a better place to bring up children, Ma," she kept saying. As if, eh? Look at you and her, both of you brought up here, and there's nothing wrong with you. I told her that. And I told her to wait until you were back. It was only a matter of days. But she said they'd made the booking, and they had to stick to it.'

Flossie couldn't answer. She went upstairs to her old bedroom and put her suitcase on the floor. She stared out her window at Lou's back garden – the window she had watched her soldier from for so long. She saw across the back fence the thick mass of net curtain she'd been contained behind for the past months. Soon someone else would be moving in, someone else would be digging the garden, harvesting the cabbages. But she would never fall in love again with someone else's husband.

Floss looks again at the words in her diary. *They left in the dead of night.* It is the dead of night now, though far from silent. Voices drift up from the street, footsteps from the stairs and the maze of corridors, the hum of the lift, working for once, probably being defecated in as she listens. A thin waver of siren, the blasting of car horns. She unscrews the lid of her pen and writes, *They took my baby.*

At first it was a relief that they were gone. There was no one to tell Flossie's secret, to let it slip out by accident over a cup of tea with the women of the neighbourhood. Flossie went back to work at the drapery, and with her soldier gone she could start to think about boys again. But they all seemed so young, so half-formed. She wanted a man who had seen life, who had known hardship and friendship, and who knew how to make her feel like a woman. After a time she stopped going to dances.

She stayed home with her mother instead, embroidering doilies and tablecloths, sewing dresses, mending stockings. She never wrote to Lou, not even a line or two at the bottom of her mother's letters. Lou seemed of another time, and was somehow too close to what had happened.

It was years before Reggie came along. Years. She was a spinster by then. And suddenly there was a future again, the prospect of having her own kitchen, her own net curtains. Her own little boy.

It wasn't until a year passed after her marriage that she began to think ill of Lou, to resent her and see the theft that had taken place that night.

'What the hell's wrong with you?' Reggie asked. 'I keep my end up. You're still as thin as a broomstick. You're not douching yourself, are you? Like a tart? You're not doing anything to stop things, are you?'

She knew that she wasn't the problem, but she couldn't say a word. That would have brought hell down on her head. He was bad enough if she forgot to buy a newspaper. What would he have been like if she'd told him?

Sometimes she dreamed about it, though. And sometimes it was so close she could hardly keep the words in. It was like a hair on her tongue that had to be removed or she would go mad. Through all his rantings and ravings she knew she had a weapon stronger than any of his. But it was a weapon she could never use. He wouldn't be able to live with it. He would desert her, and she'd be left with nothing, an abandoned wife. She would have to go home to her mother, and the shame would be worse, so much worse, than living with Reggie.

Her mother came to stay with them once. They met her in Ryde. It was the furthest she'd ever been from London.

'No baby yet?' she asked, when Reggie had gone out for a pint.

'Not yet,' Flossie said, bending her head over her needlework.

'Ah, well, not to worry. Lou took years to fall. You might be the same.'

And the next thing her mother was dead.

While Flossie was cleaning out the house a letter came from Lou. Flossie didn't even open it. She simply wrote, *Recipient deceased. Return to sender.* And that was it, the end of their contact.

Years on, Floss wonders where Lou is, whether she is still alive, whether she will make it to the steps of St Paul's in five weeks and two days. She remembers a day, before all that business with her soldier, when she and Lou went into the city. They climbed the steps of St Paul's. They went inside. They climbed the two hundred and fifty-nine steps to the Whispering Gallery. Lou was panting like a dog even though they'd stopped half a dozen times on the way. They climbed another one hundred and nineteen to the Stone Gallery. Flossie left Lou then and climbed the remaining one hundred and fifty-two to the Golden Gallery. Once outside Flossie gulped in air. London was spread before her like a toy town. It was like being on top of the world. She stared down Fleet Street, picking out the spire of St Bride's. It had inspired the modern wedding cake, and outside its circle of calm the most articulate journalists in the world hustled by, in hot pursuit of the latest stories.

Flossie had no story then. Even now they wouldn't give her more than a cursory glance. Three lines on page nineteen. The public doesn't care about lonely old women. It wants youth and beauty and scandal. What mileage is there in staying married for forty-two years? In having one's sister steal one's baby? In dreaming, fifty years on, of making some sort of half-hearted attempt at reconciliation?

Floss hated Lou for so many years – and her soldier too, for his weakness, his self-interest. But she has come full circle now. There is only one thing she wants more than seeing her sister again, and that is seeing her little boy.

[Thirty-four]

5 January

My dearest, dearest Iris

Have you survived New Year? What a fuss about nothing. I have made resolutions all the same. Nat, too, although it was only too obvious his didn't include getting a job. Entering his film in festivals and competitions, beginning another, applying for a course at the polytechnic. It seems he's almost finished his project, filming in his absent hours. What can be gained by it? Unless he is brilliant he will be just another penniless artist.

My resolutions, you're wondering. Perhaps I'm no different. To finish my quilt in time to enter the London exhibition. But I'm not so sure about beginning another. I'm too tired to contemplate it, but that may pass.

'Sweet,' Nat said when he saw the quilted cupola, stitched carefully onto the border fabric of my quilt, a silken crown. 'Sweet,' he said, touching the golden gallery, the cupola's own crown, a cupola above a cupola. Then he ran his fingers on, across the red and green sonata of pohutukawa, down the trunk in forty-one shades of brown, following a single root which diverges from the rest, and which I had yet to appliqué between the blocks. It stretched out, pinned at the edges, its point already tacked in place, a line of diminishing chain stitch meandering between the bricks of the Islington houses. Nat touched their windows, the tiny panes, the number on the door, the roofs that would have the impression of slates quilted on them. His right index finger found the curled lizard, the eggs falling off the bottom edge. 'What's this?' he asked.

I knew it would come. I knew Nat would want to know more. No one else would ask, but Nat has an insatiable curiosity.

'It represents fertility,' I said, only half lying. Fertility and infertility.

Something that was once there, and then gone.

'Why didn't you have more children?' he asked.

'Because I couldn't.'

'Oh,' he said, taken aback. What did he think? That it was a choice, in my generation. That we could stop at one because we thought more would interfere with our lifestyle?

'Have you ever thought about fertility?' he asked. 'How it's not genetic? I mean, everything's genetic. Every bloody thing. Well, you think so anyway, don't you? How kids have their great-uncle's nose, or their father's chin. I've got Dad's ears. Everyone's always told me that. I used to wonder, when I was a sprog, *Then whose ears has Dad got?*'

'He's got Eddie's ears,' I said. 'The same thing happened to him when he was a boy. *Haven't you just got your father's ears?*'

'See what I mean,' Nat said, still fingering the blocks. He was caressing the explosion, stroking the slivers of silk and cotton splaying out in a design based on the Mariner's Compass. 'We take it for granted that everything is handed on genetically. But not fertility. Or I mean infertility, really. You couldn't have more kids, but Dad's bloody prolific.'

I laughed. What was Nat doing, at his age, pondering the complexities of fertility?

'Some people have too much of it. Some people are obscene the way they pop kids out. Three mistakes at the end of the family, for Christ's sake. And others, well, I suppose all that conspicuous bloody fecundity just makes them want to curl up and bloody die.' His fingers stopped suddenly where the Double Wedding Rings intersected.

It was past eight o'clock at night and we were on the verandah, the coolest place, the roof funnelling any whisper of movement into a breeze. Nat had finished his magical cupola, the shingles glowing like copper as the sun's rays slanted. Just like the real thing. The shadows across the garden were lengthening, but the heat stood like a wall beyond the verandah roof. Mutabilis offered its single blooms in shades of apricot and pink to the sky, lending colours to the imminent sunset. Mary Rose was flourishing on Paddy's remains, taking the youth from his carcass, converting it to pink petticoats, cupped like the pillow around Fred's head.

Later, from my bed, I heard the car engine start, the tyres rattling the loose gravel as Nat directed it between the gateposts. But even so I fell within minutes into a sleep full of Fred. I couldn't forget how many times we had lain together on my bed. How tender his hands were on my middle-aged woman's skin, the creases and disasters where once a waist had been, the breasts which would have rivalled, in fullness, any cow's udder. And yet there was a reverence in his touch. Perhaps because he loved cows.

'Oh, Lily,' he said, so many years ago. 'My Lily.'

I don't rest easy with the prospect of meeting my maker. I can't decide whether I have been wicked and sinful, or merely human. Opportunities have come along, and I have taken some. Other times there were no choices. Will I be judged for having secrets, for lying by omission, for following – on the odd occasion – my heart?

Fred walked with me all night. Every time I turned over I woke and felt again his loss. The thought of his house, standing empty, filled me with gloom. His washing line with its scattering of brightly coloured pegs, two pairs of underpants, with legs, and a singlet. His compost heap, composting without him. The awful platitude, uttered at funerals, filled my head. Life goes on. Life. Goes. On.

How can it? How dare it?

I can't believe he is gone, that Fred is gone. Fred. Is. Gone.

Hugo came to the funeral, with Amelia. Joanna, he said, was looking after the Boiled Egg. Amelia took my arm and whispered, 'No hard feelings. She's the best babysitter we ever had. And she's moved on – from Hugo, I mean. She's going out with the bass player in a band now.'

Nat wore a suit he had borrowed from a friend, and we took the front pew in the church beside Fred's dry-eyed daughter. All the locals were there. Fred was a popular man.

'Such a shame,' they said afterwards.

'Such a nice man.'

'Still, he had a good innings.'

'I'd be happy to pop off about then.' As though there couldn't be new beginnings at eighty-three.

I wonder how many funerals must be endured in a lifetime. How much loss can one body bear? All this time I had been mourning Billy Brydon, and Fred was just next door.

The church committee had catered – asparagus rolls, club sandwiches and marshmallow cake in the church hall. The walls had been painted birds' egg blue by parishioners with spare time on Saturday afternoons, and the trestle tables had been covered with newsprint from reel-ends sold cheap by the local paper.

'There was that awful business,' I heard someone mumble to Hugo. 'Years ago, you know, with his son.'

Hugo looked at the floor and cleared his throat.

Jimmy Dodd's funeral was in the same church, tea in the same hall with sandwiches and cakes supplied by the school PTA in remembrance of an ex-pupil. I sat behind Fred all through the service, watching his shoulders rise and fall as he breathed, knowing he would never stand tall again. The church didn't look kindly on suicide. We sang dreary hymns and praised God for the preciousness of life. Jimmy lay at the front in his polished coffin, but his name wasn't mentioned.

'You know he bullied me,' Hugo said, back at my kitchen table afterwards. Nat and Amelia had walked down to see his creation. I could see Amelia's red blouse as she passed between the roses, Nat's arms waving as he tried to explain the lamination process, the fastening of shingles.

'Who did?'

'Jimmy Dodd.'

I stared out through the window. I felt as though I had been cut in half. All those pikelets and ginger gems. How could I not have protected him? All those afternoons, insisting that Jimmy come home to play. What kind of mother was I? I reached for Hugo's hand and he caught my fingers in a grip so tight I thought they would break. He leaned forward, over the table. He sniffed and wiped his eyes with the palm of his other hand. He stared at the old oak, the panels of veneer, the grain like magnified moths' antennae.

I always knew that Fred wasn't any kind of father. He and Eddie were cast in the same mould, standing back, curling a lip at any attempt their sons made to please them. As though they knew nothing could instil the kind of hardness they carried, the resilience, the knowledge of their own endurance. War had done that. Hell didn't frighten them. They had lived through it, come out the other end. Worse than hell. And those soft-footed sweet-faced boys danced and somersaulted for approval that never came.

I told Eddie that Hugo was mine from the beginning. There were no disputes. Plenty of criticism, but no disputes. But Jimmy Dodd didn't have that kind of protection. Fred had a free hand, and he used it for beating his son.

It was a relief when the boys left home. We didn't have to watch each other being parents any more. I knew it had been as hard for him to watch Hugo being coddled as it had been for me, seeing the cockiness in Jimmy's eyes, the cynical smirk, the fear underneath it all.

After that Fred and I became friends again, friends who agreed not to talk about their sons. And then Maisie died, and Jimmy died, and we were so much more.

'You know that I hated Jimmy Dodd,' Hugo said.

I nodded. I knew that now, too late. And there was something else I had just learned as well, too late. How much I loved Jimmy Dodd's father.

Hugo and Amelia stayed for dinner, and Nat insisted on cooking.

'The restaurant can look after itself for once,' Amelia said, winking. Hugo made a call on the verandah from his cellphone. He had discarded his tie and rolled up his sleeves. His forearms were pale despite the summer sun. Eddie always feared I was raising an indoor boy, the worst kind of boy Eddie could think of. Far, far worse than a bully.

We had fancy lettuce salad with dressing Amelia concocted, cherry tomatoes and avocado, strips of chicken breast sprinkled with cajun spices then grilled and tossed with the lettuce. We had fresh bread from the Breville with great knobs of butter. To hell with the heart for once. And afterwards Hugo and Amelia drove away.

That's all for now.
Lily

[Thirty-five]

15 January

Dear Iris

I've been living off cups of tea and my quilting things, and I stitch the day away. And the next. And the next. There seems nothing else in the world but my quilt, and yet I am tired and waste hours sleeping, wondering why I have always been such a slow learner, why so many of us are destined to make the same mistakes again and again.

The bricks of the Islington houses have slowly taken on relief, the shallow arches above the windows, the cornerstones. The panels in the door are becoming discernible, the railings taking shape. The attic windows. The roof slates. Will I make the deadline, Iris? It is everything now, to make that deadline. There is so much ahead of me, exhaustion descends as soon as I glance beyond the first block. I sleep, then I wake and stitch one or two more lengths of thread. Then I sleep again. Every time I wake I remember again that Fred has died.

My girls have said they will help me. We'll have an old-fashioned quilting, all around the table with our needles, if I don't get it done in time. Generations ago it was a social occasion, all the women of a village coming together, taking up different corners of a quilt and gossiping as they stitched heirlooms.

And, Iris, I've decided I will dedicate it to you.

Lily

[Thirty-six]

21 February

Dear Iris

It is done, gone, sent off, entered. It has used all of me, but now there is something new. It's Nat. I should have known he had come here to hurt me, and how stupid of me to allow it. I should have kicked him out that first afternoon, sent him off to the main road with his pile of rubbishy belongings. Have I learned anything in this life, Iris? Sometimes I wonder.

I won't say another word about quilts. I'm sure you've heard enough by now. Perhaps you don't even care. There was a time, so recently, when I could hardly think of anything else. Everywhere I looked I saw designs for piecing. The tiles on the back wall of the butcher's shop. The new pavers laid in the main street. The petals on a flower and the stained glass in the church windows. The palings on a fence. The treacherous red and blue stripes on an airmail envelope.

But now I can hardly think of quilts. What a waste of so many hours, cutting fabric into tiny pieces just to sew them together again. Stitching by hand when a machine is so much quicker.

'I've got something to show you,' Nat said.

'I don't know if I can take any more shocks.'

'You'll like it,' he said. 'Promise.' What was he thinking?

It was his film, apparently finished. I arranged myself on my favourite chair and fanned myself with the *Listener*. The humidity at this time of year is capable of choking old women. It's like a pillow against your face, thick and soft and impossible to breathe. The *Listener*, with its thousands of words, flapped and fluttered, whispering messages I couldn't grasp. I don't care any more about politics. Competent journalism goes in one eye and out the other, leaving no residue in the brain. Social issues, abused children, tooth decay, obesity can be someone else's fight now. Even the prospect of another war doesn't frighten me. My world has collapsed in on me. Last night all I had was the suffocating feather-down of the air, the sweet breath from those fluttering pages, and Nat, fussing about with the video player, inserting and ejecting the tape a dozen times before he was satisfied.

'For goodness sake,' I said, annoyed.

'Got to get it right. Here goes.' He pushed PLAY on the remote with an unnecessarily dramatic gesture and came to perch on the arm of my chair. 'I've got more to do yet,' he said, before any glimmer of an image was displayed. 'I have to think of a title, and do all the graphics and stuff for the beginning, and all the credits. Here it comes, here it comes.' He stood up, then sat cross-legged on the floor, pulling his calves close, wriggling with nervous energy. The first image was grey, out of focus. A thin, child's voice began a rhyme. *England, Ireland, Scotland, Wales, inside, outside, monkey's tails* ... Focus sharpened and the indeterminate black and white image became a young girl, skipping. She wore a floral dress. Her legs were scrawny, with too many taut tendons. Her knee-high socks had slipped down around her ankles, her exposed shins were bruised in the random way of children, and her lace-up shoes were misshapen, as though they had been handed down from older siblings. The girl skipped, singing. The camera rolled back and turned to focus on a door. The singing faded and the door opened. The camera traced the floorboards, old wide polished wood, a high-heeled shoe, a stockinged calf, a floral dress, a girl brushing her hair. Waverley. She looked beautiful, dreamy. She discarded the hairbrush, moved across the room, and lay down on the bed. The camera focused on a portion of the quilt, one of Marjorie's, English Ivy design. Then darkness. When it pulled back there was a soldier – Nat dressed in some moth-eaten uniform he must have scrounged from somewhere. The museum perhaps. His hair was scraped up under his hat. I almost laughed. Music started up, one of my old seventy-eights. Glenn Miller. Nat put out an arm and Waverley took it. Behind them I recognised the panelled wall of the Masonic Hall. They danced.

'See that?' Nat said. 'We've been having lessons. Thursday nights.'

My tissue was flitting about my cheeks, threatening to block out a crucial second of film. How Waverley could dance, Marjorie's bookish schoolgirl daughter turned into a siren. She spun and undulated with deftness and confidence, and each time her high heel came down onto the old floor it was with complete assurance. She caught Nat's proffered fingers with millimetres to spare. Her dress, a forties style, fluttered about her sophisticated calves, with their tantalising seams up the back. 'Nat,' I said. 'You're so suave.'

The camera swivelled suddenly to the floor, and the music stopped. An indeterminate scuffling sound became the shovelling of dirt, digging a hole, and there was Nat in his ghastly woollen shorts, a headless Nat, digging. Then a prostrate Nat in uniform lying in a hole with his eyes shut, tomato sauce on his forehead. The camera swivelled again, back to the bedroom, Waverley crying on the bed with her face covered by one arm. She turned onto her back, staring at the ceiling. Her face turned into mine.

Then the thin voice began the rhyme again. *England, Ireland, Scotland, Wales* ... The camera's eye slithered across the surface of my quilt and to the window, beyond which was a street, and the spindly girl, skipping. But this time she was barefoot, and wearing bike pants and a snug-fitting T-shirt. The image faded out and I tried to compose myself for the kind of reaction Nat required from his grandmother. Could I, as his first audience, give the desired feedback, and the confidence to take it to the world? The truth is I couldn't decide. Is he brilliant, Iris, or unscrupulous?

I hardly knew what to say, whether to be angry for stealing so much of me, or to be proud. How could someone who was nineteen have such a clear concept of the circle of life? He turned on the lamp on the television and turned off the overhead light. He pulled the ageing curtains across the open french doors to deter moths and mosquitoes. He fell into an armchair, resting his head on the back and staring up at the old pressed steel ceiling. I used to look at it too when I first arrived in the house, thinking that some early settler had arranged for it to be transported from England. How it must have arrived one day to great excitement and been installed as the crowning feature of an otherwise ordinary villa. I have thought of sewing its design into a quilt, but I don't really need a quilt of it when all I need to do is look up of an evening.

I looked at the herringbone pattern on Nat's baggy shorts. It was unlike him to be so still for so long.

'The film was great,' I said.

'Do you think so? Do you think it actually says anything? Christ, after all this work I don't even know. Months of work, Lily. Months. And what is it in the end? Five minutes and fourteen seconds. Of crap.'

'It's beautiful. Waverley is beautiful.' It was probably the heat, but he seemed suddenly flushed, his cheeks mottled in shades of rose and melon. 'It moved me to tears.'

'Probably only because you're so bloody mad with me.'

'Am I?'

'I've got a nerve, haven't I?' He turned to look at me. His hair was damp at the edges of his forehead.

'What do you mean?'

'Invading your home, your life like this. Digging out all your bloody stuff. All your secrets. I read some letters. None of my business, I know.'

'Then why did you read them?'

'Because I wanted to know everything about you, Lily. Everything. Now I feel like a bloody voyeur.'

'Which letters?' The world had tilted. Sweat cooled on my top lip. The *Listener* stopped halfway across an arc. My voice had changed, and Nat sensed it. 'Which letters?'

'Just ... some letters.'

'Old letters?'

'Some were.'

'From Billy?'

'Yeah.'

'And the rest?'

His eyes were wide. He drew himself upright on the edge of the chair. He seemed unable to answer. His mouth opened and closed, but no words came out.

I hauled myself up. In the bedroom I found the shoebox, jammed in the back of the wardrobe, its lid fitting snugly. I put the box on the bed and drew off the lid, seeing the garish stationery within, the envelopes fluttering open.

'I didn't open them,' Nat argued from the doorway. 'The gum must have been old. They weren't stuck down properly in the first place.'

'How long have you been reading these?' I asked him.

'Um ...'

'How long?'

'Well, since I got here, really.'

I stared at him. 'You had no right.'

'We've got to try and find her – Iris.'

'If I wanted to find her, don't you think I'd have done it by now? She wouldn't want me to anyway. She was the one who finished it, Nat. You don't know what happened when Ma died. All she did was scrawl across the face of my letter, return to sender. She couldn't even write to me then. She wanted nothing to do with me.'

'She might have changed her mind by now. Things change, you know.'

'*You're* telling me that. As if *you'd* know.'

'I know some things. I've written to Bree. Asked her to try and find her.'

'You've what? You mean Bree knows all about this too? Next thing you'll be telling your father.'

'He has a right to know.'

'It's dangerous to play God, Nat.'

'But isn't that exactly what you've done? You stole your own sister's kid. For God's sake, I don't blame her for cutting you off.'

'Oh, you're wise all of a sudden, are you? And you know just what things were like, and how many options we had? Back in those days, getting pregnant was a fatal mistake.'

'It doesn't matter what you say. You can't justify what you did, can you? You stole her baby.'

The words hung in the air, then formed into darts and stabbed me. 'She wanted me to. It was the answer to both of our problems. But I couldn't have stayed there, Nat. We couldn't have seen each other every day. What if she wanted her baby back?'

'What if she did?'

I looked at the quilt on my bed, the pieces sewn together with such care. I looked at the carpet, the flowers almost worn away to nothing.

'You didn't even give her the chance to be an auntie,' he said. 'Of course she would've wanted him back. Of course she bloody would've.'

He turned and I heard the kitchen door slam, the car start up and drive away. I sat on the bed and took the box onto my lap, fingering the envelopes and the thickness of the pages inside. I was gasping for a breath of that thick unbreathable air, drawing it in as though my throat had collapsed. I've told you before that he's not stupid. He had spoken out loud exactly what I have feared all these years.

So now your suspicions are confirmed. I'm a silly old woman, worse, and I've been found out. It's only what I deserve. And one of these days a skinny pierced vegetarian will come knocking at your door. I can't bear the thought. There will be so many explanations, and your life will be ruined all over again. You'll have to forgive Nat. He means well. Just as I did all those years ago. I was thinking only of you – in the beginning, at least.

The night drags on without end. I lie in my clothes on the bed, wishing the heat would diminish. The old woman in the mirror looks ill now, grey in the face with cheeks hollowed out by all that food I haven't been able to eat. My shoulder is tightening as I write, and my arm is aching. There is a pressure in my chest, a pain every time I breathe in. What could I ever say to you after all these years, Iris? What could I ever do to make amends? I won't make that meeting on the steps of St Paul's. How could I face you?

And Nat. What have I done to him, letting my anger rear up from nowhere? The sanctimonious anger of the self-righteous. I haven't felt anything like it in years, an inky blot rising uncontrollably, shattering the complacence I have cultivated since Eddie's death. I have been found out, Iris, after all this time. And Nat has gone away. I have been up the whole night, pacing the floor, gazing out at the glow from Auckland, looking for headlights and listening for the sound of the car engine, the way it rises as it climbs the hill. There are crickets, and the birds are waking, but there is no sound of Nat.

Will he ever come back, Iris? I wouldn't bother if I were him.

Your one and only, special and dearest sister,
Lou

[Thirty-seven]

Floss

One day to go, Floss writes, even though she knows it isn't true. Because it's after midnight, so the day is here. It has crept into her flat beneath the door, through hairline cracks in the reinforced concrete walls, through gaps between the window glass and the frames, as she lay awake in her bed, staring wide-eyed at the ceiling. Sleep couldn't come near her. It smelt her fear from the place where it dwelt during the day. That if she fell asleep she might not wake – she might sleep through a night and a day and another night until March the twenty-third had been and gone, and with it her meeting on the steps of St Paul's.

Spring has come too. As a child she used to think that it waited somewhere just out of sight, like sleep, until the daffodils were ready to thrust their leathery green leaves up through the grass, until the dreariness of winter had stretched the patience of hardworking housewives as far as it would go. That, if it waited a day too long, they would be halfway to the corner shop with their baskets and purses with not enough coins inside, and suddenly be flung backwards, off their feet, out of their orbits, because they couldn't take another day of cold wind without hope that it would end.

Floss knows now that spring is neither vindictive nor a calculating saviour, but a good-time girl, a harlot flitting across the globe in a constant blowsy peak of promiscuity, craving the upturned cheek, the relieved smile which always welcomes her. She is tiring of the south now that she is taken for granted there. Like Reggie, she needs a constant flood of new friends to dazzle with the same old tricks. And like Reggie, she never fails to impress.

Floss has walked among the daffodils at Hampton Court, with little Daniel in his four-wheeled throne, throwing bread for the ducks and swans, feeling the old sense of hope even though she has been betrayed by spring before.

Less than a day, she writes. *Less than twelve hours.* How will she fill the time?

She wraps a blanket around her shoulders and makes tea. The gas ring hisses, the kettle sings, the aroma leaps up at her as she pours on the boiling water. How many times is it now? Too many to count.

She takes her cup back to bed, placing it with care on her bedside table with its small inexpensive lamp, its glass of dusty water and packet of pills. She tries to read a magazine, the pages parading before her with their glossy celebrity smiles and shock headlines, but none catches her interest. Miracle recoveries from cancer seem less than miraculous. Shock fourteenth divorces have lost their power to shock. Even heart-warming fifty-year reunions hardly lift her temperature a single degree. Because she is so afraid that her own won't happen.

She takes the photos from her purse and fingers their edges. They came in letters from Lou, now and then another being tucked behind an ornament on her mother's mantelpiece. At first they held no interest for Flossie. Rather they were a reminder of her foolishness, her near miss. But over time they held a fascination with their grassy or beach backgrounds that Julie took for the Isle of Wight. The little boy grew, always with a look of his father about the eyes. He went from baby gown to sailor suit to school shorts and leather satchel in three steps. The last photo came when he was nine, his chubby face squinting into the sun, his shadow on the sand far blacker than she had ever seen a shadow, the sea behind him a monochrome horizontal which hinted at shades of tropical turquoise and leaf green.

When her mother died she gathered the curled photos from the mantelpiece and slotted them into a pocket of her purse. Her treasure from amongst all the rusty cake tins and rags of tea towels, the sheets that had been turned and the pillowcases with the embroidery worn away. The china had been divided years before, half for each daughter, gifted on their marriage. At the time Floss was not in a position to feel pity for the paucity of her mother's life. Her own was dire, made worse by the burden of not being able to speak of it. All her friends were the wives of Reggie's friends, and all were half in love with him. They swallowed his display when in public, the hand at Flossie's elbow, the fussing around her as though he always did. She would see his hand sometimes as it lay on the polished pub table, distorted through her shandy, the skin tinged a decaying nicotine gold, his fingers curved like elaborate instruments of torture. And around her their friends laughed as Reggie told jokes, the same jokes she'd heard again and again.

'What the hell's wrong with you?' he would demand later.

'I've heard them before, Reggie.'

'What difference should that make? You made me look a fool.' And then he would smile and wave as their friends shuffled off down the street, and lift his voice so they would overhear. 'Come on, my lovely. Let's get you home.'

Sometimes, as she walked with her back rigid, her neck taut with tension, she would hear snippets floating back.

'That Reggie. He's a card.'

'... life and soul ...'

Floss's clock ticks on, too slowly. She takes clothes from her wardrobe and tries them on in front of the mirror. They seem so drab. When did she start buying beige? They have all been washed so many times, ironed and repaired endlessly, until there seems no shape left, no life. Why didn't she think ahead? She could have bought something new. She could at least have had her hair done. Perhaps it's not too late. She could ring the hairdresser at nine and beg to be squeezed in. And afterwards she could go to Marks and Sparks and get herself something red, something exquisite, something flamboyant, so when Lou sees her on the steps she will know her straight away. Floss is years younger, after all. However ancient she looks, Lou will be worse.

At six she runs a bath and at seven she makes more tea and tries to eat two slices of toast. At eight she hoovers the flat and at nine she telephones the hairdresser. There is a slot at eleven if it's only for a shampoo and set. She writes it in her diary. *11am. Shampoo and set.*

At half-past nine Julie comes to the door with Daniel. 'Can you 'ave him? Just for an hour?'

Floss tries to say no. This is the most important day of her life. 'I've got a hair set,' she says. 'At eleven.'

'I'll be back before then. Promise.'

'But I'm meeting someone in town. At one. I don't have time to waste. I'll be all in a rush. Not very good company.'

'I'll be back in plenty of time. I'll just leave his buggy in case you need to get him off to sleep.'

She is gone before Floss has time to realise that she has said yes simply by not saying no. And she is angry.

At half-past ten she cancels her hair appointment. At eleven o'clock she bundles Daniel up and wheels him to the station. She buys a ticket for St Paul's. The train is empty so she wheels him straight on and parks him in the aisle.

'Never you mind,' she says when he shows a flicker of boredom, and she hands him a biscuit. A man in a suit helps her manoeuvre the buggy up the escalator from the Underground, jamming it hard against one side for the sake of those who need to travel more quickly than the escalator will take them. At the ticket barrier an attendant ushers her through the luggage gate, and she steps out onto the street. They weave between the men in dark coats and the women in their black skirts and tailored black jackets and brown paper carry bags with lunch inside. The sun shines on couples who perch on bench seats behind the cathedral, exchanging kisses between bites of baguette. Daniel points at pigeons, wiping the remains of another biscuit across his cheek.

'Pigeon,' she says, too tense to laugh, too tense even to offer the beginnings of a smile. She steers him onwards to the main steps. The sunshine has brought the tourists out, and her eyes flicker across the crowds. Cameras click and a dozen languages undulate across the flagstones. Floss drags the buggy up backwards, pausing for breath every three or four steps. At the top she looks again, down across the ethnic quilt below her, the excited faces, the coats of many colours, the flags of tour guides trying to herd their charges into manageable flocks.

Daniel chatters away, pointing at red buses and scurrying pedestrians. Floss rocks his buggy without thinking. If he would only sleep she could concentrate.

Will Lou bring the boy, she wonders? Hardly a boy now, a man of fifty. Will he come too? What will she be to him? Aunt, or long lost mother? What will he look like now, more than forty years since the last photograph? What will he look like in full colour?

She glances at her watch. Quarter to. She is early. No wonder there's no sign of Lou. She rocks Daniel, watches the crowd, looks at her watch. A minute has passed.

Clouds come in about two. The crowd has shuffled and reshuffled, formed and reformed. Daniel has gone to sleep, his cheek against the padded edge of his buggy. She rocks him still, but the movement is more to soothe herself. When the rain comes she scurries off, not knowing where, just somewhere dry, somewhere quiet, she hopes, so Daniel will sleep on. She finds a door and follows arrows to an exhibition hall. She stands in a queue, pays a pound and has a programme jammed into her hand.

'Only some are for sale,' the woman behind the desk says. 'The prices are listed on the programme.' The walls open out, and the queue dissipates.

'A red sticker on the card means it's sold,' the woman at the desk says to someone behind her.

She notices bright colours, hears expressions of delight all around her.

'Superb.'

'The work in this. Will you look at it?'

She can't seem to see or hear properly. Julie always laughs when Floss says she can't hear because she hasn't got her glasses on. But it's true. A kind of disorientation caused by the absence of one given. She needs to sit down, and the padded screens with their too-bright art form a maze through which she steers Daniel. How will she get home now? Having braved the tube once she knows what to expect, and as the afternoon progresses it will only get worse. Rush hour. She's heard of it, but now it's threatening to invade her life. How will she manage? Thousands of commuters, all getting in her way. A buggy she can't fold or unfold. Ticket barriers. Daniel almost as heavy as she is. And old-woman-invisibility. Surely she'll be trampled. There is no question. She can't do it. She simply can't get home. She's so tired, and it's all been for nothing. The waiting, the counting, the dreaming. All for nothing.

At last she sees a padded seat made from four great square footstools in a row. She parks Daniel beside it and subsides onto its cushioned expanse.

Julie will never speak to her again, and soon Daniel will be no more than a memory. She leans forward and kisses the sleeping forehead. 'I love you,' she says.

Death, she realises suddenly. People die all the time, on trains and in offices and in crowded exhibition halls. Perhaps she could die now, since there's nothing else left to live for, and someone else could get Daniel home. Break the news to Julie. She would always wonder what that mad neighbour was doing in the middle of the City, but she'd be too sorry to hold a grudge. Poor old dame, carking it in public. Should she do it dramatically, collapse headlong across the flagstones, eliciting an immediate response from those nearby, programmes flapping wildly as they look around for someone who might know what to do? But what if they didn't? What if they just stepped over her, thinking her an inconvenient obstacle, a woman who should have known better? Perhaps it would be better to simply subside, slide further and further down on the padded stools, and be found by a security guard at closing time, alerted by the crying baby.

'Bollocks,' Floss says, thinking of Julie, the word no more than a whisper as she tries her tongue around it. The consonants feel good, strong and expressive. Anger flares. Twice in one day. Anger helps her not to blame herself too much. Bloody Lou. Never had any intention of coming. And then she wonders suddenly if Lou might be dead. *I'd rather be dead than over eighty*, she'd said back then.

Floss grasps the edge of the seat with her fists, and leans forward, staring at the wall. The colours from the exhibit in front of her meld as her eyes mist up. Surely she's not going to cry.

What if she called the police? What if she told them she'd abducted the baby because she wanted one of her own? Then they'd take her home, and they'd let her off when her lawyer told them how she once had a little boy of her own that was taken away.

She conjures the police up in her mind, a young constable who has a grandma just like her at home.

'Come on now,' he'd say, taking control. And she wouldn't have to worry any more.

Through her tears, and the misty image of the constable's face, the exhibit on the wall in front of her distorts. She almost, for one misguided moment, thinks she sees her childhood home, Number Thirty-two. She stands up, takes a step closer and blinks at the red door.

[Thirty-eight]

I don't know what the date is, Iris. All days are the same now. There's no counting up or counting down. Each one is the same bland design. The tea trolley starts to clatter at dawn, and it's the last thing I hear at night too. You'll never get this, because I can't write any more, but I seem to need to go through things in my head, to settle events in place, to remember conversations and outcomes.

I have to tell you, Iris, that the wind never comes from South America. It blows unrelentingly from the west. Even the easterly has come from Australia, via Antarctica or the tropics, turning back on itself to flutter the leaves on my hillside.

And I can't have you thinking that Nat never came back. He did, soon after I finished my last letter, some time around dawn. He looked like a creature from a horror movie, and we eyed each other cautiously across the vast expanse of the dining table. He made tea and retrieved banana muffins from the cake tins, but neither of us was hungry. I could see that he was working his way up to an apology, and I was trying just as hard to tell him it wasn't necessary. He had come back. That was all he needed to do.

'I've done something stupid,' he said at last, earnest, so far from his usual jackass self – lifting a leg to make me laugh, jigging across the floor like a fool just to get a smile out of me.

'What kind of thing?' My hands were idle, lying listlessly in my lap. The news pips sounded from the radio in the other room.

'I'm going to be a father,' he said, his voice bright, brittle, his face displaying a smile which could shatter and wound us both. His eyes searched my face, looking for the first sign of reaction. I remembered you, all those years ago. 'I'm late.' Two little words that changed our lives, and here I was again. Floored, just like that other time. Totally unprepared.

'Who's going to be the mother?' I asked.

'Waverley.'

The breath went out of me. Again. I thought about the twigs in his hair when I was ill. The car creeping away in the depths of the night. And I thought of Marjorie's desire to be a grandmother. Would she be delighted, or horrified? Images passed through my head that I didn't want to contemplate. Birth control – or lack of – as practised by teenagers, one of them my grandson. The inane question, often asked, played about my lips. How did this happen? The answer was only too obvious. How it always happened.

And suddenly Nat's exposition on fertility meant something.

I remembered a room, Iris. Brown flowers contorting into infinity. A net curtain. Boiled eggs with the yolks eaten out. It was cruelty, and because of it I've looked over my shoulder for the whole of my life.

'That's the most wonderful news, Nat,' I said. And I meant it. I was going to be a great-grandmother. And I couldn't let all that happen again. Lives ruined because God made sex feel good.

Nat seemed to collapse at the words, folding randomly over the tabletop, submerging his head between his crossed arms. Then he cried. It seemed like he'd never stop. And all the while I patted his elbow and told him it would be all right. Just like I did with you. Only this time there's a chance that I'm right.

Later he played some music and pushed back the furniture. 'Let's dance,' he said, and held out a hand.

We did dance, Iris. Those nights came back to me, with Billy, just as the steps did, my clumsy old legs tapping them out. And then it happened, the stroke. I thought it was the end, Nat's strong arm throwing me into a spin, the bash on the head from behind, and I just kept going. Everything slowed, the room twirling about me, his face as it flashed past changing from delight to concern and then to fear. I don't remember landing, Iris, though the crash must have been quite something. All I could think of was that I'd taken care of him. He'd be all right in my house, heading off each day to the polytechnic, Waverley having the baby in the spring, and Marjorie never far away. I didn't think there'd be this hiatus, this pause between two worlds. I can only hope it will be short. Irony, Iris, always has the last laugh. You wait for years for your inevitable end, and it comes at you from another angle.

Here he is, Iris, striding down the ward with a bunch of autumn flowers salvaged from my garden. He tells me everything these days, even though I can't answer. He wipes my nose and my eyes and holds on to my dead hand. But the thing I most wonder about is whether Bree has knocked at your door yet.

From reviews of Bronwyn Tate's novels:

Leaving for Townsville

'An ambitious novel focusing on the difference between our dreams and daily lives and how we can step out of destructive relationship patterns ... The book's strengths lie in the successful mingling of layers of fiction and a humanistic acknowledgement of the daily struggle of living.' Mary Macpherson, *The Dominion*

Russian Dolls

'*Russian Dolls* is an original and superbly sophisticated and engaging novel from first to last.' *Wisconsin Bookwatch*

'Tate's greatest skill [is] her immense gift for creating characters ... it's a great read.' Nicola Mutch, *Otago Daily Times*

Halfway to Africa

'Tate's talent is to show the warmth of human contacts and the bonds of family ... she has the knack of articulating the awkwardness of social intercourse, as well as the level of intimacy that exists between siblings ... so easily reproduces the twists and turns of thought.' Pat Baskett, *NZ Herald*

'... a well written, thoroughly enjoyable novel.' John McCrystal, *North & North*